DEATH DATES

MADISON RUPP

MONARCH
Publishing

NONARCH PUBLISHING
Copyright © 2025 by Madison Rupp
All rights reserved.
ISBN 979-8-9909535-2-9 (print)
ISBN 979-8-9909535-3-6 (ebook)
First Edition

Cover artwork by Marcela Bolívar

This is a work of fiction.
Names, characters, places, organizations, and events are products of the author's imagination. References to real people, places, organizations, or events are used fictitiously. Any resemblance to actual events, places, organizations, or persons, living or dead, is coincidental.

ALSO BY MADISON RUPP

Liarland

DEATH DATES

1

Summer can't start until we pay our respects to the grave in the woods.

Every inch of me tingles with anticipation as we creep through the inky forest. The warm air is perfumed with damp grass and dirt. I eagerly inhale the sweet scent. It's stronger than usual—the forest's way of welcoming me back to my favorite place in the world.

For the last ten months, I've pined for this moment. Now that it's here, my head feels lighter. Breathing is finally easier. When I'm surrounded by these trees—with these people, I am whole.

My heart thrums so happily that I worry the Quinn siblings will hear and mock my deplorable joy. Not that any of them feel differently. Morbid as it may be, we all crave the high that comes with greeting a gravestone in the middle of the night.

Caleb Quinn's throaty voice shatters the silence. "Almost there."

"No shit," grunts his younger brother, Zane.

We couldn't get lost in these woods if we tried.

Their sister, Amelie, cracks a knowing smile when she

catches me ogling her eldest brother. She's always been forgiving about my feelings for Caleb. In fact, she's determined I will marry him so we can officially be sisters.

Unfortunately, I don't think she'll get her wish.

The leader of our pack, Caleb wields a snapped hockey stick as a walking aid, allowing its tip to dig into the earth every few steps. I can't put my finger on it, but something is different about him this summer. His back is broader, presumably because he's training to play collegiate hockey next fall. He walks like the world presses down on his shoulders, but this is nothing new. Caleb's always been the high-achieving diamond of the family—a role he takes far too seriously for his own good. Strands of gold weave into his tousled light-brown hair, which is likely the lingering evidence of his spring break trip to Fort Lauderdale. It's impressive he didn't lose the suntan while finishing up the school year in gloomy Boston.

So, what is it? Why does he look like he'd rather be anywhere other than here?

Stop wondering. You're not supposed to care.

I can't help being a hopeless-romantic, but even I know it's pathetic to waste another summer pining for a boy who doesn't want me back. It's time to get over him.

With that resolve in mind, I stop scrutinizing Caleb's body and focus my attention on the one we're visiting.

Unable to help himself, Zane sighs dramatically. "Poor ol' Lacy Monroe."

Amelie snorts, mussing with her black bob. "We're so sorry for your loss."

She's a good sport when it comes to maintaining tradition, but Amelie Quinn is not a fan of long hikes at midnight, or any other hour of the day for that matter. But she knows better than to outwardly complain. Instead, she's taken it upon herself to announce every single time her new (and absurdly expensive) bug spray fails her, and to humble any sibling who dares behave more dramatically than she.

"Can you try to have a soul, sis?"

"Can you—"

"Shh," says Cricket, the youngest of the family at thirteen. Despite only being at the lake house for half a day, the girl has already managed to get a sunburn. She clutches a bouquet of pink roses to lay at the foot of the grave. "What if Lacy hears you?"

Of all the waterfront properties that the exorbitantly rich Quinn family could have purchased, they settled on Lake Casper in middle of nowhere Virginia because they were certain it was haunted. Gianna Quinn, the matriarch of the family, adores anything macabre and eerie. It's a fascination she fostered within her four children, and if she were present, I think she'd be thrilled they're currently traipsing through the woods at midnight.

The property used to be a summer camp, but it closed down in 1985, which is coincidentally the same year that Lacy Monroe died. About twenty years later, Gianna Quinn purchased the land and retrofitted it into the summer house of her kids' wildest dreams, giving them the run of the place as the only inhabitants of the private lake. Ever mindful of the spooky possibilities, Gianna Quinn kept a decent amount of the old camp intact. We just have to trek a bit to reach it.

"Lacy can't hear me," Zane retorts. "Skyler said so."

The Quinns stop in their tracks to gaze at me expectantly. Caleb, Amelie, Zane, and Cricket. My favorite people in the world. All four of them are adopted. They may not share DNA, but their family is thicker than thieves.

The only time I have everyone's undivided attention is when we're speaking of spirits. "Without a sign from Lacy, I cannot confirm nor deny what she hears. But, considering she's never made her presence known, I can only assume she is not still among us."

Zane dramatically gestures toward me while staring down his younger sister. "See!"

"I'd ignore you too if I could." Cricket waves him off, continuing our hike.

I force myself to not overanalyze why Caleb's stony gaze lingers on me a moment after everyone else turns back around. My cheeks burn, but I choose to blame the long walk through the woods. It's certainly not because the most handsome boy I've ever known is staring at me.

I release a shaky breath when he finally returns his attention to the path ahead.

You're hopeless.

Despite having all the right ingredients, the Quinn's lake house is as haunted as a crappy medium's seance. I should know. All my life, I've had a knack for attracting spirits lingering in unrest. To my mother's dismay, I inherited the skill from her. However, unlike the woman, I'll never complain about my connection to the other side. Not when it's the reason the Quinns first grew so fond of me many years ago. Back when my mother was still their live-in nanny each summer.

Although I was only six years old when Gianna Quinn hired my mom, I knew it was a big deal. I wasn't so young that I didn't understand the chatter about the notable family who summered on the outskirts of town. And then Gianna was gracious enough to allow my mother to tote me along, further cementing my early adoration for the Quinn family. From that year on, we spent every summer living together.

Even now, a decade later, I'm still their sweet Skyler with a sixth sense. A haunted girl to fit right in with the rest of their oddities.

Once a trapped soul realizes they have your attention, they're keen to keep it. They tickle the hairs on the back of my neck. Whisper lonely sorrows in my ear. Flicker a nearby light. But nothing of the sort happens here. Not even Lacy is hanging around. Another perk of summering at the Quinn's lake house—it's quiet.

"I'm still convinced Robert killed her," Zane muses. Branches on the surrounding trees creak, as if laughing at his morbid theory. "Bet Lacy learned the mystery mistress' identity and her father made sure she took that secret to the grave."

We've attempted to contact Lacy countless times with every trick in the book, but she's never responded to share the truth of what happened. Not that I can blame her. Considering all the times we've poked around her grave, I wouldn't answer us either.

Amelie chimes in. "My money is on an OD."

The circumstances surrounding Lacy Monroe's death are a mystery. What we do know is that the old summer camp was owned by Lacy's parents, Robert and Winifred Monroe. It's widely known that Robert had an affair, though no one knows with who. Upon discovering her husband's infidelity, Winifred died of a shock-induced heart attack. A week later, Robert's daughter, Lacy, tragically died, as well. Cause of death? Unknown. The autopsy report came back with nothing.

Most assume the poor girl was suffering from some undiagnosed condition, like her mother. I prefer to believe Lacy Monroe died of a broken heart. But we'll never know.

Wisely, Robert Monroe immediately sent the campers home and shuttered the camp for good. Winifred was buried in a family mausoleum at the cemetery in town, but Robert chose to lay his daughter to rest at her favorite place in the world—Camp Casper.

If Robert is guilty of killing his daughter, it would explain the grand memorial she's buried beneath. The carved tombstone stands tall, curving upwards into a pointed peak. Below her name is a birthdate and a death date, both in July. She was nineteen when she died. Three years older than Amelie and I are now.

"Maybe we could dig her up and perform an auto—"

"Ew!" Amelie gasps. "Don't be gross, Cricket!"

"Little freak," Zane mutters.

"Related to you," the girl responds coolly, crossing her arms. Her strawberry blonde hair is split into two stubby braids, which makes her look younger than she actually is.

"Not by blood!" Zane's dark, angular cheeks quirk as he fights back a smile. It's clear the boy is in the middle of a growth spurt. Tall and lanky in all the wrong places. He still sports a clean buzz cut, though.

"Come now," I say as we approach the gravesite. "Don't fight in front of Lacy."

Caleb politely gestures for me to take the lead. I internally plead with my heart to exercise some self-control and pound at a regular tempo as I pass around him, but it's no use. The hint of a smile playing at his lips makes my insides somersault like I'm an acrobat flying from a trapeze.

Girl... get a grip.

Who cares if it's the first grin to grace his face since I arrived? Certainly not me.

Taking the lead, my body pulses with adrenaline. There's nothing like a mysterious grave in the middle of the woods to make you tremendously aware of your own mortality. It makes you appreciate your great fortune of walking above ground.

Pushing through the unruly brush and into the moonlit clearing, I stop dead in my tracks, a gasp escaping my lips.

"Sky?" Caleb comes up behind me, but for the first time all night, I'm too startled to take note of his closeness. "What's the matter?"

The words trail off as he takes in the scene before us. Lacy's grave basks in the moonlight, surrounded by mounds of freshly dug dirt and a gaping hole in the ground.

"That's impossible." Caleb bolts forward with the rest of us at his heels.

Amelie reaches for my trembling hand as we gawk at the sight below—or rather, at the sight that isn't below—because Lacy Monroe's coffin is open, and she is nowhere to be found.

2

Amelie accusingly whips her head toward Zane. "Is this some kind of joke?"

His palms fly into the air. "I didn't do this!"

"What's that?" I stammer, pointing to a folded piece of paper resting against the coffin's maroon satin liner. The stationary is tan with purple bell-shaped flowers ringing the edges. I recognize them immediately. Foxglove. Beautiful, but deadly.

Zane hops into the coffin amidst protests.

"Chill, you wussies," he groans, pulling himself back to ground level. "Unless Lacy rose from the dead, our body snatcher left us a message."

We gather as he unfolds the paper, only to jump back when something falls from it.

"You people are stressing me out," Zane mutters, bending over to snatch the black and white square that glints in the moonlight. He holds up what I realize is an undeveloped photograph. We all stare at it with bated breath, half-expecting an image to appear. When it doesn't, we return our attention back to the note. A brief message is written in mismatched letters clipped from magazines.

My mouth goes dry as I reread the promise. Under different circumstances, I'd find such a message tremendously romantic. But there's nothing charming about a love letter left in a coffin.

"Who wrote this?" Cricket whispers the question on all of our minds.

"What's soon?" Amelie asks, her clammy palm still pressed against mine.

"May I?" Caleb requests in a voice that's anything but asking. He stretches out his hand. After Zane relinquishes the note and photograph, Caleb's tan brow creases as he closely examines it. "Why didn't the image process? Instant film pictures are supposed to develop well in dim lightning."

Amelie scoffs. "And it's pretty dark six feet under."

Caleb continues like he didn't hear her. "This dirt smells fresh."

I'm the first to catch his meaning. "Someone stole Lacy recently."

The boy glances up, those ocean eyes locking with mine before he nods once.

A cool breeze rustles through the woods, making the back of my neck prickle. It's the same sort of sensation I feel when a spirit is lurking about. My head swivels like an owl, anticipating a ghost drifting through the trees. It's been ages since I've encountered the afterlife. My mother isn't exactly fond of our shared sense of the spiritual realm and prefers to keep our interactions with the other side to a minimum. We aren't out here helping spirits pass on in our spare time, although I've secretly always wanted to do some good and give it a try.

The wind dancing through the trees is unsettling. Foreboding. When nothing reveals itself, I anxiously fiddle with a strand of pale blonde hair.

"This has Mom written all over it," Amelie says, regaining my attention.

The Quinns may have come to accept their lake house isn't haunted, but that's never stopped Gianna Quinn from doing everything in her power to spook her children.

"That makes sense," Cricket hesitantly agrees, rubbing her arms.

"Does it?" I ask, not eager to accept such a silly explanation. The tech mogul may have a thousand people at her beck and call, but I doubt a single one of them would steal a body for her. That's heinous, not to mention illegal. "Where is Lacy's body?"

"If Mom isn't behind this, perhaps some sicko took Lacy," Amelie says far too casually for my liking.

"And we're okay with that?"

Zane remains unbothered. "Chill, Skyler. The sooner you realize that this world is full of freaks, the better."

"Those freaks shouldn't be here. We should alert—"

"Security?" Amelie questions, her onyx eyes bugging out at the suggestion. "We're not supposed to be anywhere near Lacy's grave. I'm not getting a lecture because we were the first to find her missing."

"Everyone knows that rule is only stated out of respect for Lacy's father. No one actually upholds it." My brow furrows as I glance back at the gaping hole in the ground. "This doesn't feel like something we should ignore."

"This isn't our problem, Skyler," Zane retorts. "If security is doing their job right, they'll notice in the morning."

"You can't be serious." I'm not afraid of calling out his dumb ideas. The fifteen-year-old might be infinitely richer and more powerful than me, but I've seen him jump into the lake in only his underwear. He stopped intimidating me a long time ago.

"Our family receives thousands of threats a year. If we paid attention to everyone who tried to daunt us, our empire would fall."

Only Zane Quinn refers to his family's technology conglomerate, TeQ, as an "empire." The rest of his siblings prefer to pretend it's not a big deal to come from one of the most influential families in the country. It's the healthiest mindset to have when you're on the inside. Living rent-free in the minds of the masses is actually pretty costly.

Gianna Quinn is the founder and CEO of TeQ. She credits the Earth itself as her top collaborator and inspiration. TeQ always seems ahead of the curve in the development of environmentally friendly products, whether it be cars, phones, or appliances. Of course, said advancements come with a hefty price tag. The only TeQ gear I possess come as Christmas gifts from Gianna herself.

"So what?" I ask incredulously. "That's it? Tough luck for Lacy?"

Zane waits for any of his siblings to protest. When no one utters a word, he shrugs at me, like this is the most obvious course of action. "Yep. We leave it."

"And we're not telling anyone?"

"Nope," he says with a pop of his lips. "This is someone else's problem. Are we all in agreement?"

Helplessly, I turn to Caleb. He has the strongest moral compass of the lot. Surely he will protest this awful plan. But that stony expression is back as he gazes upon the grave, clearly lost in thought.

Without their eldest brother to change their minds, the others nod their heads in unison. I'm the last to comply. Nothing about this seems right, but what choice do I have? I'm a guest who's fortunate to be here at all. It's not my place to press this further.

"Maybe we'll see ya on the other side, Lace," Zane declares, turning his back on her empty coffin.

3

I'M NOT sure what makes me wake up—or how I even fell asleep in the first place—but whatever the cause has me slowly blinking up at the dark ceiling of my bedroom in the Quinn's lake house. Wishing my skin didn't still prickle from our midnight rendezvous in the woods, I readjust to lie on my side.

That's when I see her.

Sucking in a breath, I shrink under my duvet at the shape of a girl standing beside the door. She's alarmingly pale, her skin shining with a slightly bluish sheen. The edges of her figure are hazy, like she's made of mist. Stringy-white strands of hair hang in her face, covering almost everything but her eyes, which stare blankly into mine.

Realizing she's gained my attention, the girl's head slowly cocks to the side, sending a chill down my spine. Those hollow, unblinking eyes have me completely frozen in place.

It's never real.

I've experienced night terrors for as long as I can remember. My mother believes they come with the territory of having a sight for the other side. Lucky us. Apparently, she didn't have them before her near-death experience as a teen that granted her newfound ability.

Unlike the trace of a lonely spirit, there's nothing real about the hallucinations that haunt my sleep. They don't tickle the hairs on the back of my neck or pebble my skin with goosebumps. My eyes might be open, but I have to remind myself that what I'm seeing isn't really there, no matter how convincing the vision may be. Sometimes, it's a faceless ghoul looming over my bed. Or a thousand spiders climbing on my pillow. These petrifying visions paralyze all but my vocal cords. My screams are usually what wake me up.

This nightmare is a new one. I squeeze my eyes shut, willing myself to awaken without screaming. *It's never real.* The last thing I want to do is wake up the whole house. *It's never real.* Slowly reopening my eyes, I draw another sharp breath.

She's still staring at me, those persistent eyes refusing to blink. My pulse quickens as I wait for something—anything—to happen. It's pounding so loudly that I'm sure she can hear.

My vision is deceiving me. This girl is a figment of my imagination.

I need to wake up.

A knocking sound makes me startle. My eyes cut to the door for a split second, and when they return to the figure, she's gone. Vanished. The hair on my arms stands on end.

Another knock, this one more urgent, has my body jumping back to life. Finally, I'm awake and able to move my limbs. I snap on a bedside light and carefully pad over the rug to crack open the door.

Apparently, tonight is full of surprising guests.

"Caleb?"

For years, I've dreamed that Caleb Quinn would turn up in the middle of the night. He'd curse at how he'd been so ignorant before wrapping an arm around my waist and drawing me closer. But considering his bloodshot eyes and deep frown, it's safe to assume the reason for his visit has nothing to do with realizing we are meant to be.

"Can I come in?"

Judging by the way his gaze is respectfully trained to my face, I can tell he's noticed my nighttime attire. Of all the nights to only wear a ratty, oversized t-shirt to bed...

Thank goodness the hem reaches my knees.

Still, I catch his attention drift slightly before he clears his throat. "If you're comfortable with it, that is. There's something I want to show you."

Making room for him to enter, I'm careful to close the door as quietly as possible. I'm not letting a single other nosy Quinn spoil this moment for me.

This isn't a romantic gesture, I remind myself. *It's a conversation between two friends. In a bedroom. At two in the morning.*

Geez, I'm hopeless. My mom always said I was a lost cause after developing a crush. My heart possesses me and there's nothing my head can do about it.

In the golden glow of the lamp, Caleb starts pacing around my bedroom. An emerald rug covers most of the wood flooring, masking his frenzied footsteps as he paces to and fro. His golden-brown waves look like they've had a hand raked through them one too many times and the deep bags under his eyes make me wonder how long it's been since his last full night of sleep.

It's rather unnerving to see Caleb so frazzled. What happened to the boy who was perpetually cool, calm, and collected?

"Is something wrong?" I ask him.

He answers my question with another. "How can everyone fall asleep after finding Lacy's grave empty?"

His mood was sour long before we discovered Lacy missing, but I know better than to press the matter. It's clear he doesn't want to talk about whatever else is bothering him.

"Pretending it's not a big deal is the easiest way to cope," I respond, carefully studying him as he crosses the length of my room again.

"Well, while they're *coping*, I'm losing my shit."

"I can't get it out of my head either," I agree, perching on the edge of the plush, cream-colored duvet. The night terror still lingers in the back of my mind, but at least the warm light has my breathing slowly returning to normal.

"Obviously, everyone on property is aware of the grave," Caleb says, moving to lean against the wall by the door. I try not to think about the demon that had just occupied the space in my dreams. "But why would someone take her body and leave a note behind?"

"We're sure this isn't a prank?"

His jaw clenches. "It could be. You know Zane and his antics."

"You don't sound very confident." My voice is barely louder than a whisper.

"Because I'm not." Hesitantly, Caleb meets my gaze, his pink lips pursed. As he anxiously stuffs both hands into the front pocket of his purple and silver Brackenridge Academy hoodie, I realize he's carefully selecting his next words.

"The picture developed," he finally mumbles.

My eyebrows raise. I didn't even realize he kept it. "What's it of?"

Not breaking our eye-contact, he pulls the photograph from his front pocket and holds it out.

Hesitantly, I pluck the picture from his grasp, though it only stays in my hand for a second. As soon as I see the image, it drops to the rug. Blood drums in my ears as my lips part with disbelief.

"I don't understand—"

Worry creases Caleb's forehead as he helplessly runs a hand through his hair. The fear on his face mirrors mine. "Neither do I."

Gaping at the picture resting at my feet, my own face stares back up at me.

"What is my picture doing in Lacy's grave?"

4

"Do you remember this picture being taken?" Caleb questions as I attempt to regain control of my breathing. The look on his face says it all. Something is seriously, seriously wrong.

"No," I manage.

That's the most-terrifying part. I never saw a flash or a cameraperson.

And yet, that's me in the picture. Dressed in the same clothes I wore earlier today. Standing outside the lake house. The picture could only be hours old.

"I don't understand..." My voice trails off as I kneel to pick up the photo. I loathe how defiling it feels in my hands. Someone planted a picture of me in an empty coffin. Who put it there? And why? Did they expect me to find it?

My head begins to pound, making my temples ache. This is worse than any night terror. *It's very real.*

After working up the courage, I scrutinize the image for more clues. It depicts me getting dropped off at the outskirts of the property. Hazy-green foliage rings the picture, leading me to assume that the photographer was hiding in a bush. My side is to the camera as I load my suitcase onto the golf cart, completely oblivious that someone is secretly watching me.

"Can you recall any details from when you arrived?" Caleb asks softly, trying and failing to not sound concerned. "Did you see anyone? Was anything out of the ordinary?"

My lips pinch as I recall the peculiar afternoon.

Like every other summer, my mother drove me over. However, instead of a chipper commute ahead of a happy reunion with the Quinns, Mom spent the entire thirty-minute drive in complete silence. She's always been guilty of prioritizing the families she nannies, but I know better than to complain about what pays the bills in our single-parent household. I guess Mom was eager to get rid of me for a few months so she could focus on work and forget the reason she has extra bills to pay in the first place. It's not like I asked for her to get knocked up by some stranger she met and never saw again, but that's neither here nor there. In two years, when I turn eighteen, I won't be her problem anymore.

Still, it was unlike my mother to be so openly detached. Our lukewarm relationship is usually cordial.

Working for the Quinns was obviously a phenomenal gig. Maybe she missed spending the warm months at the lake house too.

After the Quinns grew out of needing a local nanny for the summer, I thought that was the end of my friendship with the most incredible family in the world. Being invited to return as Amelie's guest remains the greatest joy of my life. Amelie swore she couldn't enjoy the lake house without me. All I can do is hope she never changes her mind.

Not keen on dissecting my mother's oddities with Caleb, I tuck my hair behind my ears, before shrugging. "Everything was normal. My mom dropped me off. Samuel gave me a ride to the security base before taking me up to the lodge."

Samuel Rivers is the Quinn's head of security. He doesn't

grant most guests a personal welcome, but the Quinns have always made it clear I'm not just any guest.

Suddenly, a detail from my quick visit to the security office pops into my mind.

"There was a boy being questioned by a member of Samuel's team," I say at once.

Caleb's head swivels in my direction. "A boy?"

"About our age," I describe, forcing myself to picture him in my mind. "He had copper hair and a stud in his ear."

"What was he doing?"

I recall a cardboard box sitting on the desk between the boy and the security guard. "Making a delivery, I think."

"But you didn't see a camera?"

I shake my head, already feeling like we're back to square one. "It's probably nothing."

"You're right to leave no stone unturned," he offers encouragingly, moving to sit on the bed beside me.

His closeness would make it hard to breathe if I weren't already fighting off a panic attack. Still, that doesn't stop my nose from detecting a hint of citrus in his cologne. Did he spritz himself before coming in here? Before I can get myself off-kilter by overanalyzing that, I return my attention to the photograph in my hands.

A stranger hid in the bushes with a camera. They presumably dug up a grave, stole a body, and left a picture of me in its place. Who the hell could do such a thing? And why photograph me? I'm the least important one here.

"You can't think of any reason why someone would leave a picture of you in Lacy's coffin?"

I blink at him incredulously. "Obviously not. This is either one of your brother's dumb pranks or someone is really trying to scare me, though I have no clue why."

"Regardless, we won't stand for it." Caleb is so close that I can feel his warm breath on my face. "We're not allowing someone to upset you and get away with it. We'll get to the bottom of this together."

Something inside me swells at his use of *together*. Caleb Quinn could easily brush this off like the rest of his siblings. When his lips spread into an encouraging smile—a real one that finally reaches his eyes—my insides become jelly. Being on the receiving end of that smile will always feel like a reward. Finally, it feels like the old Caleb is back.

"You really want to find who did this?"

"You know I do, Sky. It's been a few summers since we've had a good mystery to solve."

As children, one of our favorite pastimes was playing detective. We'd turn anything into a mystery. Every question needed to be answered with the help of a magnifying glass, blacklight, and fingerprint kit.

My face falls. "This doesn't feel like a game."

"I know it's not." He nudges me, waiting until I meet his sincere eyes before adding, "You're family, Skyler. We're not going to stand for someone messing with you."

Like a balloon with a puncture, I drift back down to earth. His words are tremendously kind, but the polite wake-up call rings in my ears. Caleb's trying to let me down easy. He's going to help me, but only because we grew up together. I'm family.

Why does it suddenly feel like there's a hole in my chest? I'm supposed to be over him. This shouldn't matter.

I force myself to redirect my attention, standing to pace the length of the room. Moving helps me think, as does a little distance from that cologne. "It's time to find out what really happened to Lacy Monroe. Maybe there's a connection that'll point us toward who did this."

Caleb's forehead creases skeptically. "We've already exhausted all our leads."

When Mom was still around, she'd shut down our bold attempts to learn more about Lacy Monroe's untimely death, calling our interest "morbid" and "out-of-line". I can practically hear her knowing voice in my head now. *Let the poor girl rest in peace. If Robert wanted to revisit his daughter's death, he'd visit her grave more.*

Last I heard, Robert was out west, hopefully living every day with regret. No man who can host more than one lover in his heart deserves peace.

The heart isn't so easily controlled.

I shake my mother's voice from my mind. The last person I'd ever seek out for love advice is the most unromantic human I know. It's a miracle I'm even here.

My arms cross as I look down at Caleb, who still sits on the edge of my bed. "Please. Our investigations were elementary at best."

"We were in elementary school at the time." His eyebrows raise in challenge as he leans back to rest on his elbows. He sure is making himself at home.

Focus.

"You're a Quinn and I see ghosts. I think we can do better than a quick internet search and asking a few security guards if Robert Monroe seemed shifty during his visits."

Caleb won't free me from his disorienting gaze, so I continue pacing in an attempt to keep my thoughts from getting jumbled.

"But now is not the time to ignore any thread of information," I say. "We need to unearth everything. How Lacy died, if she had any lovers, what her time at Camp Casper was like. Hell, maybe we need to learn the identity of Robert's secret mistress. There must be some connection we don't know about."

"You don't sound afraid anymore," Caleb points out, his expression darkening as he moves to sit back up. His calloused hands fold together in his lap.

"I'm here," I remind him, and myself. "There's no place safer than with your family."

That smile is back. "Very true, Skyler Pierce. Quinns stick together. No matter what."

My insides warm at the promise. I'm one of them. No matter what.

The thrilling sensation of having a plan with Caleb wears off after he slips out of my room with the promise that we'll start investigating tomorrow. As soon as I'm alone, reality returns. Someone took my picture and put it in a coffin.

As I attempt to fall asleep with the lights on, I'm suddenly aware of every creaking branch and rustling breeze in the distance. Haunting goosebumps still prickle my arms. But the demon from earlier was only a dream.

Right?

This place isn't haunted. It's eerie, but ghosts aren't suddenly floating about. Not unless someone died here recently.

Or their grave was disturbed.

The girl. Could she be—

I slam the brakes on that train of thought. I'm allowing myself to spiral like a paranoid sissy. But no matter how hard I try to redirect my mind, three words run on repeat in my brain.

Soon, my love.
Soon, my love.
Soon—

5

THE AGENDA for the first full day at the lake house is always the same. Mackenzie, the family's private chef, starts everyone's morning with an incredible feast. It's the only breakfast the siblings eat all together, because after the first day, everyone wakes up when they want.

I'm feeling better now that I've rested. Thoughts of creepy pictures and misty figures are long gone as I breathe in the sweet morning air. There's nothing better than waking up here, and I owe it to myself to enjoy every single second.

The back patio smells of warm syrup, scrambled eggs, and crispy bacon. Amelie and I are the last to arrive after she spent eons debating which bandana best complimented her outfit. In the end, she settled on a fuchsia one from some designer I've never heard of.

"It's from a few seasons ago," she'd remarked, tying it over her black bob.

I sighed with mock sympathy. "Practically vintage."

"I knew you'd get it!"

"Get over yourself," I scoffed, dragging her downstairs.

I think the main reason I remain Amelie's chosen guest is because I remind her of what a normal life is like. Well, that and the fact that Amelie's girlfriend, Camila, always spends the summer backpacking across Europe with her family.

I like to consider myself a suitable plus one for my friend. I understand her story but never sell it. I accept her wealth but never ask for anything. Every summer, we check-out from the world together. We're just kids at camp.

Sliding into our normal seats at one end of the outdoor table, I wait for Amelie to begin filling her plate before reaching for a lemon-ricotta pancake with a strawberry compote.

Mackenzie squeezes my shoulder. "Made 'em just for you, love."

"My guardian angel," I coo affectionately.

Mackenzie's been on the staff since I was a kid. After my mother was let go, Kenzie promised to keep an eye on me when I returned alone. With a wink, she disappears back into the lodge, chirping something about squeezing more orange juice.

The lodge is aptly named due to the fact that it's practically the size of a ski lodge. The two-story home looks like an enormous log cabin with vast, angular windows and an evergreen-colored roof. This is the true meaning of glamping. We're surrounded by nature without relinquishing our comforts.

Gianna Quinn won't fly in until the end of the month, so we have a few weeks to enjoy the place by ourselves.

Digging in, I find the other houseguests have arrived. There's Zane's friend, Diego, and Cricket's bestie, Phoebe. A boy I don't recognize sits across from me.

I eye him curiously. Newcomers are a rarity around here. He must be Caleb's plus-one, which is another surprise in itself. Preferring to reserve summers at the lake house for family time, Caleb rarely brings a guest.

They must know each other from school, judging by the boy's silver Brackenridge tee. Probably from hockey. He must be special if Caleb invited him. Unfortunately, Caleb is too busy zoning out and pushing scrambled eggs around his plate to introduce us. Looks like he woke up in a bad mood again.

Noticing he has my attention, the stranger cocks his head to the side curiously. The intensity of his gaze has me swallowing nervously. I've never had someone look at me with such interest before.

Accepting the challenge, I return his inquisitive stare with one of my own. He has a rounded jaw, shaggy black hair hanging nearly to his ears, and equally-as-dark eyes that glint like the night sky.

I have to stop myself from breathing out a curse aloud. He's gorgeous.

Have some self-control, Sky. You don't even know the guy.

I force myself to make more diplomatic observations instead. He must be an early riser because his plate has already been cleared. And judging by the way his bronze skin glows, he has a decent skin care routine. There. Two totally normal details to note about a stranger.

The newbie offers me a smile that shines against his sun-warmed skin. "I'm Mateo," he murmurs in a voice that's breezy-cool and whispers through my hair. "You must be Skyler Pierce."

My reputation precedes me? Immediately, I wonder what Caleb says about me when I'm not around. Am I the girl he loves to spend every summer with? Or am I nothing more than his sister's silly friend who yearns for him?

Before I can respond, our heads snap toward the other side of the table, where Zane is leaning back with a satisfied groan. "Boat time?"

"Already?" Amelie takes a delicate bite of egg. "Do you want us to puke in the lake?"

"So long as it's not in the boat, I don't care what you do."

Amelie wrinkles her pale nose. "It's too early for you to be this gross."

"It's never too early for Zane to be gross," Diego points out. He's buzzed his bleached hair. It only accentuates his round, rosy cheeks.

Zane started bringing the boy around a few summers ago, and while they've never made it official to any of us, we all suspect they're privately dating. If it's true, they make a cute couple.

"I barely started eating!" Amelie complains.

Zane shrugs. "It's not our fault you slept in!"

The pair both turn to Caleb, instinctively waiting for their eldest brother to step in as the authoritative voice of reason.

Caleb sighs deeply, like the last thing he wants to do is make a decision on the matter. Eventually, he shrugs. "Sorry, sis, but tradition is tradition. First day has a full agenda."

No one points out that Caleb sounds like he couldn't care less about tradition. Nor does anyone mention the dark circles under his eyes. It's obvious the boy is barely keeping it together. I'm dying to ask what's wrong, but I don't want to upset him further by bringing it up. It's obvious Caleb is doing his best to maintain the usual motions of life at the lake house.

Everyone abandons their plates, because around here, what Caleb says goes. However, that doesn't stop Amelie from silently protesting by taking her sweet time changing into a bikini.

"Wear the red one," she determines after glancing at my swimsuit drawer. "If you put your hair in a ponytail, you'll give off major hot-lifeguard vibes."

Before I can respond, she's reaching for a hair tie and pulling my hair back.

I don't mind when Amelie styles me. She's one of the most fashionable teenagers in the country. Using her family name as a springboard, she solidified her own brand in the fashion influencer world. There are some places where Amelie can't walk anywhere without the flash of a camera. She pretends like she doesn't mind because it "comes with the territory," but I know better than to believe her. That kind of attention—scrutiny—is enough to wind anyone too tight. A picture holds a lot of power.

I understand that now more than ever.

We've never been shy, so I change into my red bikini with little blue flowers right there. While I do so, Amelie delicately rubs sunscreen into her legs. She's the type of human to make even the most mundane task look glamorous.

"Gorg!" Amelie grins once I'm dressed, surveying her handiwork. "My little doll."

"The longer we take, the harder Caleb's going to try to throw us off the tube."

She pinches my cheek. "And you'll still love him for it."

I roll my eyes with a scoff. "I told you I'm over him."

"Sure you are," she says, flicking the brim of the ivory hat I'm currently pulling my ponytail through. It's stitched with an alligator, which is the mascot for some hockey team I don't even know the name of. All I do know is that it's not Caleb's team and will certainly get a rise out of him. Not that I would ever do that intentionally.

"You know," Amelie says meaningfully, "he's been asking a lot about you recently."

It takes all my effort to not look like this news affects me. "That's sweet of him."

Amelie laughs, immediately clocking my coyness. "Maybe this is the summer you actually make a move on him."

I shake my head. "It's like I said, I'm over him."

"Whatever you say, Skyler," she says with a click of her tongue and wag of her eyebrows.

I should prove my point by asking about Mateo, but before I can, Amelie is strutting from my room. Straightening my hat, I hurry to follow.

So what if Caleb was talking about me or showed up at my room in the middle of the night? For years, I've allowed my hopes to rise over any little indication that he may have feelings for me. I can't put myself through that anymore. If he truly cares for me, it's up to him to make the first move.

Still, it's easier to not overanalyze that nugget of information once we're back outdoors. The vast lawn is soft beneath our bare toes as we skip toward the glittering lake. It's a cloudless day, and the water reflects the sapphire-blue sky magnificently.

The main lodge is built on the refurbished side of the lake and features all of the luxurious amenities the Quinns could want. There's sand volleyball, a basketball court, and a rink for roller hockey. At the water's edge is an enormous boat dock, a dozen chaise lounges on the shore, and comfortable rafts that are tethered to the bottom of the lake.

The other side of the water is what we refer to as "Old Camp." It's exactly how it sounds. Old Camp is the preserved remains of Camp Casper. Most of the original cabins still stand deeper into the woods, and from here, you can see what used to be the large mess hall, craft cabin, and canoe racks. There's another dock on this side of camp, but it's so rickety and missing a few planks, that we all tend to avoid it. Gianna's response is to scoff when asked why she doesn't fix it up.

"I don't imagine Camp Casper will continue to be so welcoming to us if we do not respect its glory days," she likes to remind us. "Best to tread lightly."

Gianna Quinn had a habit of referring to anything and everything like it was sentient, but especially Camp Casper. I suspect it's because her brain is pulled into so many directions with work. Without any documented lore to base our campfire stories on, Gianna took it upon herself to make up her own. I think flexing her imagination keeps her sane. Well, as sane as a tech CEO can be.

Aside from the family's four jet skis, the Quinns own two vessels. One is a pontoon boat, which is perfect for lounging.

Today, we're taking out the other, a speedboat the color of a fire-engine.

The mini marina is maintained by a chirpy crew, led by a woman named Tara Vargas. She has the extraordinary skill of predicting which vessel the Quinns will be wanting before they even have to ask.

The helm is Caleb's usual spot aboard the scarlet speedboat. His tan back is to us as he confidently pulls away from the dock, waving goodbye to Tara when he's ready to pick up speed. There's nothing Caleb loves more than being out on the water. I can only hope it improves his mood.

While Zane and Diego get cozy at the stern, Cricket turns on a playlist she and Phoebe curated—a bold mix of indie-rock, country, and early-2000s pop.

"Cute hair, Pheebs," Amelie compliments the girl. "Lavender is totally your color."

Phoebe's face brightens at a compliment from Amelie Quinn. "Cricket said you'd teach us how to French braid this summer?"

"Pinky swear," Amelie promises.

There may only be a few of us, but here, we're the camp counselors for the younger girls. Like my mom cared for us when we were blossoming, it's our duty to care for them.

I find a spot next to Mateo and settle into my seat as Caleb steers the boat into the center of the private lake. Turning my face into the wind, I welcome the cool mist that meets my cheeks. I've never minded the smell of lake water, even if it is a little fishy. When I catch Mateo studying me, the sun seems to burn a little brighter. Apparently, he has no intentions of getting in the water, because he's still wearing his black athletic shorts and school t-shirt from breakfast. Something tells me this boy has perfected the art of being a mystery. It's certainly working. I just met him and I'm already dying to figure him out.

For the first time, I believe moving on from Caleb might actually be in the cards.

Putting the vessel in neutral, Caleb lowers his aviators to wickedly eye his victims. It's nice to see this side of him return. "Who's first?"

Cricket and Phoebe call dibs as Diego shoves the neon-orange inner tube into the lake. A long yellow cord keeps it attached to the boat, but we all know Caleb will be testing the tether's strength in a matter of minutes.

"Life jackets!" Caleb calls after them, earning small groans from the girls as they stop to grab bulky vests from the storage beneath a seat. He mocks their pouts. "Aw, does your mean brother not want you to drown?"

Cricket sticks her tongue out as she clips the buckles on the life jacket. "If you didn't want us to drown, you wouldn't try so hard to throw us from the tube!"

His jaw drops with mock-offense at the suggestion. "I would never!"

"Look whose good mood is back," Amelie mutters with a sniff.

Despite holding on for dear life, the girls don't last five minutes before Caleb knocks the tube against the wake and flings them into the air. They swim back to the boat, cursing and sputtering, before asking when they can go again.

Zane and Diego are next. Their spindly muscles tense as they tightly grip the handles on the tube. The pair last a decently long while, but Captain Caleb always succeeds in the end. He steers the boat in tight circles, creating gnarly waves that best the boys.

Diego gags as he climbs the ladder onto the boat. "I think I swallowed a minnow."

"Think a kiss turns him into a frog?" Mateo whispers into my ear, making me giggle.

This earns Caleb's attention as his head snaps in my direction.

"Skyler's up," he announces. Those sapphire eyes narrow as he appraises me with a sinful grin. "I wanna knock that abominable hat off her head."

Accepting the challenge, I pull the cap lower onto my forehead, making sure my ponytail is securely looped through the back. "Bring it on, Quinn."

"After it sinks to the bottom of the lake where it belongs, I promise to give you one for the Brackenridge Bats." Caleb actually winks, causing my stomach to flip.

Um, what was that?

Nope. Do not even go there. It's just a playful wink from a friend. We will not be replaying that in our head over and over and—

"May I join?" I hear Mateo inquire behind me.

Relieved to realize I was wrong about him not wanting to participate, I nod for him to follow us onto the tube.

"No mercy," Caleb calls after us.

Mateo laughs over his shoulder. "I'd expect nothing less!"

"Being on the lake turns Caleb into a ruthless monster," I warn Mateo.

"You have no idea," Amelie snorts.

Mateo takes this in stride. "He's gotta get his aggression out somehow now that the hockey season is over. You should see him at the rink."

I can think of few things I'd enjoy more than watching Caleb play. It's too expensive for Mom and me to travel to Boston and catch one of his games.

One by one, we hop onto the unsteady raft. Amelie takes her place at the center, leaving Mateo and I to hold on at either side of her. It takes all my willpower not to ogle Mateo's large biceps as he situates his grip. What are they feeding these Brackenridge hockey players? Are they all this handsome?

Caleb whoops, revving the boat. "Time to drown!"

"Oh, great," Amelie moans. "Your dumb hat is gonna get us killed."

"Hold on, ladies!" Mateo bellows.

"No shit!" My giggle turns into a shriek as the boat begins to move.

Our arms lock as the tether tightens and we pick up speed. Caleb stays true to his threats, dramatically swerving the vessel so the tube flings every which way. We scream as we dip in and out of the wake, holding on as tight as we can. A vicious bounce sends Mateo flying into the air with a howl.

Determined to throw us, too, Caleb leaves Mateo to float in the middle of the lake as he careens nearer to the shore opposite of the house, where the trees are thicker and remnants of the abandoned camp still stand.

"I'm not going anywhere!" I scream at the boat in a tone that is certainly not flirtatious.

Caleb barks a laugh from the helm, urging the vessel to go even faster.

Amelie shrieks, "Do you have a death wish?"

"I'd like to see him try and—"

But it's at that moment something catches my eye, and I nearly lose my grip.

"Who's that?" I cry.

Amelie whips her head in every direction. "What?"

I blink mist out of my eyes, attempting to relocate the shadow I'm sure I saw on the shore.

"There was someone standing by the old craft cabin!"

"I don't see anyo—" Amelie starts to say, but her words turn into a scream as she slips down the back of the tube with a splash.

I crane my neck to get another glimpse. There was someone there. I'm sure of it.

"Hey!" I try to alert the others on the boat, pointing toward the shore. Long gone is my attempt to best Caleb. All that matters now is capturing their attention.

Not noticing, Caleb steers me over a precarious string of waves. With only one hand holding on, I'm immediately doomed. I fly through the air, barely remembering to suck in a breath before I plunge into the freezing lake. I feel the hat wrench off my head as I go under, but that's the least of my worries. I fight to the surface, screaming for anyone to radio security.

Someone's on the property, and judging by how fast they disappeared, they aren't supposed to be here.

6

Only Caleb took my concerns seriously.

He immediately called for the security team to check things out before returning everyone to shore. The others complained that our boating was cut short, but as soon as they started lounging by the pool with one of Mackenzie's watermelon smoothies, they quickly moved on.

I didn't. While they tan on the deck and float around the crystal-blue pool, I can't find it in me to relax. Every breath is charged with dread, for what exactly, I'm not sure. I think that makes the horrible feeling worse.

The security team promised they didn't find any evidence of someone breaching the property, but I know what I saw. Someone was there.

I think back to the picture unknowingly taken of me. Was this the same person? What do they want?

Lost in my thoughts, I sit at the edge of the pool, dangling my feet into the cool water. The afternoon sun beats down on me, but my body appears to be incapable of soaking in the warmth. A persistent chill welcomes goosebumps up my arms and legs. The unnerving sensation is so thorough I can't even appreciate the warmth of Mateo as he sits beside me.

If I hadn't known Amelie for most of my life, I'd be concerned by her lack of care for the situation. But this is just how Amelie is nowadays. It's easier for her to dissociate and trust Samuel to do his job.

But just as I know her, she knows me. I'm not used to feeling like someone's watching me—someone alive and unwanted, that is. I'm in no state to simply move on and work on my suntan. I require more time to collect my thoughts and calm down.

Taking the hint that I need space, Amelie is currently on the other side of the pool deck, helping pose Phoebe so Cricket can capture a picture worth posting. I have no doubt Amelie will be up next. She posts less frequently when we're at the lake house, but it's been a few days since she reminded her followers of her existence.

Zane and Diego relax on pool rafts, never floating too far apart. Mateo quietly sits near me at the edge of the pool. Caleb started swimming laps, his favorite method for when he needs to work through a mental puzzle such as this.

If I weren't so freaked out, I'd likely admire the toned muscles of his back that flex with every stroke of his arms. But, alas, my fears keep my brain preoccupied. Even I'm wise enough to know that two alarming encounters in less than a day cannot be explained away as a coincidence. My intuition refuses to grant me the peace of mind by blissfully accepting otherwise.

Someone is trying to scare me. It could be a prank. It could be worse. But someone is intentionally messing with me, and regardless of their reason, it's working. I'm scared.

Mateo doesn't say much, which I appreciate. He must be able to tell I'm not in the mood to be comforted. Instead, he focuses on swaying his legs through the water in time with mine. Every now and then, our feet nearly brush, and we'll wrinkle our noses at each other in pretend offense. Then it's back to staring at the water, both of us zoning out.

Who was here? What do they want?

I startle out of my thought spiral when Mateo moves to stand up. "I'm going to give him a moment with you."

Puzzled, I turn to find Caleb swimming up. My lips pinch when I see the scowl on his face.

Guess his bad mood is back. Although, I can't blame him for it right now. I'm not exactly my chipper self either.

Treading water before me, Caleb frowns while watching Mateo disappear into the shade of the house. Then his attention snaps back to me with such an intensity that I find my own lips drooping even lower. I thought these boys were friends? Why does it feel like Caleb doesn't want me talking with Mateo?

"So what's the story with you and—"

At the same time, Caleb says, "About your hat—"

I sigh and accept the inevitable conversation about earlier today.

"You know that's not what I'm worried about," I mumble. We haven't told the others about the developed photo. Caleb doesn't want to scare them until we have an idea as to why there was a picture of me in a coffin. If she knew the whole story, Amelie would be packing her bags right now and our summer would be over before it even started.

He pushes his wet hair out of his face. "Security said there was nothing, Skyler. They checked to see if Robert Monroe decided to pay his daughter a visit, but I guess he's out in Nevada."

My heart sinks. A piece of me truly hoped the shadow belonged to Lacy's father. But he hasn't visited his daughter in years, and when he does, it's never when the Quinns are on site.

Caleb continues. "Security couldn't find any footprints in the sand or—"

"This wasn't a ghost."

Years ago, when everyone had abandoned the campfire

aside from us, I revealed to Caleb I had a special sense for when a spirit is present. He took the news similarly to his sister—like this was the most normal secret a human could share. It was easy for them to accept my oddities, because they were experiencing life in a peculiar way, as well. I saw spirits and they saw strangers obsess over their family.

"Are they kind to you?" It was his only question when he first learned.

"Yes," I answered without hesitation. "I think they're just happy to have someone finally notice them."

The first time I encountered a spirit, I was four. Mom and I were staying at a bed-and-breakfast in upstate New York so she could attend her college reunion. Apparently, the inn was under new management, but unbeknownst to anybody, the late previous owner was still hanging around. The poor old woman was so relieved to be seen by my mother and I, but unfortunately, Mom wanted nothing to do with her. She checked us out an hour later and moved us to some crappy motel instead.

I'll never forget telling this to Caleb and finding him blinking at me through the flames with awe. "They're lucky to have you."

Those five words fueled my crush for years. I'll always cherish how he grinned at me as firelight danced across his face. At that moment, I felt like the lucky one.

Even now, I still feel lucky that Caleb respects me enough to take my concerns seriously. He believes me when I say the lake house isn't haunted. He also trusts me when I say I saw something.

"You think it was the photographer?"

The way he says it—*the photographer*—sends a chill down my spine, despite the ridiculously-warm sun beaming down on us. All I can do is nod and fight the urge to look over my shoulder. Ever since the photo developed, I've felt the itch of a thousand eyes trained in my direction.

Caleb takes this confirmation in stride, like he expected it. His face purses into a frustrated scowl before his determined eyes meet mine. "I'll check back in with Samuel's team to have them do another sweep and comb through the security footage again."

"Are you going to tell him about Lacy's grave?"

"They already know."

"What about the photo and message?"

"Do you want me to bring them up?"

A resounding "yes" should tumble out of my mouth, but I find myself biting my tongue. If any of the adults catch wind that someone is targeting me, my mother will whisk me away before I can even finish packing my bags. The last thing I want is to be stuck in an empty house all summer.

"Let's keep it between us for now," I respond instead, hoping I'm not making the most foolish decision of my life. "Until we know more."

He nods in agreement. "We don't want to ruin our secret so soon."

When a coy grin toys at his lips, I decide I regret nothing. Having a secret to share with Caleb makes any risk worth it.

This is a terrible idea. Do not put yourself in danger to bond with a boy who sees you as a sister.

But I'm not really in danger, am I? I do trust Samuel's team to keep any unwelcome guests away from the house.

And what about your picture in an empty coffin?

For all I know, Zane planted it there to give us all a good scare, but when the photograph didn't develop, he chalked his prank up as a failure.

I'm so busy debating myself that I don't properly relish in my victory of earning another smile from Caleb before it disappears from his face. His lips stretch into a thin line as he ponders me with what appears to be trepidation.

"We won't be able to keep it a secret forever," he reminds me. "I'll never forgive myself if something happens."

My pulse quickens at the thought. I've always felt secure here. Even with everything that's going on, I still feel safe. Between the highly-trained security team and surveillance gear literally invented by Gianna herself, I can think of few places safer than the Quinn's lake house. If or when we clue Samuel into what's been going on, I don't doubt his ability to protect me.

"Nothing's going to happen to me, Caleb."

He offers me a weak smile. This one doesn't reach his eyes. "Of course not," he agrees before shaking his head at the bleak turn our conversation took. "It's our first day back at the lake house. Some creep shouldn't ruin that."

I want to tell him to listen to his own advice, but it feels unwise to allude to the cloud that's darkening his mood. Like prodding it will release a storm.

So, I try to push thoughts of shadows and photographs from my mind. Even if it's a little forced, Caleb's grin certainly helps as he drags me into the water for a game of volleyball.

I stay present for the rest of the sweltering afternoon, sunbathing with Amelie, Caleb, and Mateo, having dinner with Amelie on the deck, and enjoying a scoop of Mackenzie's homemade chocolate-cherry ice cream with the family as the sky burns in blazing shades of orange.

After Amelie finally finishes licking her cone, Zane sits up in his chair. "About time."

Cricket and Phoebe are already out of their seats, disappearing back into the house, only to return a moment later. Each burdens an armful of flashlights.

"Everyone remembers the rules?" Caleb asks the group in a far-too-chipper voice that doesn't reach his hollow expression.

From the way his siblings are warily eyeing him, I wonder how long he's been in this funk. He's like a ghost. A shell of the boy he once was. It's obvious he's pretending everything is normal when something is clearly bothering him. The Caleb I know would be elated to round out the first day of summer with a game of flashlight tag. It was a tradition he started and holds each of us to every year.

"Obviously, but will that stop you from reciting them anyway?" Amelie retorts.

"Hey!" Mateo pipes up. "I have no clue what's going on!"

"No going indoors," Caleb begins, earning a groan from everyone but Mateo. "Anything beyond the property line is also off-limits. No arguing if someone tags you."

"You hear that, sis?" Zane asks Cricket and she sticks a finger up at him.

"Mind your manners," she warns, "or I'll give you the flashlight that flickers."

Zane immediately opens up his flashlight for inspection, flipping the batteries around and ensuring the light's beam is satisfactory.

"Switch with me," Diego offers sweetly.

Zane grins widely while the rest of us share knowing looks.

"Once you get out, you help tag." Caleb regains his audience. "Last one standing wins."

I test my flashlight, flipping it on and off. The golden light is decently strong, and the switch doesn't stick. I grip it tightly, moving to wait at the bottom of the deck with the others. We draw into a circle on the soft grass, the air suddenly charged with anticipation. The sun has nearly diminished for the day, leaving a sliver of pinkish light in the distance. Any minute now and we'll be masked by darkness—exactly how we like it.

"Lights," Caleb orders, and we all immediately switch on our flashlights, keeping them pointed at the ground. "On my count. One, two, three!"

Everyone but Mateo—who's still struggling to keep up— raises their flashlights, pointing to a person. I aim my beam at the poor boy, grinning cheekily when I find him hastily trying to locate his flashlight. I suspect he forgot it on the deck. He better hope he's not tagged. Mateo only stops fumbling at the sound of Phoebe's groan. We both turn to see three lights cast on her. With the most votes, she is most-decidedly "it".

"Bitches," she mutters, glaring at Amelie, Zane, and Cricket. "I know who I'm hunting down first."

"Bring it on," Cricket says confidently. She may be short, but those legs of hers are powerful and strong. I'm sure she'll be halfway around the lake before Phoebe's even finished counting.

On cue, the girl plops onto the wooden steps at the bottom of the deck. "One-hundred, ninety-nine, ninety-eight..."

Immediately, the rest of us scramble like ants after their home is disturbed. Cricket sprints into the trees. Caleb and Mateo take off together in the direction of the boat dock, playfully racing each other as they fight to be first to the boats. As Zane and Diego vanish to the right of the lodge, I grab Amelie's hand, silently forming our usual alliance.

Night envelops us as we disappear into the trees. Most hunters assume their prey has escaped as deep into the forest as possible, which is why Amelie and I prefer to hide around the edge of the woods. We each pick a sturdy-looking oak with leafy branches perfect for hiding.

"Ready or not!" Phoebe cries in the distance.

"Get going, girl," Amelie orders, already halfway up her tree.

"I'm going, I'm going," I mumble, finding what appears to be my safest starting point and jumping. I climb as high as I dare. Hugging the trunk, the leaves should mask me from Phoebe's searching light. There's nothing more humiliating than being the first tagged.

We freeze at the sound of a crunching branch somewhere to the left of our trees.

Not breathing, I spy Phoebe wildly swinging her flashlight, hoping to land on a target.

My eyes widen at the sound of cracking wood coming

from Amelie's tree. The light flies in our direction. I almost fall off my branch when Phoebe's twinkling laugh rings out.

My friend curses. "Are you for real, Pheebs?"

Daring a peek through the leaves, I find Amelie hanging upside down, barely clinging onto a branch that's snapped in the center.

"Please, blame the tree, not me," the girl cackles. "Now where's Skyler?"

I wince, but before I can reveal my location, Amelie says, "Not with me."

"Really?" Phoebe asks suspiciously. Her flashlight darts over the foliage, causing me to press myself even tighter against the trunk.

"Yeah, she ran off with Caleb."

Phoebe snorts. "Poor girl is hopeless."

"And predictable." Amelie laughs, illuminating her light. "Bet they're at the docks."

She's a scary convincing liar, but it's to my benefit so I'm not complaining. My friend's a loyal ally until the end, willing to say anything that'll allow me to escape undetected. Even if it's to say I'm a predictable, swoony mess when it comes to her brother.

"Sweet, let's go."

As soon as the woods fall back into darkness, I carefully drop back to the dirt. This is the first time I've been alone with these trees this summer. Forcing myself to forget the unnerving events of the last twenty-four hours, I suck in a deep breath. This is where I belong. I'm going to be okay.

I allow the rustling branches to soothe my thoughts. Humming insects add a harmony to the tune. If my mother was here, she'd tell me to stop scaring myself with my dramatics.

"Fear is fuel," she'd remind me. "Don't give it the power to paralyze you. Use the adrenaline to your advantage."

It was the only advice of hers that felt worthy of remembering.

So, I got a little scared earlier. Someone pulled a prank on me, I had a bad dream, and then I saw a weird shadow. Am I really so skittish that I'm going to let that stop me from enjoying my favorite place in the world? We're all getting older. Caleb is going off to college in the fall. We only have so many of these summers left together.

Maybe this is the year I finally win flashlight tag. As long as I keep moving, I have a shot. I just need to take advantage of my fears and allow them to propel me to victory.

Once I'm completely at ease, I make my escape.

Keeping a steady pace as I run, I sprint deeper into the woods that I know like the back of my hand. At first glance, they appear massive and consuming, but after years of playing between these trees, they're not all that imposing.

I remind myself that I'm genuinely safe in these woods. Here, I'm totally free to be myself. I'm not the weird girl who is always staring off into space, seeing things my classmates cannot. Alternatively, I'm probably the most normal person currently running around the forest.

Crashing into a clearing, I pause to catch my breath and plan my next hiding spot. Climbing another tree feels safe but uncomfortable. Not able to completely shake the shadow from earlier, I'm not keen on heading toward Old Camp, even if the best hiding spots are over there.

Before I can decide, a snap of white light flashes behind me, making me freeze.

7

Turning as the light disappears, I search the dark trees for one of the girls.

How did I not hear them coming?

Another flash to my left has my head whipping around. Blinking against the harsh light, the world spins in incorrect shades as I frantically try to locate whoever is turning their flashlight on and off. Why isn't anyone appearing to victoriously tag me?

"Who's there?" I hate how my voice quivers like a child. These woods shouldn't scare me.

Another flash.

My mouth grows dry. It finally occurs to me—this isn't from a flashlight, *but a camera.*

The photographer is here.

Heart lurching, I fight to keep it from beating out of my chest.

"Who are you?" I say, trying and failing to not sound terrified. "What do you want?"

Another flash.

This one completely takes out my vision. The world shines white as I plead with my eyes to cooperate. There's a faint rustle through the underbrush and a snap of a twig. Frantically spinning, I attempt to follow the sound.

"Come out!" I scream, whipping my head around to search the dark trees for the stranger. "Tell me what you want!"

"Skyler?" I jump at the voice behind me.

A new light appears, this one golden. The beam remains on. As my eyes adjust, I breathe a sigh of relief when I spy Caleb sprinting toward me.

I meet him halfway, pulling him from the clearing. "We need to get out of here. Turn off your flashlight. Hurry!"

"Whoa, whoa," he says when he sees my face. "What's wrong?"

"There's someone here," I whisper frantically. "Taking pictures with a flash. It's *them*."

Caleb's eyes widen as he snaps his flashlight off, whispering for me to stay hidden.

"Where are you going?" I ask wildly.

"To find this freak."

I grab his arm, trying to keep him in place. If someone's here, Caleb Quinn is the last person who should be wandering the woods alone. The heir to TeQ, it was always the family's intent that Caleb takes over one day. His life is worth far too much to prowl around the woods and hunt down a stranger. "We need to call Samuel."

"And let them get away?"

Maybe he's right. This might be our one shot at finding this photographer's identity and discovering what they want with me.

"Fine." My head shakes with disbelief. "But you're not going alone. Horror movie 101."

Caleb looks like he's going to argue, but after meeting my hard eyes, he concedes with a nod. We've watched enough scary movies to know the rules and he's lived through enough stalker scenarios to avoid foolish mistakes.

In sync, we snap on our flashlights, scouring every shadow for anyone who may be lurking. I'm suddenly aware of every creaking tree and gust of wind. Staying together, we round the clearing once, but it's apparent our perpetrator did not linger.

A determined jolt clenches my stomach. This creep isn't going to ruin my summer. They've had their fun. I'm done being taunted. I've spotted this stranger once before, and right now, it's the only lead we have.

"We need to go to Old Camp and see if Sam's team missed any clues as to who this is."

I worry Caleb will shut me down when his lips pinch, but then he agrees. "Let's get 'em."

That's when the unthinkable happens. Caleb's free hand slips around mine, tightly interlocking our fingers. My pulse begins to pound in a new type of way. Horrified heartbeats are replaced by hopeful ones.

I need to get a grip. This should not be my priority right now.

But that doesn't stop my head from humming as he pulls us through the trees. It keeps up as we approach the far side of the property. Relics of Old Camp cling to this side. Trail markers and wooden directional signs. They point toward a walking trail, the lake, and the run-down ropes course that we're not allowed to enter. Faded bandanas are tied to low-hanging branches, each signed with a camper's nickname. Fallen leaves and twigs litter the roofs of the decrepit cabins, each painted with a group name like "Green Sasquatches" and "Purple Squirrels." Dirt turns to sand as we approach the lakeside. Dark water gleams like a sheet of black glass, and across the way, the lodge looms. Something about the home snaps me back to reality.

I whisper, "Have you seen the others?"

They shouldn't be out here. Who knows what this stranger wants and how far they're willing to go to get it.

"You were the last to get out," Caleb explains. "We were all looking for you, but then I got this feeling that something was wrong and sent the others back to the lodge."

I blink with surprise. "You could feel it?"

"I guess we're just in-tune together." A sheepish expression crosses his face. "It makes sense, when you think about it. For us to be on the same page after all these years."

I swallow with surprise.

What page would that be? I don't have the courage to ask it aloud.

Caleb's eyes flit over to the craft cabin, which rests on the edge of the tree line. "No matter what, we stick together." He turns back, waiting for me to nod in understanding, before leading the way across the shadowy shoreline. His warm hand never leaves mine.

Shining my flashlight over the sand, I allow it to dance over the tire treads left by the security team's golf carts. The tracks are accompanied by sets of large footprints that roam every which way. It's impossible to tell if any belong to our suspect.

I trust that Samuel's team was thorough, but I want to see things for myself. At this point, I'll do anything to feel in control of this situation even a little.

Crossing the sandy terrain, I'm careful to not kick the scratchy granules into my sneakers. I'd rather swim across the lake than walk all the way home with sand in my shoes.

Giving his hand a squeeze, I release it before ducking around him to creep toward the old craft cabin. An unfamiliar breeze nips at the nape of my neck, encouraging me to approach.

"Do you feel that?" I ask, already knowing he doesn't.

"Feel what?" His head whips in every direction.

My mouth goes dry when the pull only intensifies. Something—or someone—is beckoning me inside the cabin. Never in my life have I ever felt such a desperate tug on my soul. This isn't like any eager spirit I've encountered before. Something is off.

Caleb hurries after me. "Sky, wait—"

"I have to go in," I say, transfixed.

Groaning, he grabs my elbow, stopping me from opening the door. "You're not going in first," he orders, locking our eyes. "Get behind me."

I'm too mesmerized by the mysterious pull to properly process Caleb's sweet protectiveness.

Wordlessly, I allow him to shift ahead of me. Flashlights at the ready, I suck in a breath as he hesitantly pulls the cabin door open. I frown, peering around his large frame.

It's empty.

"I could've sworn," I whisper to myself, completely bewildered. The chill still tickles my skin. I must be missing something.

The small room is lined with shelves of bins filled with dusty crafting materials like bandanas, beads, twine, and paint. When we were younger and the days felt impossibly long, Amelie and I used to sneak in here to make friendship bracelets.

Nothing appears to be out of order. I'm not sure why that disappoints me so much. The less contact with this creep, the better. But it does little to ease my spiraling thoughts. I need answers. Something that'll make any part of this—the pictures, the shadows—make sense. And why can't I shake the feeling that something in here *is* out of sorts? What am I missing?

"Skyler?" I hear Caleb say. He's by the far wall, inspecting sagging shelves of supplies. He pulls a beige shoebox from the shelf, and I immediately realize why it's out of place. It's the only container not held together by tape. No one would realize it was wrong, unless they'd spent their childhood sneaking in here. "It's kinda heavy."

Caleb waits until I join him at the center of the room to pull the lid off.

We gasp as the box falls to the floor between us. My eyes squeeze shut, but nothing will ever scrub the image from my brain.

"What the hell," he gags.

"Is this real?"

Daring a peek back into the box, I'm repulsed at the sight of a heart. The decayed organ is purple and gray, and I'm forced to fight with my stomach to keep a hold of its contents.

With a shaking hand, I reach for the folded paper tucked against the side of the box.

Clipped magazine letters are pasted onto the foxglove stationary to form five words that make my head spin.

MY hEaRt is
YouRs, SKYlER

8

"WHERE THE HELL WERE YOU TWO?" Amelie demands when Caleb and I approach everyone waiting on the back deck.

We returned empty-handed because the last thing we were going to do is lug a literal human heart up to the house, so we left it and the note back in the craft shed. That freak can take the organ back if they want. The message was received loud and clear.

Soon, my love. The message wasn't for Lacy. It was for me.

My heart is yours, Skyler. But whose heart?

Despite being the biggest lovesick fool I know, my romantic prospects have never been anything to boast about. In sixth grade, while in one of my classmate's basements to celebrate a cast party for the fall musical, a boy named Oliver asked to kiss me goodnight. For a full year, I didn't shut up about that little peck on the lips, even if whenever I retold the romantic tale, I pointedly left out the fact that we never spoke again.

It wasn't until freshman year of high school that someone else displayed any outward affections for me. A boy from my biology class named Spencer. He asked me to go watch some quirky indie film at the local cinema. I thought the whole ordeal was tremendously romantic up until the moment the movie started and he gently put his arm over my shoulder. I'd dreamed of that moment all my life. Cuddling during a cute movie date. Yet here it was, finally happening to me, and I felt nothing. That's when I realized just how in-deep I was for Caleb, because all I could think about was having his arm draped around me instead. Everyone else paled in comparison to him. They always had, and if I didn't get over my dangerous crush, they always would.

I highly doubt that either Oliver or Spencer is secretly harboring any lingering feelings for me. Certainly nothing so intense that would lead them to trespass onto private property, dig up a dead body, and leave a heart for me to find.

No—we're dealing with someone entirely new.

A secret admirer.

But who?

My heart lurches at the thought. I've always longed for someone to adore me from afar, but not like this. There is *nothing* romantic about this.

They must be a stranger. No one I know is this sick and twisted.

"We were on the other side of the lake. Took us a while to trek back." Caleb's explanation comes so easy—like we didn't just witness the most gruesome, hand-delivered threat of our lives.

Caleb may hide it well, but I know he's internally panicking. Back in the woods, when I couldn't give him any leads on who could love me so violently, his face hardened with fury. He didn't have to say it aloud, but I knew he wasn't going to allow whoever was behind this to get away with it. That truth is the only thing keeping me from running away screaming right now.

The excuse isn't good enough for Zane. "And why did the rest of us have to stay at the lodge?"

"I was the lead tagger!" Phoebe's arms cross. "You don't always have to take charge."

Maybe they do need a little dose of fear. Anything to keep them from making unsafe decisions. So, I say, "I thought I saw someone in the woods."

"Again?" Amelie asks, her eyes cutting to the dark trees.

Caleb and I agreed we'd share this with the others. Hopefully, it's enough to keep them out of the woods until Samuel's team can set up more cameras around Old Camp. Caleb already called the head of security and insisted it happen as soon as possible. When Samuel demanded to know why, Caleb promised to call him back and explain everything once I was safe in the lodge.

"You think it was the same person from before?" Mateo asks me, his forehead creased with concern. His response is touching. We just met, and yet, it's so easy for him to care.

I nod. "They were taking my picture."

This earns a unified gasp from the others.

Amelie whispers, "Are you serious?"

Because they were not present to witness the undeveloped photograph in Lacy's grave, Mateo, Diego, and Phoebe don't know the full extent as to why this revelation is truly terrifying, but they've been in this world long enough to understand that a stranger taking photos is never a good thing.

"That's messed up," Diego mutters, crossing his arms with disgust.

Mateo agrees, his face hardened with anger. "You don't deserve this."

"We should get inside," Amelie says, already hurrying up the wooden stairs. She turns back to me and holds out her hand. I immediately leave Caleb's side to take it.

She's right. Lingering out here is the last thing we should be doing.

"Why can't people just leave us alone?" Cricket whines as she and Phoebe follow us.

"They'll never leave us alone," Amelie mutters under her breath. "Not ever."

It's the cruel reality of being a Quinn. As long as their mother's legacy stands, there will always be people drawn to it. For better or for worse. Like moths to a flame, power will forever attract the public.

That's why the lake house has always been so special. It's the one place the Quinns can act like real kids. Fool around in the outdoors, safely tucked away from judgmental eyes. Until now.

The safety of this retreat shattered, we solemnly retire into our separate bedrooms. Before heading off into her own, Amelie pulls me into a tight hug.

"I'm so sorry," she murmurs, squeezing me closer. "People shouldn't be following you in the woods because of me. If you want to go home—"

"No," I insist. "I'm not letting some stalker steal our summer from us."

I mean it, too. Our time together is too precious. No one is tarnishing this place for us.

Besides, Amelie has no idea this stalker isn't tormenting me because of my association with the Quinn family. At least, I don't think they are. This feels personal.

My heart is yours, Skyler.

That night, it takes ages to fall asleep. Every time I close my eyes, white-hot flashes from a camera startle them open. Tossing to my side, a pale-blue light has me sucking in a surprised breath.

Jerking upright, I stare into the hauntingly alert eyes of the girl with stringy-white hair. She's wearing the same attire as before: a loose-hanging sundress with lace trim, which appears to be muddied at the hem.

Lacy?

As if reading my mind, the girl's head cocks to the side in a way that confirms my worst nightmare.

That's when I realize there's a hole where her heart should be.

I suck in a horrified breath.

What kind of dream is this? In the past, the lifelike visions I see are never real-life people, but projections from my worst imagination. Faceless monsters, crawly insects, or ambiguous shadows.

But I'm confident this is Lacy, or at least, what she looked like when she was alive.

As soon as I begin doubting her to be a night terror, a familiar chill dances down my limbs, confirming everything I need to know.

This is real.

The lake house *is* haunted, and after all these years, Lacy Monroe is in my bedroom. As I accept that truth, the blue mist glowing around her intensifies as she takes the form of the other spirits I've encountered. A wayward soul not of this world, but not of the next, either. The edges of her figure seem to pull away from her, before pushing back into place. Like she's trying her best to pass on, but something is stopping her from doing so.

No wonder her expression is marred with agony. She's trapped here.

"What do you need?" I hear myself whisper.

Lacy stares blankly at me, as if the answer is obvious.

"Please," I moan. "Why is this happening, Lacy?"

At the sound of her name, the girl's face twists with rage, her colorless lips widening into a silent scream. She takes a furious step toward me. And then another.

That's when I start screaming, too, only mine echoes throughout the room. I scream and scream, pleading with myself to wake up, but it doesn't work, because this isn't a dream. Lacy continues to draw nearer as my throat grows raw.

Someone in the hall bellows my name, causing my scream to get lodged in my throat.

My eyes snap to the door and back to the space where Lacy once stood, but she's gone now. Disappeared like the flash of a camera.

Gasping for breath, I attempt to collect myself as I return to reality. Still, even as my eyes desperately search the room for anything out of the ordinary, my fears aren't quelled in the slightest. No matter how hard I try, I can't convince myself who I saw wasn't real.

That was Lacy, not a vision from my imagination. She's here and she's furious.

The caller bellows my name again, more frantic this time.

My entire being protests as I abandon the safety of my bed, but the promise of help has me hurrying across the room. Maybe Caleb has come to comfort me.

Yanking open the door, I startle as I come face-to-face with the last person I expect to see.

9

My head jerks back at the sight of Mateo. I never anticipated he would come rushing to my aid. I mean, he barely knows me.

But he came. My heart pounds at the implication.

His dark eyes are wide as they rake over me. "Are you okay? I heard screaming."

I swallow hard, immediately feeling guilty for waking him up. But only a little. "Yes, sorry, just a bad dream."

But that doesn't send him away.

"Mind if I come in?"

I'm a different kind of awake now. His sincere expression has me opening my door enough for him to slip inside. My eyes widen when he settles himself upon my bed. He pats the spot next to him, inviting me to sit like it's not the very bed I've spent countless summers in.

Once I'm beside him, he says, "Not that it's a competition, because I'm sure your bad dream really sucked, but I have a literal sleep paralysis demon messing with mine."

This morbidly piques my interest. "Do you now?"

He dips his chin. "True story. Ever since I was ten."

"What do they look like?"

His eyes cut to me as a grin plays at the corners of his lips. "Promise you won't laugh?"

I nod.

"An old-timey scuba diver."

I fight from smiling. "Is that so?"

"Hey!" His mouth drops open with offense. "You promised!"

"Do they wear one of those fish tank helmets?"

"It's not funny, Skyler."

"But do they?"

Mateo groans, throwing his head back against the headboard. "Unfortunately."

"Damn, that's rough." I breathe out a laugh. "If it makes you feel better, I see ghosts."

The confession slips out so easily that I take both of us by surprise.

My eyes as wide as his, I clear my throat uncomfortably. "Not that it's a competition or anything."

What is wrong with me? I've only ever told the Quinns my family secret, and yet, I reveal it to someone who is practically a stranger?

Mateo absorbs this information with a slow nod of his head. "Well, if it were a competition, I guess we'd be tied."

My lips part with surprise. "You—"

"See them, too?" he finishes for me. "Yeah. Bit of a newer development for me, isn't that fun?"

Like I'm seeing him for the first time, I gape at him with shock before stammering dumbly. "How—"

"How did I start seeing dead people?" He winces playfully. "Kind of a personal question, don't you think?"

As soon as I start apologizing, he interjects with a warm smile. "I'm just playing with you. I had a near-death experience, and I guess something like that will open your eyes to the things you didn't see before."

I blink at him with wonder. Other than my mother, I

haven't met another person with the sight. It's likely there are many of us out there, but a majority are too afraid to believe what they see, and therefore, do not make themselves known.

It's tempting to pry about this "near-death experience", but I suspect he would've provided more details if he wanted me to know. Instead, I say, "My mother had a brush with death when she was a teenager, too. It must be hereditary because I inherited my sight from her."

Like Mateo, my mother preferred to remain aloof when detailing the event that had her greeting the Grim Reaper. "All that matters is I survived. Without fate's intervention, you wouldn't have been born," she'd say to silence my nosy questions.

I used to suspect Mom's dance with death froze her heart, but now that I'm in the presence of someone as kind as Mateo, I realize the woman was just born that way.

The boy cocks his head to the side. "Lucky you."

We stare at each other a long time, both of us measuring up the other. I'm inclined to believe him. I mean, why lie about such a thing? However, that doesn't stop me from asking, "Since you've been here, have you felt anything?"

"Yes," he responds immediately. "From the moment I arrived, I felt this tug on my soul. It's like there's a thick, icy rope tied around my being, and whoever is pulling on it can't be ignored. I was already halfway to your room before you started screaming."

Now I know, without a shadow of a doubt, he's telling the truth. Mateo sees the world like me, and by proxy, he sees me. A warming sensation swells over my body, and it takes me a moment to pinpoint it as comfort. "I feel it, too. It started the night before you arrived."

Hearing the fear in my voice, Mateo's brow furrows. "Let me guess—you haven't felt anything in years past?"

I nod.

His lips purse as he considers this, before asking, "What do you think that means?"

"I don't know yet," I whisper, and that's the truth.

I'm confident the pull is due to the disturbance of Lacy's grave, but it's clear something far more sinister is afoot. I'm not sure I want to divulge the terrifying details right now. If I do, I may never fall back asleep tonight, or ever again for that matter. When I say as much to Mateo, he ponders me intensely. The concern etched on his face makes my stomach tingle nervously.

"I don't know anything about walking among the afterlife," I hear myself confess, my voice low with shame. "My mom doesn't like keeping paranormal company; she doesn't want to understand more about how we might be able to help them. So, I'm just stuck here. Seeing things I can't do anything about."

Mateo ponders me curiously. "But you want to know more?"

I nod earnestly. "They don't deserve to be abandoned by someone who can finally see them."

"Well," he admits with a modest shrug, "I'm no pro, but I've picked up a thing or two since I started seeing the other side."

I eagerly shift myself to face him, ready to absorb whatever knowledge he has to impart.

He grins at my enthusiasm, maneuvering himself to face me, too.

"Where to start?" His eyes dance over my face. "You already know the sight is usually hereditary. Your mother's brush with death started a new line of seers."

"I'll make sure my children are better equipped," I interject.

"I don't doubt it." Another warm smile graces his face. "Oh, I bet you didn't know this. Apparently, the dead haunt their killers."

I shiver at the thought before nodding with understanding. "Good for them."

Mateo laughs under his breath at my reaction. "Normally, I'd think a murderer would be undeserving of our gift, but it seems only fair that their victim gets to mess with them from beyond."

"What about helping a spirit pass on?" I finally inquire, unable to wait any longer.

He nods like he expected me to ask. "To assist a spirit with passing on, you need to help them find peace. Some are trickier than others, but nothing soothes the soul like freeing another."

"Have you ever done it?"

"Not yet, but I've met enough experts to know what to do when the situation presents itself."

"Maybe one day," I wonder aloud before I can think better of it, "you and I can help someone pass on together."

Mateo's firm gaze bores into mine. "I'd love that."

My insides flutter shamelessly. Before I can help myself, an entire future with Mateo paints itself in my mind. One where we have a mobile home full of adorable, sight-gifted children. As a family, we'll drive in a van across the country, helping the restless find peace.

As if imagining the very same future, Mateo gently nudges me with his knee. "I have to ask. What's up with you and Caleb?"

"What do you mean?"

"Well, Caleb seems to think you've had a crush on him for forever." Seeing my face fall, Mateo hastily adds, "But that's kind of Caleb's thing. I love the guy, but he thinks everyone orbits around him. I guess it's the byproduct of being a Quinn."

So, this is what Caleb says about me. I'm nothing but a pathetic girl he puts up with every summer. Likely one of the many to have feelings for him.

Hoping my next words make it back to Caleb, I pointedly say, "I used to have feelings for him."

Mateo raises his dark eyebrows. "You don't anymore?"

"Definitely not," I assert. "Actually, I'm actively doing everything I can to move on. Unrequited crushes are excruciating. I'm ready to get him out of my mind."

Maybe with you, I finish internally. I want to move on with a boy who comes running for me.

Working up the courage to return my gaze to Mateo, I find his deep-brown eyes studying me in a way that makes me wonder if he heard that last part aloud.

Carefully, he brushes a loose strand of hair behind my ear, causing a new kind of chill to dance down my spine. His eyes widen at the contact, like he can't believe this is happening.

I cannot believe it either. For the first time in my life, my silly love-at-first-sight crush is reciprocated. It's another kind of sight we share.

Mateo inches closer as he whispers, "I can help with that, too, if you want."

A flurry of butterflies flutter through my body when I catch his gaze darting to my lips before returning to my eyes. I raise my chin, making my intentions equally as clear.

"I'm glad it was you who came to my rescue tonight." With every word, I draw nearer, until our faces are nearly touching.

"Me too, Skyler Pierce."

And then his lips are pressed gently against mine. Careful and respectful. He waits for me to push closer before his hand rises to cradle my cheek.

All at once, I'm swarmed with the glorious scent of cool spearmint, maple trees, and a musk that simply can be described as Mateo.

Mateo.

Mateo.

My heart sings his name with every brush of his lips.

"Are you still thinking about him?"

"Who?" I respond breathlessly before squashing Mateo's laugh with a deeper kiss.

I've never kissed a boy like this. Content and slow, like we have all the time in the world. I may never walk out into the sun again so long as this never ends.

"Do you think you can fall asleep without bad dreams now?" He murmurs against my lips, and when I happily nod, he rises from my bed. Spying the disappointed expression on my face, he laughs again. "We have all summer, Skyler. Let's take our time."

He's right. Some wanting spells aren't meant to be broken right away.

"We're going to make this summer something to remember," he promises, heading for my door. "The bad dreams stop now."

I open it, resting my head against the side as he departs. "You think?"

Mateo offers me one final smile. "I know."

He doesn't, but I'm too lost in my bliss to care.

That's how he leaves me, with a whole colony of butterflies darting around my stomach. I think that's exactly what he intended. To leave me wanting more.

And it worked.

For once, Caleb is far from my thoughts as I drift off to sleep. When I do finally let go, I don't dream of Lacy, empty graves, or camera flashes. I dream of Mateo and it's the best night of sleep I've had in years.

10

The following morning, Amelie opens my door without knocking.

"What the hell is this?" she demands.

I'm perched on the edge of my bed, tying the laces of my sneakers. "What's what?"

She holds up the last thing I expect to see. A folded piece of stationary. Tan parchment with foxglove flowers.

My breath hitches, any ounce of euphoria from the night prior evaporating into the ether. "Another one?"

Amelie uses the tips of her fingers to hold it out for me to take, like it's poisonous to touch. I unfold it, already bracing for the photograph waiting on the inside.

It's the same type of film as before. White borders rim an out-of-focus image. I shouldn't be surprised when I see myself. I know someone took my picture last night in the woods. What I didn't expect was how terrified I'd appear. Like a deer in headlights, staring directly into the light, completely frozen in place. But there I am, completely lost in the dark forest, trying to find a face behind the flash. Words composed of cutout letters are pasted onto the stationary.

63

A Love for a Love. Pick Wisely.

My stomach clenches as I reread it again and again. What does it mean? A love for a love? Like an eye for an eye? And what am I picking wisely? Familiarity with the phrase tugs at the back of my mind, but I cannot seem to place where from.

Mateo and Caleb enter my mind, but only briefly. They don't fit into this puzzle because I'm not picking between them. How can I be when one of them has made it abundantly clear they aren't an option? Caleb has never been on the table. Not that I want him to be anymore after the night I shared with Mateo.

So then what does this sender want me to pick wisely? Them? But who are they? Judging by Amelie's perplexed expression, she hasn't a clue, either.

"Where did you find this?" My voice is barely louder than a whisper.

Her petrified gaze meets mine. "On the floor outside your door."

My mouth grows dry. "They were inside the house."

Fear courses through my body. How could they get so close without anyone noticing? This monster is keeping their distance, but for how long? What happens when they decide notes are not enough and they want to converse face-to-face?

"I know," Amelie responds darkly.

"We need to tell Samuel."

"Like that'll help," she mutters, taking me by surprise. Amelie never talks poorly of the people who work for her family, least of all the ones keeping them safe. "Shouldn't his team be stopping this freak from coming inside in the first place?"

I don't want to throw Samuel under the bus, but I can't help but agree. A real person left this at my door, not some midnight spirit messing with my sleep schedule. At any moment, they could've twisted the knob and gotten to me. Something is keeping them at bay, but I'm not betting my life on whatever it is lasting forever.

"Do you have a secret boyfriend I don't know about?" Amelie asks with a frown, rereading the note. "Or two?"

"No," I sputter, holding up the ominous letter. "You think I'd date a guy like this? Someone so unhinged they'd break into your house and dig up a body?"

Amelie sniffs. "Obviously not, but you've been moping around ever since you got here, and I wondered if that was because you just broke up with some weirdo."

I force myself to remain patient. She wouldn't be saying this if she knew everything, so I guess it's time to clue her in.

"There's something I have to show you," I mumble, turning to dig into the bottom of my drawer for the first photograph.

As soon as Amelie lays eyes on it, she gasps. "Is this the picture from—"

"Lacy's coffin?" I finish. "Yeah..."

"When did it develop?"

"Later that night."

"How do you even—"

"Caleb kept it. As soon as he saw the image, he shared it with me."

Her eyes cut to me accusingly. "Why didn't you say anything before?"

"We didn't want to scare you."

She can't argue with this and we both know it. Nothing upsets Amelie more than someone evading her family's security. Her mother has received far too many death threats for her not to be.

So, instead, she asks, "You and my brother are a 'we' now?"

I scoff. "You and I both know he doesn't like me like that. He's just looking out for me. Come on, you don't think I'd inform you the second something happened?"

Her glossy lips purse. "I just don't want him toying with you."

"He's not," I insist. "Trust me. Nothing is happening between us."

She studies me for a long moment before offering me a pitying shake of her head. "Well, if something does happen, try and finish whatever you're doing with my brother before you come running to tell me, okay?"

I release a shaky laugh. "Deal."

I'm tempted to tell her about my midnight rendezvous with Mateo but decide to keep the news to myself for a while longer. Being boy-crazy is what ruined my chances with Caleb. I don't want to blab anything prematurely and spoil everything.

We return our attention to the photographs in our hands, and the gravity of the situation brings us back to reality. It's strange that both are pictures of me and not her. Yet another mystery I can't make sense of.

"It's a good thing my girlfriend doesn't have cell service right now. If Camila knew everything going on around here, she'd judge the hell out of us for staying," Amelie says wryly, chewing on her bottom lip.

I don't know what to say to this. The last thing I want to do is leave. If I'm not here, I'm spending the summer at home alone. Sure, I have some friends from school I could meet up with, but they don't get me like the Quinns. To them, the world is mundane. We're not even adults and they've already settled into the lives they plan to live forever.

Always reading my mind, Amelie takes the photograph from my hand and shoves both back into the bottom of my drawer. "Screw this. We're not letting some creep ruin our summer. Caleb has Samuel on it?"

"Yeah."

"Good. This is the last second we're wasting on that freak. They've stolen too much of our energy already."

With that, she grabs my hand and pulls me downstairs. This is what I'll always appreciate about Amelie. She's spectacular at acting like everything is normal, which is exactly what I need.

However, I don't get to pretend everything is fine for long, because shortly after breakfast, Caleb comes jogging in with Mateo. It appears the boys arose early for a morning workout. Although, neither of them seems to be huffing and puffing too strenuously. Mateo doesn't even look like he's broken a sweat when he grins at me.

"Good morning, ladies," he says, not taking his eyes off me.

"Morning," I chirp back, fighting off a revealing smirk of my own. I'm glad we're on the same page of keeping our blossoming feelings to ourselves for a while longer. It's exhilarating to share a secret of our own. "Where'd ya run?"

"Twice around the lake," Caleb answers, earning an amused expression from his friend.

"That explains the smell." Amelie's nose wrinkles. "Next time, try jumping in the lake before coming inside."

Caleb ignores his sister as he directs his attention toward me. It doesn't make my heart beat uncontrollably, which is a startling realization. The tender butterflies from last night are still floating inside me.

"Samuel wants to speak with us."

I should've seen this coming. Samuel Rivers is tasked with keeping the Quinn kids safe—a role he takes unbelievably seriously, especially when Ms. Quinn isn't around.

"You two are going off again?" Amelie fidgets with the

pool towel hanging over her shoulder. "We were going to sunbathe."

"I'm going to freshen up," Mateo excuses himself, but not before shooting an apologetic look in my direction. Even as a newbie to the lake house, he must sense the argument brewing between the siblings. It's a shame he can't whisk me away, too.

Caleb says to his sister, "Samuel needs Skyler to go over some details from last night."

"I'll meet you on the pool deck as soon as we're done," I promise my friend, feeling bad for ditching her.

"Make sure you tell Sam about this morning's note," she remarks, watching as her brother's face twists with confusion.

"What note?" Caleb demands.

As I fill him in on the latest letter left outside my door, Caleb's expression grows more and more concerned.

"Why didn't you come to me with this immediately?"

"Please," Amelie chastises her brother. "She doesn't have to tell you anything if she doesn't want to."

"But I'm the one helping her!"

"So am I!" Amelie snips back.

"I just haven't had the chance to speak with you in private yet," I placate Caleb before blinking between the two of them. The Quinn siblings love to bicker, but they should know this is absolutely not the time or place.

"Don't let Samuel interrogate you for too long. We agreed to not let this freak ruin our summer and I'm holding us to that," Amelie says with a pointed look at her brother before heading off to the pool.

"It shouldn't be too long, right?" I ask Caleb.

He frowns. "We can take as long as you want."

Those words ring in my mind as we drive a golf cart to the security hut at the front of the property. Why did he have to say it like that? Like he wants us to linger. I'm starting to wonder if Caleb has a sixth sense for whenever I'm pulling away. But he has no reason to reel me back in.

Even this early in the morning, I can already tell today is going to be a scorcher. Perspiration plays at my hairline, making me want to get back to the pool as soon as possible.

The security hub is located in a small office near the front gate. Parking the golf cart outside, I blink at Caleb when he doesn't immediately hop out.

"Is everything okay?"

His eyebrows raise.

I hastily tack on, "Other than all the scary stuff going on?"

"I just want to get on the same page here."

It's my turn to frown. "About what?"

"I didn't tell Samuel everything last night. Do you want him to know about the photographs, because as soon as he does, Ms. Sue is coming to pick you up."

"Not if he catches this freak before she can," I respond optimistically, earning a wary expression from Caleb. "Samuel needs to know everything to keep us safe."

"Whatever you want to do, Sky," he finally says. "I just really hope you don't have to leave."

Mateo flashes in my mind. "I don't either."

The inside of the hut is filled with televisions displaying various angles of the property. In a matter of days—maybe hours—the feeds will multiply. Soon, every inch of this place will be monitored. It sucks, but even I know it's a necessary precaution for the time being.

Three guards don't look up from their computers as Caleb and I walk through the space, beelining for Samuel's office in the back. Caleb raps on the door twice, not waiting before he pushes it open.

"Morning, Sam."

Samuel is a muscular man with hair that's graying far too early for his age. He looks like he hasn't slept in twenty years, which is coincidentally how long he's worked for the Quinns. No one takes their job more seriously than Samuel. To him, the Quinns are family, and by association, so am I.

"Hey, kids. I'm sorry to interrupt your morning. Thanks for coming in." Samuel gestures for us to take a seat across from his desk, which houses a bunch of papers and the latest TeQ monitor. There's not much else in the space other than half a dozen filing cabinets and some framed pictures of his dog—a rescued pit bull named Willow.

I already anticipate getting straight into it. Samuel is not the kind of man to make small talk about the weather.

"Sky, hun, can you elaborate on the person you saw in the woods?"

"Which time?"

The man clicks his tongue. "Both."

I recount everything about the figure with a camera. Where we were, the color of the camera flash, and how many times I think they took my picture. Samuel takes diligent notes on a yellow legal pad while asking countless follow-up questions. With each response, the creases in his brow deepen, and I get the sense my nondescript answers aren't satisfactory. But what am I supposed to say? It's not like my stalker walked up and shook my hand. I don't know what's going on here.

Eventually, Samuel leans back in his seat, taking a long sip from his *World's Best Boss* mug. "It's not a lot to work with, kids."

"We know," Caleb says. "That's why we're hoping the additional camera feeds will catch them. Maybe we can bring on some extra guards to patrol the perimeter."

"There's also more," I interject, ignoring the stoic expression on Caleb's face.

Samuel grows more and more flustered as I explain the strange notes and pictures. Meanwhile, Caleb is busy fidgeting with a worn piece of bandana tied around his wrist.

"Where'd you find these letters? And where are they now?"

"This morning's was left outside my bedroom door, which is where I've kept them stashed."

The man sucks in a breath, realizing our perpetrator has breached the house.

"Then there was one in the craft cabin at Old Camp. It was hidden in a box alongside a heart."

"Excuse me?"

"A real heart," I confirm.

Samuel immediately picks up his radio and sends a team to comb through the craft cabin.

"The first," I say, feeling Caleb's eyes cut to me, "was at Lacy Monroe's grave."

Samuel chokes on his coffee. "You're not supposed to be near there," he reprimands me between coughs. "When was this?"

"We went on a walk they day we all arrived," Caleb cuts in, trying to rein me back in before I confess to our midnight ritual at the burial site, "and didn't realize how far we'd gotten, but I guess it's a good thing because we wouldn't have found the note otherwise."

The pair share a look. Caleb's face conveys innocence, while Samuel's is beet-red.

"You kids need to stay away from Lacy Monroe's grave." Something about the severity in Samuel's voice has the back of my neck prickling. "We have a deal with her father to keep it protected."

"Protect it?" I scoff under my breath. "Her body is missing."

The man sets me with such a stern expression that I cower in my seat. Meanwhile, Caleb is also shooting me daggers for admitting we're aware of Lacy's disappearance. Until now, no one suspected us kids knew a thing about the empty grave. Security has yet to mention a word about it to us.

"Exactly," Samuel says curtly. "So stay away. I've got more than enough problems to work through without you kids loitering around my other crime scene."

I'm so shocked by his reaction that I find myself nodding

despite understanding nothing. Who cares if we were near the grave? Someone is stalking me!

Samuel's face twists with hurt and frustration. I hadn't realized I said that last part aloud.

"Of course that's my main concern, kid," he groans. "And I am gonna catch this freak taunting you, but it would be a lot easier to keep you safe if you obeyed the house rules. If this admirer is also our grave digger, we don't want you anywhere near it."

"Understood." I tuck a strand of hair behind my ears as I lie, because I don't understand. Nothing about this conversation—or for that matter, this entire morning—is unfolding in any sort of understandable fashion.

"Can you think of anyone who might be targeting you, Skyler? Disgruntled ex-boyfriend? Someone you talk to online?"

Now, it's my cheeks that are burning. This is the last conversation I want to have in front of Caleb.

"I've never had a boyfriend," I mumble. "And my mom's really strict about what I do online, so I'm not DMing anyone. I don't even post all that much."

"Maybe boyfriend is too serious of a label for you kids. But what about dates to school dances? Anyone you thought was flirting with you?"

Sinking further into my chair, I worry I might die of humiliation before this freaky secret admirer can get to me. Giving Samuel the embarrassingly brief overview of my nonexistent love life, I don't dare glance in Caleb's direction. Mercifully, I don't feel his eyes on me. Still, his tense posture tells me he is enjoying this conversation about as much as me. He grows more agitated and uncomfortable with every passing minute.

As I reach the end of my short list of suitors, I wonder if now is when I confess to kissing Mateo last night. But this is not how I want Caleb to find out I spent the previous night making out with his friend, so I keep that detail to myself. It won't help Samuel, anyways.

The head of security writes down all the relevant names, promising to look into each of them. I mentally apologize to Oliver and Spencer.

"I really don't think any of them would ever break into the lodge to scare me."

"Let's not make any assumptions just yet. People are prone to making terrible decisions when in love. You might not think about any one of these boys, but we cannot guarantee that neither of them still thinks about you.

"However," he continues, "there's a very good chance this is someone obsessed with the Quinns who sees you as an effective target to capture their attention."

Caleb lifts his head. "If that's the case, we won't give this freak the satisfaction of thinking they've succeeded."

"Never," Samuel asserts while rifling for something in his desk. "One more question. Have you ever seen this boy before, Skyler?"

He holds up a security-feed picture of the copper-haired boy with the ear piercing. My brow furrows at his acne-ridden complexion and bushy eyebrows.

"I mean, I guess I saw him here when I first arrived at the lake house."

"But you don't know him otherwise?"

"No? Should I?"

"This boy is named Logan Lewis, and he's a grade below you at Casper High School."

I frown at the picture again. "I don't think I've ever seen that boy in my life."

"Casper High has a student population of 800." It's not a question, but Samuel intends for it to be one.

"I guess I don't really pay attention to the boys at my school," I admit as my cheeks grow pink. *I've been preoccupied obsessing over a boy who doesn't want me back.*

Or at least, I don't think he wants me back.

"Logan Lewis attempted to make a delivery directly to the front door of the lodge. Obviously, that is a breach of security, so we pulled him in for some questioning."

"What was he trying to deliver?"

"Groceries for Mackenzie."

I immediately feel dumb for assuming it would be something nefarious, like a box of poisoned chocolates. Or a heart.

"It seemed to be an innocent mistake on the boy's part, so we let him go." Samuel stuffs the photograph back into his desk. "He's likely not our suspect, but I wanted to be sure you didn't know him."

"Okay," I mumble, feeling anything but. It's clear Samuel has no viable leads, which means there's little to no chance this situation is solved before sundown.

"I'm gonna get to the bottom of this, okay? I don't like how close this weirdo has gotten. I need to get with my team, because clearly, our current protocols are not satisfactory. But I'd appreciate it if you stayed close to the house in the meantime. Can you do that for me?"

"We can," Caleb answers for us, the two words clipped.

After saying he will send one of his guards up to the house to collect my notes and pictures, Samuel dismisses us from the office. I leave not feeling any better than when I walked in.

"You really opened up in there," Caleb grumbles as soon as we climb back into his golf cart. He doesn't turn the key in the ignition, angrily swinging the lanyard instead. "You know we don't talk about visiting Lacy."

"Are you upset with *me*?"

Caleb's nostrils flare. His frustration catches me off-guard. What did I do wrong here?

"Come on," I snap, not afraid to push back. The last thing I'm in the mood for is to be on the receiving end of Caleb's newfound bad attitude. "Since when is keeping the secret of our annual ritual at an off-limits grave more important than informing Samuel of every last detail? He can't keep me safe and alive if we're hiding things from him!"

Caleb frustratedly rakes his fingers through his hair. "It's not more important but—"

"And did you hear how suspicious Samuel sounded? He about popped a vessel when I brought up Lacy, when moments prior, I told him someone broke into the house! What's up with his priorities?"

"How can you turn on him so fast? Of all the people around here, I thought you'd be the last to judge a member of the staff."

My cheeks burn. I know he doesn't mean it to be an insult, but that doesn't stop my insides from twisting with a mixture of hurt and shame. Caleb has no right to control how I react to a scary situation. But am I just as wrong for distrusting Samuel's reaction?

Before I can weed through my emotions, Samuel comes sprinting out of the building, followed by everyone else working inside.

"What's going on?" Caleb calls, but they're too busy jumping into golf carts to answer.

Samuel's screaming into his radio. "Spread out! Start at the edge of the perimeter and work your way in. She's fourteen, about 5'4" with purple hair. Answers to Phoebe Tanner."

I cry, "What happened to Phoebe?"

But Samuel and the other guards are already taking off in opposite directions.

Caleb frantically fumbles with his keys, but when I jump out, he screams, "Where are you going?"

"I'll only be a minute!" I sprint back inside the security office. This may be my one chance to comb through Samuel's office for any information about Lacy Monroe.

Caleb groans as he chases after me. "Have you lost your mind?"

"Shut up and help me look so we can go!"

I want to see what's happened to Phoebe as fast as possible, but this might be our one chance to enter the office unsupervised.

The phone in Samuel's office is dangling from the receiver on the desk, filling the space with the faint beeping of a dial tone. I head for the first filing cabinet and yank it open. The drawer is heavy and completely filled with carefully organized files of papers.

"What are we even looking for?"

"Anything to do with Lacy Monroe," I say, my fingers dancing over the labeled tabs for each file. There's a thick file for every summer. Leafing through some pages, I realize they're a log of every threat made to the family while they're at the lake house. Each incident comes with a dozen pages of background on the suspect, police reports, and restraining orders. There are too many to count. Any one of these people could be behind this.

Feeling overwhelmed by the number of people who hate the Quinn family, I head for the next filing cabinet, which is labeled as "Guests".

My lips pinch when I realize there's a file for everyone. As tempting as it might be to take a peek, I ignore mine in favor of withdrawing Robert Monroe's.

The thin file doesn't fill me with optimism, but I flip it open nonetheless. On the inside is a photograph of Robert, a weathered old man with blotchy skin and white hair. A wiry beard covers most of his jaw. Beside it, there's the contact information for a nursing home. No wonder he hasn't visited the last few years. The next page details when Robert may visit the grave and that he may only do so while supervised by a member of the security team. Under no circumstances is Robert allowed to enter the lodge.

Under this, a note has been scrawled in red ink.

Per the boss, Miriam Davis may not accompany Robert on site.

Miriam Davis?

I recognize that name as someone who lives back in Casper. She owns a unique shop in town that sells all sorts of oddities, like tarot cards, crystals, and palm readings. Mom never let us walk in there, claiming Miriam was selling people a mystical dream that's actually a nightmare.

But what does Miriam Davis have to do with Robert Monroe? Unless...

Could she be the famed mistress? After all these years, her identity's been sitting in this file?

"Oh shit," Caleb breathes out and I'm at his side in an instant.

From the back of his filing cabinet, he pulls out a photograph. The image has faded, but it's still clear enough to see the group of seven teenagers smiling at the camera. They're all dressed in high-waisted shorts and grimy tanks that say "Camp Casper." A guy in front holds a wooden plank painted with the words "CC Counselors."

I squint at this boy for a moment before it dawns on me. "That's Samuel." The smile looks unfamiliar on his face, but the closer I look at him, the surer I become. The shape of his face is the same, as are those brown eyes. My suspicions are confirmed when I squint at the bandana tied around his bicep, which has "SAM" written on it in black marker.

Caleb points to another figure in the top left corner. She has sharp blue eyes, a confident smile, and raven hair. I don't need the bandana around her forehead to recognize this woman. I'd know Ms. Quinn anywhere.

"My mom was a counselor at Camp Casper with Samuel?" Caleb breathes out. "She never told us that."

But I can't focus on the image of a young Gianna Quinn because I'm too distracted by who she has her arms around.

This girl has sunken eyes and stringy white hair that hangs to her waist. My pulse quickens as I study her face. The very same face that's been haunting my dreams. Except, no longer is she a figment of my imagination. I've had night terrors for as long as I can remember, but never have they appeared when I was awake. Not until now.

Last night, I thought I was making a silly leap by assuming the figure was Lacy's ghost, but now I'm more certain than ever.

Frantically, I search the figure for a name, squinting when I see the bandana tied around her belt loop. She was a counselor at her parents' camp. The confirmation sends a chill down my spine.

Then a new face draws my attention—this one more startling than Lacy, Gianna, or Samuel. But now that I've spotted her, I'm not sure how she wasn't the first face I noticed. It's a face I'd recognize anywhere because it's been frowning at me my entire life.

The face of my mother.

11

WE CAREEN through the forest as fast as the golf cart will take us.

"Our mothers have known each other for years and never let on," I utter in disbelief. "Since they were practically our age."

Caleb appears to have forgotten his previous frustration in the security hub, replacing it with pure disbelief at our most recent revelation. There's something else, too. An emotion that I can't identify, bubbling below the surface. Is it hurt? Fear?

I know I'm experiencing all of the above.

Not once has Ms. Quinn ever hinted at knowing my mother. As far as I was concerned, they met when Mom interviewed to be a nanny. Never once did my mother mention being a counselor at Camp Casper before it closed, nor did she allude to the fact that she held the position with the woman who later became her employer. Why keep their past a secret?

I mentally comb back through everything I know about the shuttered camp. Mom always made it very clear that no one local to Casper ever attended or worked at the camp. Camp Casper was invite-only, and said invitations were exclusively shared with the country's best, brightest, but mainly, the wealthiest. Robert and Winifred Monroe treated Camp Casper like their exclusive little island. Untouchable.

"Rich kid summer camp," Mom always called it. Her opinion of the place was much like that of every other excluded local. Shared with a skeptical sniff and an eye roll.

But I guess that was all for show. Does anyone even know she worked at the camp? Or did she simply disappear for the summers and no one cared enough to ask questions?

Kind of like I do now.

"They were all counselors here," Caleb says with a shocked shake of his head. "Both our mothers and Samuel."

"And Lacy," I tack on.

Caleb about drives the golf cart into a tree. He veers back onto the dirt road in the nick of time. "What did you just say?"

"She was in that photo, too."

He doesn't press me for more, and I'm not in the mood to further ruin his day by revealing this place is finally haunted. I'd rather talk about ghosts with someone who will fully understand, like Mateo.

"Who wasn't in this photo?" Caleb grumbles.

Both at a loss for what to say, the golf cart's motor fills the silence. As guilty as I feel for not rushing home immediately, we needed to see that picture.

"So, your mom never mentioned working at Camp Casper? Because mine certainly didn't."

His eyes cut to me for a moment before they return to the worn path. "Never."

I can hear it in his voice. The bitterness and confusion. For as long as he's been alive, Caleb has spent every summer here. It's hard to believe that his mother's history with the property never came up once over the years.

My mother *knew* Lacy and never let on. Does she know how she died?

Why was everything kept secret?

Neither of us says it aloud but we're both thinking the same thing. Gianna Quinn clearly doesn't want her history with the camp out in the open. She's the most influential of the three of them. Knowing her, I wouldn't be surprised if it was somewhere in Mom and Samuel's employment contract to never bring it up. The Quinns are known for their air-tight NDAs. Hell, I even had to sign one when my mother started working for them.

One thing is for certain: our investigation of Lacy Monroe is screwed. If this isn't something Gianna Quinn wanted out in the open, she'll have done a clean job of it. She can afford to wipe any mention or photograph of her, the others, or the camp from the internet. No wonder we could never find anything online. Fact can become fiction if you're rich enough.

But what happened at this camp? How did Lacy Monroe die? How is my mother mixed up in all this? And most pressing—who is taunting me now?

A sudden chill overcomes the forest. Puzzled, I glance up to find a cloudless sky beyond the trees.

"Do you feel that?" I call over to Caleb.

"Feel what?"

Oh no.

"Stop driving!" I shriek, and Caleb immediately slams the breaks.

"What is it?"

"It's Phoebe," I breathe out. "She's—"

My words peter off as the forest grows colder. No, no, no, no. How did I miss it before? I'm such a fool for not rushing after her immediately.

"I think she's dying."

Caleb's mouth drops open with shock. "How do you know?"

I'm too busy throwing myself out of the golf cart to

answer. Running every which way, I frantically feel which direction is coldest. I find my answer when I near the path that cuts deeper into the forest, toward Old Camp.

Suddenly, it hits me. The seemingly familiar phrase, "A love for a love." Lacy's body is missing. What if this monster plans to exchange it with another? I've been so distracted assuming this freak is obsessed with me, I didn't even think one of the others were at risk.

"Lacy's grave!" I cry, jumping back into the golf cart.

Caleb's still trying to catch up. "Huh?"

"Drive to Lacy's grave! Hurry!"

Without any further question, Caleb takes off.

Wind whips in my face, but I know this thing can go faster. "Step on it!" I urge him.

"I'm trying to get us there in one piece," he grunts, bouncing in his seat as we drive over the rough terrain.

"Please let us not be too late," I plead. "Please, please, please."

But it only grows colder as we draw nearer.

Dirt flies as the tires skid to a stop just beyond the frigid clearing. We're on our feet in an instant.

We don't have shovels, but as we approach the freshly overturned earth, it's clear we won't need them. Whoever did this wanted to ensure their handiwork was discovered.

Caleb curses, blinking in horror at the mound of soil beside the grave. It's me who makes the first move to look down the hole because I already know what—*who*—I'm about to find.

Still, I should've better braced myself.

The monster who took her from this world didn't bother closing the coffin lid because they wanted us to find her. They left Phoebe's lifeless body in a heap. The poor girl's limbs are bent every which way, like she's a rag doll forgotten at the bottom of a toy chest. Scarlet blood seeps into the satin liner.

A note on that damned stationary rests on her chest. The last thing I want to do is read it, but I have to know.

PICK FASTER

Those two words make my vision blur as I wobble on my feet.

Phoebe's dead because of me.

This sick freak killed her to make a statement to me.

My ears start to ring as I feel arms wrap around me and pull me away from the grave. Caleb tries to turn me from the horrific scene, but I slump out of his grasp and onto the grass. As he crouches beside me, trying to brush the hair from my face, I see his lips ask if I'm okay, but I still can't hear a thing.

Phoebe's dead because of me.

Because of me.

12

I WISH the next few hours were a blur, but I was acutely aware of every single second that ticked by.

Slumped against a tree trunk, we waited for security to arrive. As soon as they did, my stomach finally emptied itself onto the roots of a maple tree. Samuel had Caleb bring me back to the lodge.

Afterwards, on a too-plush couch in the living room, Amelie and I consoled Cricket. Each of us held one of her shaking hands as Samuel disappeared to call Phoebe's poor parents. It was clear this matter would be handled like any other of the Quinn's sensitive affairs. With discretion.

And then it came time for the family meeting. Ms. Quinn left an appointment early and was en-route. Until she arrived, it was only Samuel and us kids sitting around the heavy dining room table. I cannot remember the last time we actually sat in this formal room, considering most meals are taken on the deck. From the walls to the decor to the angular rafters, everything in the dining room is constructed of glossy, auburn hardwood.

Mackenzie tried to supply nourishment, but everyone

shook their heads at the platter full of fresh fruit and energy bites. I'm not sure any of us could stomach a thing right now.

By this point in the day, the whole family was looped in on the horrific messages I've been receiving. Cricket hasn't met my eyes since. Not that I can blame her. I'm the reason her best friend was brutally murdered. With that knowledge, I can barely stand to live in my own skin.

My only solace is Mateo protectively standing behind my chair. Every now and then, he'll covertly fiddle with a strand of my long hair, reminding me that I won't face this nightmare alone. Only once do I think Caleb notices, his brow furrowing as he darts his eyes between Mateo and me.

"I don't know what to say, kids," Samuel begins softly, pulling a tattered cloth from his pocket and wiping his brow. "I take full responsibility for the loss of your friend. Somewhere today, my team failed you, and I swear, it will be made right. I can assure you that myself and a team of trusted members of the local force will be launching a full investigation as to what happened here. Until we know more, I'm going to ask you kids to stick close to the lodge. I know your time at the lake house is precious, so if you must venture outdoors, stick to the areas close by. Until further notice, Old Camp is off limits."

The Quinn siblings are so dazed that they don't bother arguing. These days, it's not often someone tells them what to do, but it looks like Samuel is going to get away with it.

His gaze barely brushes over Diego and Mateo before landing on me. "I've already looped in your parents. I assured them you're safe here, and now I'm going to say the same to you. A horrible accident has occurred. One that I'll never be able to erase. But I swear, you are safe under my care. I will keep you safe no matter what. All of you."

So, Samuel already spoke to my mom and told her everything. I'm shocked she didn't immediately call me afterwards and tell me to not bother packing my bags. Maybe she truly trusts Samuel's word. They are childhood friends, after all.

I haven't found it in me yet to text her. I barely have the energy to sit through the conversation happening in this very room.

I slump down into my seat. The people who are supposed to be keeping me safe have been keeping secrets from me for my entire life. I'm not sure how I'm supposed to feel comforted by anything they say or do.

After today's events, there's a very good chance I will never feel comfortable ever again.

"Thank you, Samuel," comes a powerful voice that startles me back to upright.

Gianna Quinn's black hair swishes as she struts into the room. She always swears the long hair keeps her looking young. Between that, fillers, and a well-tailored pantsuit, Ms. Quinn successfully presents herself as a youthful entrepreneur, not a single mother of four in her fifties. It's all a crucial part of the TeQ plan to stay relevant as a top technology player in a crowded market. They're the brand for the younger generations. Hip, affordable, and sustainable.

At her appearance, Samuel abandons his seat at the head of the table, holding out the high-backed chair for her to slide into. No longer the ringleader, he respectfully relocates to a corner.

He's not the only one in the room to change in the presence of Gianna Quinn. All four of her children sit up straighter. Well, all except Caleb, whose shoulders seem to be curling in on themselves. My nose wrinkles at the sight. I've never seen him appear so meek when around his mother.

A shorter woman follows after Ms. Quinn, not bothering to look up from her TeQ smart phone to acknowledge the family. Her manicured nails furiously tap against her phone screen, like Phoebe's death put a real damper on her day. We all warily eye her as she takes up residence in the corner opposite Samuel.

"Just who we needed," Zane mutters under his breath.

We shouldn't be surprised that Ms. Quinn dragged her head of publicity to the middle of Virginia in the midst of a PR crisis. Usually, the lake house is off-limits to company personnel, but I guess this place stopped being our safe escape a few hours ago so what does it matter?

"Hi, Mom," Amelie says, not even bothering to keep the bitterness from her voice. "Sorry you had to cut your business short in San Fran."

Gianna Quinn clucks impatiently. "You know I'd drop anything for you kids. Even an unbelievably important meeting with investors."

Amelie rolls her eyes but miraculously bites her tongue. Ms. Quinn may "drop anything" for her family, but that always comes at a cost. In a family like this, everything does.

"Cricket, honey, I'm so sorry about your friend."

"Are you?" Cricket snaps tearfully.

"Of course I am," Gianna says, her voice ringing with hurt at her child's accusation. "I am incredibly disappointed by today's events."

"Give me a break. You toting Pamela along is all I need to know about your so-called disappointment." Cricket groans, shoving her chair back from the table and stomping out of the room.

We all watched her departure with wide eyes. It's a rarity to see one of the siblings disrespect their mother.

Gianna sniffs with frustration but isn't the first to speak.

Instead, Zane fills the void, sarcastically saying, "Not that we don't love you and your life advice, Pamela. Who wouldn't want someone calculating their every move in order to keep the TeQ board pleased?"

"We won't be discussing business at this family meeting," Gianna asserts while pinching the bridge of her nose.

"Don't lie," Amelie retorts, moving to follow Cricket. "Every single one of our family matters is *business*."

Zane makes a show of loudly clearing his throat before meeting Diego's eyes and jerking his head toward the door. "Yeah, we're going to go with them."

Only Caleb, Mateo, and I remain. Just when I thought this day couldn't get any more uncomfortable. Mateo stays behind my chair while Caleb fervently studies the grain of the table.

My posture stiffens when Gianna Quinn turns her attention to me. "Skyler, you have no idea how disturbed I was to learn about these notes you've been receiving."

I don't know what I'm supposed to say to that, so I settle with a single duck of my chin.

Unfazed by this, Gianna continues, "I only wish you kids had told us sooner." I don't miss her stern gaze cutting to Caleb. The way his jaw clenches makes my stomach flip with guilt. This isn't his fault.

"I'm sorry for how long I foolishly believed the notes were a prank." My voice is hoarse after a full day of crying.

Gianna responds like she doesn't hear me. "I had a call with your mother on the way here."

This takes me by surprise. Sure, I expected Samuel to contact my mother, but someone as busy and important as Gianna Quinn?

"I assume she's picking me up soon?"

Gianna considers me thoughtfully. "Only if that's what you wish."

I frown. "Mom is leaving it up to me?"

That's so unlike her. Though, come to think of it, this whole day, she's been acting out of the ordinary. She hasn't called nonstop, nor has she barged through the door to check on me, and more importantly, her other honorary children.

Gianna nods. "While discussing the matter of these

concerning notes you are receiving, I assured her there is no safer place for you than here."

"And she agreed with you?"

Another nod from the woman.

I feel the eyes of everyone in the room studying me intently. Why does it feel like I'm the one being scrutinized when the adults are the ones keeping secrets?

Before I can think better of it, I hear myself ask, "And why do you think that is?"

"What do you mean, dear?" Gianna responds inquisitively.

From across the table, I notice Caleb subtly shake his head, silently making it clear now is not the time to bring up our mothers' secret history.

Maybe he's right. There are more pressing matters at play right now. Phoebe is dead and I'm in danger.

Choosing to trust his judgement, I offer Gianna an innocent shrug. "I was just curious what you said to her that's kept her so calm. You know my mom."

"I do," she says in a tone that makes me want to ask my initial question all over again. "But your mother trusts Samuel—"

I bet she does.

"—and understands the safest place for you is here. At least until we have more information about who is bothering you."

"How do we plan to get that information? Because, so far, this person has broken into the house, evaded all security guards and cameras, dug up a body, and buried another in its place."

"It's hard to keep everyone safe without knowing the full extent of what I'm dealing with," Samuel defends himself.

My mouth grows dry because he has a point. This is all my fault.

"Come on, Sam," Caleb interjects on my behalf. "That's

not fair. She didn't ask for some freak to become obsessed with her."

One stern look from Gianna silences him. Any ounce of conviction in the boy evaporates under that stare. Whatever is bothering him, I highly suspect his mother is somehow linked to the situation.

Samuel huffs before eventually offering me an apologetic nod. "I've stationed a guard to patrol your wing of the house during all hours of the day. And a few others outside the entrances to the house."

"Thanks," I mumble.

"Unfortunately, those notes you've been receiving came back clean, not that I expected our culprit to be foolish enough to leave prints. The stationery is sold widely online and the magazine clippings are a dead end." He winces at his choice of words. "I also had the heart analyzed."

This has me sitting forward. "Who does it belong to?"

"It was a realistic prop," Sam responds in a voice that shuts down any further speculation that it might belong to Lacy Monroe.

I blink with surprise. "The heart was fake?"

My mind must be messing with me because I could've sworn the spirit who visited me last night had a gaping hole in her chest.

This secret admirer hasn't half-assed anything else thus far. Why leave a fake heart for me to find? Could they not get their hands on a real one?

"I've also looked into those boys you mentioned earlier. Both came back clean. Oliver Hainsley is currently on an Alaskan cruise with his family and Spencer Young is at church camp in Michigan. I still think we're dealing with someone more interested in the Quinns, than you, so I'm going back through my files to make a new list of suspects."

"You're saying it could be anyone."

After a long pause, the man nods. "That is what I'm saying."

My thoughts return to our only other potential subject. The copper-haired boy with the earring. Logan Lewis.

Reading my mind, Samuel sighs. "We haven't been able to locate Logan Lewis since his delivery a few days ago."

My brow furrows. Surely, Samuel's highly-trained team hasn't been outwitted by a fifteen-year-old boy. "Do you not have his address?"

"We do, but he hasn't gone home since."

"And his parents aren't worried sick?"

"Apparently not."

I slump back in my seat. This has been the least-assuring family meeting ever.

"Regardless, you won't see another one of those damn letters," he grunts. "I swear it."

I hate that I don't believe him.

"We all do," Caleb promises, his eyes glossy.

"Agreed," Mateo says firmly, resting his hands on my shoulders and giving them a squeeze. "No one scares you and gets away with it."

The severity of his tone is the only one that brings me comfort. Then I catch sight of Caleb's frown at our closeness and the nerves start right back up. He has no right to deny me a relationship with his friend. Not when it's the only thing keeping me sane.

"You do feel safe here, don't you, Skyler?" Gianna asks quietly, reaching across the table to hold my hand in hers. Her thumb gently rubs over the top of my hand.

It's always startled me how easily she can "turn it on." One moment, she's all business, and the next, she's a maternal saint. I don't doubt that both come naturally to her, but when you've been faced with CEO-Gianna for so long, the appearance of Mother-Gianna always catches you off guard.

Gianna continues with, "Because, if you'd rather go home,

we can go call your mother together. I don't want you sticking around here if you don't think it's what's best for you."

Caleb begins to interject, "Mom—"

"No matter what my son—or any of my children—want from you. The decision to stay must be yours."

My breathing spikes as I feel the pressure of the room build. Everyone's eyes are intensely locked on my face. There's a clear right answer and wrong answer, and everyone seems to know it but me.

"I-I need to think about it."

Gianna Quinn releases a breath I feel like everyone was holding. "That's understandable, my dear. Take as long as you need. I completely understand if you do not wish to remain."

Now, I'm confused. Does she want me to stay or go? Does she even care?

Surely, she doesn't want me around if it means the lives of her children are at risk. Even if Samuel promises the lake house is the safest place for me, my presence alone makes it unsafe for the rest of them.

Maybe this is all a mind game, designed to make me think she wants me to remain here, when in actuality, she needs me to leave.

My head begins to spin painfully. I'm completely lost on what I'm supposed to do. All I know is I don't want anyone else to get hurt.

"I think I need to go to my room, if that's okay," I say softly.

"Of course. Let us know when you decide." Gianna dismisses me.

I shakily rise from my seat. The boys move to walk out of the dining room with me.

"Not you," the woman says firmly. Looks like CEO-Gianna is back. "Excuse us, Skyler, but I need to have a word with my son."

With hardened eyes, Caleb drops back into his seat. I offer

him an apologetic expression and he returns with a helpless shrug of his own.

Gianna Quinn has always treated her eldest son as a liaison for the whole family. She sets the expectations, and in turn, he ensures his younger siblings stay in line. It's clear by Pamela's presence that this entire situation is extremely delicate, and they plan to use Caleb to keep the others in check.

I find the answer to my impossible predicament in his bleak expression.

My presence is only making life harder on Caleb Quinn, and I refuse to be the reason his world gets any more difficult. He might not be the boy for me, but that doesn't mean I've stopped caring for him completely.

There's no other choice. I have to leave.

13

MATEO, who trailed after me into my bedroom, frowns when he sees me pull out my suitcase.

"You already decided? You're leaving?"

Shushing him, I quickly close the door. I don't want this decision to become a family affair because my mind is already made up. Unzipping the suitcase, I hurry to the dresser to retrieve all the shirts and shorts I only folded away a few days ago.

"Skyler, will you just talk to me?"

I whisper back, "And will you just keep your voice down? The others will hear."

Sparing him a stern expression from over my shoulder, I find him running his hands down his face in exasperation.

"No one is safe as long as I'm here," I explain, returning to shoving clothing into my luggage, "and I cannot live with myself if anyone else gets hurt because of me."

"Skyler—"

"You won't change my mind," I assert, rushing past him to the conjoined bathroom to grab a few toiletries. If this murderer is after me, there's no way I'm going home to my mother and putting her at risk. I cannot bear the responsibility of willingly endangering anyone.

Where exactly I'll go, I haven't yet decided. Maybe the police station. Maybe a motel. Maybe I can ask Amelie to help me buy a plane ticket to the other side of the world. She'd do it. She's the most sensible of the bunch when it comes to safety.

Tossing my hair care products and toothbrush into my toiletries bag, I hurry back into the bedroom and stuff that into my suitcase, too.

"Skyler!"

I continue to ignore him, hands on my hips as I glance around the room and ponder what else I might need.

"Will you please just look at me?" he pleads, coming to stand behind me.

My eyes squeeze shut as his scent envelopes my space. Like I'm frolicking through a patch of wild spearmint growing in the forest. I know if I turn around, my whole resolve will wash away, so I whisper, "Please, don't try to change my mind."

"I'm not," he promises. "Your choices are yours to make. I just want the chance to say goodbye."

Heart swelling, I spin to face him. I find his eyes glossed with relief.

"You understand why I have to go, right?"

"Of course I do," he whispers, bringing his hands to either side of my face, "but that doesn't mean I have to like it. No one's ever seen me like you do, Skyler."

I melt in the rasp of his voice. No one has ever seen me like him, either.

When his thumbs begin to trace my cheeks, I know he's going to have to lock me outside of this house, because all I want to do is ignore the cruel reality and stay with him. Only Mateo has the power to push away those haunting images of mangled friends and suffocating secrets.

Judging by the way Mateo is looking at me now, he wants to do the same. I catch his eyes flick down to my lips, only briefly, before returning to bore into my own. He's questioning himself. Wondering if we dare continue what we started last night.

I certainly want to. I'm ready to add a layer of new memories on top of today's horrible ones. Lessen the pounding in my head and replace it with a different kind of pulse. I need my last experience at my favorite place in the world to be one worth remembering.

"This isn't goodbye forever," Mateo swears, tucking a strand of hair behind my ear before sliding his thumb down my jaw. Gently, he lifts my chin toward him so his lips brush mine as he says, "One way or another, we'll find each other again. In this life or the next."

"I hope it's both," I murmur, winding my fingers through his shaggy hair and drawing him closer.

Finally, his lips fully press against mine, and for the first time today, my aching heart finds peace. So what if we just met? Time does not dictate fate—and fate is the only logical explanation for this. I never thought my heart could beat like this for anyone else. Who am I to ignore such a sign?

When I breathe his name against his lips, his roaming hands squeeze my waist, sending a shiver down my spine. I didn't think anyone else was capable of making me feel this way.

The door flies open, making us jump to opposite sides of my room.

"Um, come on in?" I exhale breathlessly as Caleb and Amelie burst inside.

With a devastated moan, Amelie darts across the room, obliviously cutting between Mateo and I as she drags me to sit at the edge of the bed. Sniffing, she rests her tear-streaked face on my shoulder. This is exactly what I was hoping to avoid. An under-the-radar escape was the only way I was peacefully getting out of this house.

"Don't you dare go," she mutters against me.

After carefully closing the door after him, Caleb's eyes suspiciously dart between Mateo and me. My insides sink with guilt at the perplexed crease on the bridge of his nose.

No—that's not fair. I'm guilty of nothing other than moving on from an unrequited crush. He cannot mourn what he never had, nor does he have any right to dictate how I move on.

Before this summer, I would've thought that to be a relief to him. After years of me wanting, it was his choice to never give us a chance. It's too late now. We have to live with that.

Mateo clears his throat uncomfortably. I only hope that he's not going to give us up to appease his friend. Not that it matters much now.

"I have to," I murmur. "You know I do."

Caleb looms in the doorway, surveying the state of my bedroom. Finally, his disappointed gaze lands on me. He doesn't say anything. He doesn't have to. His opinion on the matter is clear.

Unlike her brother, Amelie is desperate to vocalize her thoughts. "No, I don't understand." She lifts her head to look me in the eyes. "Why would you leave? It's not safe for you out there."

"None of us are safe if I stay here!"

"Told you," Caleb grunts, still at the door.

My attention snaps to him. "Told her what?"

"I told her you'd think it was for the better of the group if you left."

"Do you not agree?" I ask back. Caleb is the smartest, most-rational person I know. He rarely gives his emotions the reins. If anyone understands my decision, it'll be him.

Or so I thought.

Caleb crosses his arms, leaning against the doorframe. "No, Skyler, I don't think you should leave."

I challenge his nonchalant expression with one of my own. "And who do you think will die next because of me?"

Amelie squeaks, giving my hand an angry squeeze. "Don't speak like that."

"Why not?" I ask the room. "Why are we acting like we're all suddenly going to be okay when we all know that's not the case? Everyone knowing I have a murderous stalker doesn't negate the fact that I have a *murderous stalker*. They're clearly willing to do anything to make me 'pick them,' whatever that means."

"I think it's very obvious what it means." Amelie glances up at her brother, testing to see if he has reached the same conclusion. "You have a toxic secret admirer who wants you to love them back."

She puts it so plainly, as if these notes aren't accompanied by a missing corpse, a heart, a break-in, *and* the death of our friend.

"Sure, that part is obvious, but their identity is not, which is reason enough for me to leave."

I helplessly glance at Mateo for support, but he's taken a step back, making it clear this is my conversation to navigate. I guess I can't blame him for not wanting to push me to stay or go. The guilt of making the wrong decision is enough to eat anyone alive.

"I think that's reason enough for you to stay," Amelie disagrees. "You don't know who is doing this. None of us do. This is the safest place for you until we can dig up the truth."

"*We?*"

"Dig up?" Caleb says at the same time.

Amelie waves him off. "Poor choice of words. The point is Skyler isn't going to feel safe until she knows who is obsessed with her, so we're going to work together to figure it out."

"No, we aren't," I immediately interject. The last thing I want is the Quinns hunting down a murderer. Caleb and I decoding the mysterious letters and Lacy's missing body was one thing. That was before Phoebe died. The last thing we are doing is turning this into a group project. It's too dangerous.

"This isn't the time to play detective," I shut her down. "We're letting the professionals take over."

"The professionals won't take over if you leave! Is this because you don't trust Samuel anymore? Caleb told me about the picture you two found."

Of course he did. I shoot him a frustrated look. He made sure to prepare his sister ahead of coming in here. She knows every single one of my reservations before they even come out of my mouth.

"It's a weird secret to keep," I say, my tone clipped. "One would wonder why they bothered keeping it at all."

She eyes me fiercely. "If you stay, we can figure it out together."

Why can't she just let me go? For once, why can I not get my way?

"Please," I whisper desperately. "Please, don't put this burden on me."

"You're not a burden, Skyler," she insists, growing frustrated with the back and forth. It's not like us to bicker about anything for longer than a few minutes.

Helplessly glancing around the room, I find Mateo's hard eyes on me. I silently plead with him for help. A slight shrug of his shoulders tells me it's my decision.

Caleb's brow furrows when he catches this exchange. Clearing his throat, he says quietly, "I need to speak with Sky alone."

14

It's NOT a question and everyone in the room knows it.

My eyes roll. No one around here is taking orders from Caleb.

But then Amelie squeezes my hand once more before rising from my bed.

"I'm right across the hall if you need me," she murmurs, and I wonder if the reminder is more for me or her brother. "If you choose to leave, please say goodbye first."

With that, she's obediently out the door.

Now she starts listening to her brother?

"This is important," Caleb mutters. I note he doesn't meet Mateo's eyes.

There's an uncomfortable stand-off between the two of them. One that's completely silent but still manages to say a lot. I thought these two boys were supposed to be dear friends and teammates? Caleb doesn't dole out invites to the lake house to just anyone.

My insides burn when I realize what—or rather, who—is coming between them.

But I thought Caleb didn't think of me in that way? He's not supposed to care if Mateo does.

Mateo glances my way, waiting for me to stop him. I offer him the same expression he just gave me. The one that says *this is up to you*.

"If you say so," Mateo grumbles, heading into the hall.

My lips pinch. I was hoping he'd put his foot down and refuse to leave. Maybe he's no better than me when it comes to giving the Quinns whatever they want.

Closing the door with a sigh, Caleb turns on his heel before resting against it. Staring at his sneakers, he carefully ponders his next words. I settle back onto the bed, knowing this will take a moment. Caleb isn't the type to spit words out without measuring their weight. It takes almost a full minute for him to drag his eyes up to me.

"Since when do you not feel safe here, Sky?"

The Quinn siblings are well aware their lake house is my favorite place in the world. I've always regarded it as my escape. There's nowhere I feel more myself. This is the only place I don't hide the truth about my awareness for souls trapped in this world. My mother's hatred for our sight aside, it's unwise to be public about such a gift. Skeptics would label us as demonic and likely treat us as such.

But now, my safe place is just as dangerous.

"Do you really need an answer?"

He takes a step toward me. "You know I'd never let anything happen to you."

"Did you say that to Phoebe, too?"

His head rears back like I've slapped him. "You know I would've done anything to protect her had I been around. But instead, I was with you, making sure you were safe."

I swallow hard, immediately feeling guilty. Caleb isn't the bad guy here.

But who is?

"Sorry," I mumble. "That wasn't fair."

We fall quiet, both studying the weaving details of the rug

as we think of something to say. I've always felt nervous around Caleb, but never at a loss for words.

"Sky," Caleb says, and when I glance back up to him, I find he's a step nearer. "I swear, you *are* safe here. You're safe with me. You know that, right?" Those last words rasp in his throat as his gaze locks onto mine.

A new kind of shiver shoots up my spine when I realize how he's looking at me. There's something different behind his eyes. This isn't only him being a protective friend. This is more.

Since when has it been more?

After years of pining, hoping my feelings would be reciprocated and wanting him to look at me the way he is now, it finally clicked in his head. The pull I've felt all along. The inevitableness that is us.

The universe and its timing are cruel. Why does it have to be now? I was finally moving on.

But when Caleb Quinn stares at me like this—those misty blue eyes blinking like they're seeing for the first time—I find myself questioning if I could ever truly move on from this boy.

"Sky?" He murmurs my name again, and I realize I never answered his question.

"I know, Caleb," I whisper. It's an answer that meets a lot of questions—including some I'm not sure he even meant to ask.

A comforting haze settles over my mind as my heart reclaims the reins. Possessed by love, my thoughts grow lighter. This boy—*this boy*—has always been my greatest weakness. The most intoxicating drug of them all.

"Does that mean you'll stay?" Again, it's a question that comes with a few left unspoken.

I answer them all with one word. "Always."

Caleb's shoulders begin to rise and fall with relief, like he was incapable of breathing before hearing my answer.

"Hey," I say, finally standing to close the gap between us, "it's okay. You know I was never going anywhere. Not really."

How swiftly my resolve washes away when in the presence of the boy I've loved all my life. I cannot believe I ever considered packing my bags.

"If there's really some freak out there, one set on harassing you, I don't want you out there on your own," he mutters, coming to bring his hands to rest on either side of my face.

It's my turn to suck in a breath as the reality of our situation sinks in. This is real. I'm not looking for invisible signals that aren't really there.

Oh shit.

My heart skips erratically as Caleb cradles my face, his eyes dancing between mine.

"I swear to keep you safe, Sky. Nothing from this world or the next will touch you."

"Except for you?" I ask as he gently tucks a strand of hair behind my ear.

Caleb's eyes widen, as if he just realized the position we've found ourselves in. "Is that what you want?"

My heart lurches like a ship lost in a tremendous storm. Never have I faced such a dastardly predicament as this. After years of nothing, two boys—both worthy in their own right— yearn for me.

What a mess, I helplessly think to myself. It's like I'm in one of my romance novels, but something tells me this trope doesn't play out so neatly in real life.

Pick wisely echoes in my mind, but my heart shoos it away before I can consider the implication.

After all my years of waiting, how can I ignore this fork in the road? What if this is the truly fated path that leads to happily ever after?

I'll never know if I don't take the first step.

My lips quirk. "I think you've known what I want for a while now."

His nose scrunches sheepishly. While I never outright professed my feelings for Caleb, I know my crush was obvious. I always hung on every word that left his lips. Attempted to catch his eye. Embraced every one of his interests, from hockey to rare card collecting to hiking.

"Perhaps." Caleb's eyes lock onto mine, his voice firm, ensuring I hear the truth in his words. "I think there's a part of me that always figured we were inevitable."

"Then why keep us waiting?"

His expression darkens slightly. "I'm a difficult guy to be with."

I actually laugh at the absurdity, the sound ringing around my bedroom walls. "That's not true."

"It is." His gaze hardens, making my heart pang with sadness because he genuinely believes it to be true. "I know you understand the baggage that comes with my family. The expectations. The micromanaging. My mother. But that's not what I'm talking about. I'm far from a perfect person. I'm not good enough for a girl like you. I've never been."

I balk at his words. Caleb's always been a model human. Kind, just, and clever. He could make anyone pale in comparison. "What are you talking about?"

He swallows hard. "I'm not without my sins, Sky."

"Who is?"

His head shakes but he doesn't back away. We're still toe-to-toe at the center of my room, both waiting for the other to give first. "You don't understand—"

"That people have problems? Trust me, Caleb. I'm more than aware of that. And coming from someone who has known you most of your life, I can assure you that yours aren't worse than anyone else's. You've always been good enough for me. More than enough."

His eyes glaze over as he allows my words to sink in. I start to wonder how long he's been needing to hear them.

Certainly, everyone in his life should regularly be shouting his praises.

He releases a relieved breath. "Why was I avoiding the inevitable again?"

I spy his gaze flick to my lips before returning to my eyes. Silently asking for permission. I lift my chin in response. A moment ago, I may have done the same for another boy, but how can I deny myself the chance to truly know the one my heart has always wanted?

And then, the very thing I've hoped for all my life occurs.

Caleb Quinn kisses me.

The polite brush of his lips against mine is exactly how I imagined it would start. Caleb isn't the sort of boy to push things too quickly. But also as I suspected, when neither of us pulls away, he draws me closer. His hand curls around the back of my head, fingers knitting in my hair. He breathes me in like I'm the only oxygen in the room.

I let him kiss me deeply, while my insides scream with fireworks. This is all I've ever wanted. This. Him. Caleb.

Caleb.

Caleb.

I'm unable to fight back my smile, making him laugh against my lips. "It's been a long time coming, huh?"

I pull back to meet his eyes, but a shadow behind him captures my attention.

His brow creases slightly. "What is it?"

But I'm too stunned to speak. Instead, my lips part with horror at the familiar figure looming near my door. It's a miracle she's standing upright because the limbs of her short frame are bent in all the wrong directions. Her jaw, which also appears to be broken, is hanging slack. But her eyes, wide and unblinking, stare at me like they've witnessed the greatest terrors this world—and the next—has to offer.

It isn't Lacy.

"Phoebe?"

Her skin doesn't glow like the other spirits I've encountered. Probably because she's so new to this cursed state of existence.

"What?" Caleb gapes, swiveling around to search my room for any sign of the girl. Turning to follow my train of vision, he stares right at Phoebe, but I know he doesn't see her.

"Sky," he murmurs, chest heaving, "is she really here?"

I nod, still unable to articulate a single word. Until now, every lost soul I've encountered was a stranger to me. I far prefer it that way. Seeing Phoebe, so close to how I remember her, yet undeniably unlike herself, puts new meaning behind the word "haunting".

You poor girl. Who did this to you?

As if reading my mind, her slack jaw trembles, attempting to articulate a single word. A name. Like her tongue's been ripped from her mouth, she's incapable of uttering a sound.

"Try," I plead with her, feeling guilty for how easily I find my voice while she struggles. "Who hurt you?"

The child's entire frame begins to shake from exertion.

"I'm so sorry!" I cry, growing nauseous with guilt. She is this way because of me. This is my fault.

And then, as quickly as she appeared, she's gone.

I gasp, startling back a step. I should feel calmed by a spiritless room, but the contrary occurs. I'm more scared than before.

Someone stripped her from this world. She was so young and innocent. There was so much life left unlived.

How could anyone kill her in such a gruesome manner? Who is capable of such a monstrosity?

Phoebe came to me for a reason. She knew I'd be the one to see her. She's leaving it up to me to discover who did this to her. To make sure they can't hurt anyone else.

The sound of my name snaps me out of my daze. I'd nearly forgotten Caleb was here. His arms squeeze around my waist protectively as he searches for any sign of threat.

I turn to him, blinking the horrified haze from my eyes. "She was here."

"You're certain?"

I meet his gaze, nodding once.

His eyes grow hard as he carefully articulates his next question. "Have-have you seen anyone else?"

Swallowing hard, I search his face for why he'd ask me such a question. For as long as we've come to the lake house, I've asserted this place is anything but haunted by lingering spirits of campers or counselors. No matter how much the family hoped, I couldn't lie to them.

Just like I cannot lie to Caleb now.

"Lacy."

He sucks in a breath through his nose. "Where?"

"Here. In my room."

"That's how you recognized her in the picture so fast," he says, piecing it together.

"This is all connected, but I don't understand how. There's something the adults don't want us to know about Lacy, and I think it's somehow related to why I suddenly have a secret admirer with a penchant for dead bodies."

"And you can't think of anyone who might suddenly be so in love with you? Someone from school? Or who works on the property?"

Another shake of my head.

"If you still choose to stay, we'll do whatever it takes to find them. Sneak back into security, hunt around my mom's office, break out the Ouija boards, hell, even hold a seance. Anything to find out who's behind this."

My heart swells with relief. I've always known Caleb had my back, but I'm asking him to dig into his family's history. To uncover a time of his mother's life that was clearly kept a secret for a reason. It's bound to be uncomfortable. We'll likely learn things we wished we hadn't. But if it's the only way to unearth the truth, we'll have to wade into those

murky waters. I'm fortunate that Caleb wants to swim alongside me.

His eyes bore into mine. "I swear, Skyler. I'll keep you
safe."

"I know you will."

"And you haven't seen anyone else?" Caleb asks. "There
aren't any other clues haunting these halls?"

"No," I say with a slight shake of my head. "Thankfully,
there aren't any other murder victims stopping by to say hi."

The boy's shoulders sag with relief. There's been enough
death already. "Let's keep it that way."

15

I EXPECTED to wake up full of joyous butterflies.

Instead, my skin itches beneath a thousand insect legs. Even if I lie to myself and pretend I'm safe inside the lodge, this sickly feeling refuses to leave.

It doesn't take me long to realize what's wrong. Guilt. I'm wracked with guilt after kissing Caleb. I never expected to feel so horribly after finally experiencing a moment I've looked forward to my entire life.

What have I done?

Mateo was so clear with his intentions. He never made me wait. He doesn't deserve someone who shares a moment with him and then proceeds to kiss his friend not fifteen minutes later.

I've read countless romance books. Swooned during every rom-com—good or bad—I could find to watch. Wished over and over for my own love story to come to fruition.

I never anticipated a plot twist like this. Chapters upon chapters of nothing, and then all at once, everything from everyone. The last thing I want is to be the villain in Mateo's story, but after last night, how can I ever reclaim the title of leading lady?

For as long as I can remember, I've yearned for Caleb. But even after the boy of my dreams kissed me last night, it doesn't completely push Mateo from my mind. It's this specific dilemma that's making my skin crawl. My heart beats in double time and my head is doing its best to keep up.

If I've learned anything from my romance education, it's that I'm totally screwed. I'm in too deep and unable to erase the inevitable ending I'm barreling toward. People will be hurt. There's no avoiding it.

Just what this summer needed.

In a daze, I dress for the day. It isn't until halfway through brushing my teeth that I realize I've donned a mismatched bikini. Changing my bottoms for the matching violet pair, I pause, wondering if I'm a fool for wearing such casual attire when we're in the middle of a crisis. How can we easily lounge by the water after Phoebe was found dead on the other side of the lake? Hurriedly, I pull off the swimsuit altogether and change into denim shorts and a black t-shirt.

I should go find Amelie. She'll know what to do. I don't know Mateo well enough to anticipate how he will react when he learns of the development between Caleb and me. Should I confess right away? It's not like one kiss makes Caleb and I a couple, but Mateo deserves to know he's not the only boy pursuing me.

Flinging open my bedroom door, I jerk back at the sight of the very boy standing on the other side.

"Mateo," I breathe out.

His expression is unreadable, and I immediately fear Caleb got to him first. Not that I deserve to break the news before his friend, but how did Caleb present such delicate information?

"Morning," he murmurs. "Sleep well?"

My head shakes. "You?"

He shrugs.

I internally curse. He definitely knows.

"Listen—"

"It's okay," Mateo responds before I can explain.

I blink at his calm expression, surprised when I realize I might actually believe him.

"Really?"

"Really," he says with another casual shrug. "I'll respect your wishes when you make them clear, but until then…"

Mateo trails off as I nod with understanding. He's going to fight until the bell. My cheeks flush at the very thought.

At this moment, I wonder—should I be making my wishes clear? What are my wishes? Looking into his deep-brown eyes, I find myself suddenly incapable of articulating a single thought.

"I just think it's interesting," he tacks on under his breath.

"What's interesting?"

"You've known Caleb for years. *Now* he decides he's interested?"

I bite my lip. Should I find the timing peculiar?

Mateo shrugs again. "It is what it is, I guess."

"Yeah, I guess."

But now that the seed's been planted in the back of my mind, I can't stop it from taking root. Is it strange for this to be the summer Caleb finally develops feelings? Or is it completely understandable for current events to bring his feelings bubbling to the surface?

To make matters worse, I don't trust myself to correctly see through my eagerness and properly scrutinize the situation before me.

My stomach churning, Mateo and I move down the hall, stopping outside Amelie's door so that I can knock.

"Come in," she groans from the inside.

"Are you decent?"

"Does it matter?"

"Kind of?"

Amelie pulls the door open, and thankfully, she is fully clothed. Her eyebrows raise. "Since when?"

The boy standing beside me should be answer enough. I clear my throat. "How'd you sleep?"

"Fan-freaking-tastic," she mutters, pulling the door open a little wider to reveal Cricket curled up beneath the duvet. Amelie lowers her voice. "Poor thing didn't fall asleep until three."

I grimace. "Anything I can do?"

"Let's give her some space so one of us can get some sleep."

"What about you?"

Amelie's shoulders rise and fall in response before she shuts the door behind her.

The upstairs of the lodge is as grand as the floor below. Every bit of it is constructed from shining wood. Along the walls hang sconces with tin shades pounded with depictions of woodland creatures. A long rug the color of a spruce tree extends down the floorboards. The soft carpeting is a blessing for bare feet on cool mornings.

We pass down the corridor in silence. It's a numbing kind of quiet. One that makes my mouth go dry and my head feel fuzzy. These halls used to feel safe.

The morning transpires at an achingly slow rate. There's more security patrolling the grounds than ever before. We spy them passing by the large windows of the lodge and disappearing into the woods. Samuel relocated his headquarters into the house, setting up shop in Pamela's already-cramped office. I'm sure the woman just loves that.

Almost all the staff has been sent home, and aside from the security team, the house is operating with a skeleton crew. Mackenzie remains, but without her assistants, she is manning the kitchen herself. Gone are the gardeners, marina crew, and cleaners.

No one seems to want to be around each other for long. Amelie departs to try and reach her girlfriend. Mateo also disappears upstairs, muttering something about Caleb having the right idea by holing away in his room.

Caleb hasn't shown his face once today. Does he regret last night? Is he avoiding me?

The nerves are eating me alive.

I resolve to return to my room, praying there aren't any unexpected visitors within. Although, when I open the bedroom door and find the space empty, I don't find myself even remotely relieved.

Lacy and Phoebe are trapped here. Tethered to where their bodies were stripped of their souls. They know I can see them, so why aren't they here, demanding my help? Don't they want to pass on and finally find peace?

What am I missing?

Exhausted from having more questions than answers, I think of the first one I can solve. Turning on my heel, I march back down the hall to Caleb's room. Two words beat alongside every footfall. Why now? Why now? Why now?

After being the reason I remain, I think he owes me a conversation.

Rapping on the heavy wooden door, I pause for a few moments before knocking again. I can envision Caleb sitting up at his desk, waiting for confirmation that someone is indeed disturbing his sulking, before crossing his room to fling open the door.

But there's no telling creak of floorboards beneath his feet.

I knock again, more firmly this time to make it abundantly clear someone is here to see him.

The door doesn't open.

Where is he?

Why now?

Biting the inside of my cheek, my hand drifts to the doorknob, twisting it before I can think better of my actions.

Sunlight streams into Caleb's empty room. The bright light cascades through the open window, falling over the navy-blue duvet crumpled atop the enormous bed. Bookshelves line one wall, covered with an equal number of novels and knickknacks. First edition bindings of old-school mysteries sit alongside model sailboats and insect displays. On the far wall, trophies from hockey tournaments and debate competitions sit on a shelf above his desk. There's a new one from this past season.

Caleb's always been perfect at anything he decides to pursue, and hockey is no exception. It's widely known Caleb could've gone after a professional career, but that's not the future Gianna Quinn envisioned for him. Not after she spent his entire childhood and adolescence priming him to be the perfect successor for herself. He could enjoy the pastime while at school. Allow it to build character and endurance. Then, when the time came, he'd use those skills to lead a company.

My gaze shifts back to his unmade bed. Caleb's not the type to leave his room disorderly. Not even on his lowest of days does he forgo tucking his sheets and pulling up the duvet. Perplexed, I blink at the messy sight. Yet another change of behavior in the boy I've known all my life. How many new habits did he develop over the last year?

Why now?

The repetitive question has my eyes darting around the rest of the room, like it'll provide me with an answer.

I shouldn't be snooping. It's not my place to steal the explanation from Caleb.

But something feels... off.

It's a different kind of prickle that toys with the hairs on the back of my neck. I can't explain how or why, but I need to know why Caleb is acting so differently. I need to understand before it's too late and we go down a road both of us regret.

Before I can reconsider my actions, I begin combing through the room, hunting for anything out of the ordinary. There's nothing odd in his desk drawers. Nor his closet. After failing to find something of note on his bedside table, I turn to the bookshelf.

Studying the rows of books, I read title after title. A

Quinn through and through, Caleb has a fondness for murder mysteries and ghost stories. It isn't until I'm standing on my toes that I spy the spine of a worn, brown-leather notebook.

Not to doubt Caleb's sensitivity, but I've never seen that boy journal a day in his life. There's no way this belongs to him. It's that assurance that emboldens me to carefully slide the book from the shelf.

Barely larger than the palm of my hand, the notebook is pocket-sized. I'm immediately reminded of a field journal. Something intended for on-the-go scribbles. It feels fragile in my hands, like the binding is hanging together by threads after frequent use.

Carefully opening the cover, I'm disappointed to not find an author listed.

However, the lack of an owner isn't the only thing out-of-the-ordinary.

As I flip through the pages, my brow furrows when I realize each page features a different style of handwriting. How many shared this journal?

Heading back to the first page, I hastily skim the entry. There's no date, adding to my growing madness. Whoever wrote in this journal, clearly didn't intend to make it easy for an unwelcome reader to comprehend.

That doesn't stop me from trying.

It took two weeks for us to prep camp for the kids, but parents were pleased when they dropped them off. We've given the campers the run of the place. Figured they'd be less tempted to nose their way around if nothing was labeled "off-limits." That—and a few well-intended ghost stories—

keep the kids in their cabins after curfew.
Most of them, at least. Some counselors
are convinced a few punks are sneaking out
in the middle of the night. Even the
soberest of us swear to have seen unexplained shadows lurking between the trees.
Mr. Rob says "Kids will be kids. So long as
no one gets hurt, let 'em sneak around and
have their fun."

Skimming through the next few pages, which detail the locations of poisonous plants and instructions for closing up cabins at the end of the summer, I realize what's in my hands. A counselor's log from the Camp Casper days. How did Caleb get his hands on this? Did he swipe it from his mother? Or Samuel? Perhaps he unearthed it at Old Camp, considering it was sitting out in the open on his shelf. Judging by the amount of dust on it, I doubt Caleb ever cracked it open.

A new question pops into my head. Did my mom ever write in this? The idea has me rapidly flipping through the pages, searching for any sign of her handwriting. It isn't until halfway through the notebook that a curious entry catches my eye. It's not her script, but the details capture my attention, nonetheless.

This morning, we found three more holes
dug up. Had to keep the kids from the
west-side of the lake until we could fill

them in. Can't figure out what kind of animal can dig a hole that deep and wide. The kids should know better, but just in case, we locked up all the shovels. I keep expecting us to find something at the bottom, but the hole is empty every time.

Mr. Rob says to stop worrying about it.

Holes? Who dug them? The familiarity leaves an uneasy feeling in my stomach. Whoever stole Lacy Monroe left a massive hole—and then tossed Phoebe's body in it for us to find.

The empty holes are mentioned in the counselor's log a few additional times, but never alongside an explanation. It's simply documented, alongside camp duties, maintenance guides, and maps of the surrounding forest. There's some mention of Robert sneaking around the camp with a woman, but never her identity. Though one entry on the matter has me pausing to read.

The red-haired lady is back. No counselor can come up with a better name for her than that. Mistress doesn't seem fair. We don't know why Mr. Rob invites her here whenever Ms. Winifred runs errands in town. But if it is what it looks like, Ms. Winifred deserves the truth, and Lacy has a plan to help her find it.

And on the next page, a hastily scribbled entry provides further insight.

> Lacy's plan went to shit. Ms. Winifred returned to camp early, just like we wanted, but she lost her mind when she saw the red-haired lady. We couldn't hear much of what was being yelled in their cabin, but she screamed the name "Miriam." Ms. Winifred dragged that lady out of the owner's cabin by her red hair. Made it pretty deep into the woods before they started fighting.
>
> Mr. Rob doesn't know we were lurking and we're gonna keep it that way. Counselors took a blood oath to keep it a secret, so if you're reading this, consider yourself inducted. Just know, none of us trust what we saw.
>
> Ms. Winifred was furious at her cheating husband, but she attacked the red-haired lady first. Knocked her clean out with a shovel and was half-way finished with burying her in the woods when Mr. Rob finally found them. He worked Ms. Winifred into a tizzy. It was hard to tell exactly what happened, but she started gasping for breath and then collapsed dead. Mr. Rob dumped her in the same hole as the red-haired lady. Then he helped the red-haired lady out.
>
> Maybe the red-haired lady wasn't completely dead like we thought.

Robert killed his wife and got away with it. Everyone in town assumed Robert closed the camp after his wife tragically died of a heart attack.

Not only did he kill her, but the counselors knew. Did my mother?

What made the counselors stay quiet? Because it was their plan that led to her death?

An itch at the back of my mind tells me I'm missing something.

My lips purse when I flip and find the next pages torn away. It isn't until I've reached the last few pages that I pause again.

I'd know that neat scrawl anywhere.

Mom's handwriting.

Camp Casper will have you, but ya better watch out
Play by its rules, it's what this song is about
A camp with a curse, a fire to sit 'round
Heed our wise warning or you won't be found

Camp will have order, everything in place
If you enter a buildin', leave with no trace
A tool shed unkempt, a mess all around
Heed our wise warning or on your head they will pound

The water will tempt ya, a counselor fulla air
You go skinny dippin', enter if you dare
A lake with a secret, lurkin' vines that can bound
Heed our wise warning or you will be drowned

A love for a love, a heart for a heart
One sweetheart to have, the other to depart
A land with a legend, a hole in the ground
Heed our wise warning or sleep under a dirt mound

Camp Casper will have you, but ya better watch out
Play by its rules, it's what this song is about
A camp with a curse, a fire to sit 'round
Heed our wise warning or you won't be found

As I read, the song comes rushing back to me. A chirpy little tune I thought my imaginative mother had made up. She had a rotation of nonsensical jingles she sang under her breath while doing housework. There's a good chance she did create this one, considering the lyrics are documented in her handwriting.

Straining my memory, I realize the last time I heard this specific song, I must've been about seven. The same age as when she secured a job nannying for the Quinns.

The lyrics sounded so incoherent as a child. Most children's songs are gibberish, after all. As far as I knew, my mother had nothing to do with Camp Casper and was entertaining herself with a silly story about it. But as I read them now, I realize they aren't meaningless words in a song. They were actual warnings designed to help future Camp Casper counselors learn from the mistakes of those who came before them.

Rereading the verse, I attempt to make sense of it.

A love for a love, a heart for a heart
One sweetheart to have, the other to depart
A land with a legend, a hole in the ground
Heed our wise warning or sleep under a dirt mound

It sounds like a warning to sway counselors from fraternizing with too many of their colleagues at once. Or maybe they were singing about their two-timing boss, who literally killed one sweetheart to continue life with another. Whoever the intended audience, the message is clear: If you welcome more than one suitor, prepare to choose one over the other.

When I realize the lesson applies to my current situation, I begin to gnaw on the inside of my cheek.

But what's this about a legend? For as long as I've lived in the area and summered at the lake house, I've never heard anyone allude to something of the sort.

I need to get a hold of myself. I'm spiraling over a silly song and some vague accounts in an old notebook. It was clearly left behind to inform new counselors and keep them in line. It's highly probable this doesn't pertain to my current situation in the slightest.

But when I turn to the next page, my stomach flips with fear.

> *Today, a counselor drowned. Mr. Rob told us to use Lacy to revive her.*

Use Lacy? How?

Below this cryptic entry are only two words, written in a handwriting I immediately recognize as Ms. Quinn's.

> *It worked.*

I frown at the entry. What worked? Did Lacy rescue the counselor?

My mind races to catalogue this new information and make meaning of it. The counselors thought the red-haired lady, supposedly Miriam, was dead, but Robert Monroe pulled her out of the hole. Lacy was *used* to revive the drowned counselor. Whatever that means, it worked. But we all know how that summer ended for Lacy. It was her body buried in the ground.

A love for a love, a heart for a heart. One sweetheart to have, the other to depart.

What if this warning isn't about cheating lovers, but... sacrificing one heart for another?

Surely, they can't mean literally.

Right?

"Forget your library card?'

16

I JUMP at the sound of Caleb's voice.

Shit. I was so distracted by the journal that I completely forgot I was snooping in the middle of Caleb's room.

Forcing an innocent grin across my face, I turn on my heel, covertly tucking the small notebook into the back pocket of my shorts.

If Caleb notices, he doesn't say as he saunters over to me. In fact, judging by the amused glint in his eyes, he's anything but perturbed that I'm in his bedroom.

"Waiting for me to get back?"

I happily take the out provided, cocking my head to the side. "Took you long enough."

Where has he been all day?

His hand reaches for mine, tugging me away from the shelf and toward his bed.

Visions of last night spin and swirl around my mind. His soft lips. Those strong hands. It wasn't a dream. Caleb finally kissed me, and it was everything I wanted it to be.

Looking up at him now, my heart flutters at the expression on his face. For over half of my life, I longed for Caleb to look at me the way he is now. Like I'm the only soul he wants to see.

Suddenly, every instinct turns off as I gaze into the face of the boy I've always adored. The world goes quiet and there's only him.

Maneuvering himself to sit on the edge of his bed, I find myself standing between his legs. Now, we're eye level with each other.

"I haven't stopped thinking about last night either, Sky," he whispers, pulling my chin toward him.

My stomach flips. Last night wasn't a fluke or a mistake. This is real. Caleb wants *me*.

In an instant, his hands are squeezing my waist as his lips find mine. My fingers weave into his hair, tugging until he murmurs my name. It makes my insides crackle like a campfire. I no longer care where he's been all morning. All that matters is we're together now.

Kissing Caleb Quinn is a glorious blend of familiar and new. I'd know the smell of his lemongrass shampoo anywhere, but I never realized it made his hair so soft. I was always aware he had a birthmark where his neck meets his collarbone, but now I know what that part of his skin tastes like. Kissing Caleb is countless birthday cake candles and 11:11 wishes rolled up into one. He's all I've ever wanted.

Why now?

Mateo's voice in my head takes me by surprise. I'd completely forgotten the initial reason for my visit. I'm supposed to be demanding answers.

As if he can sense my distraction, Caleb kisses me deeper, tangling his fingers into my hair.

I need to stop kissing him, but I can't. There's a part of me that worries we'll never find our way back if I pause us now.

And so, I allow myself to be swept away by Caleb's ocean, relishing this moment before the waves inevitably pull away. I become lost in his lips, pressing myself closer to him. His hands comply eagerly, feeling down my sides, exploring whatever he can reach.

"What's this?" he murmurs in my ear as his hands graze my back pocket.

I instantly tense, knowing I've been caught. A thousand excuses get lost on their way to my tongue, leaving me stammering like a fool.

"You really did forget your library card." He chuckles, raising his eyebrows at me in playful accusation as he pulls the counselor's log from my pocket.

I scrunch my nose helplessly. "Sorry, I was—"

"Curious about the bleak history of Camp Casper?"

My lips purse as I nod.

"I figured you'd want to dig up everything you could after we found that picture of our moms." Tossing the notebook onto the bedspread behind him, he pets the sides of my face with a knowing shake of his head.

"Have you read it?"

"I skimmed the first few pages," he responds in a casual tone that tells me he didn't get far enough to note anything significant.

"You didn't notice our mothers' handwriting in it?"

He glances back at the journal with a puzzled expression on his face. "I guess I wasn't looking that closely."

"You probably also missed the part where Lacy and the other counselors hatched a plan to reveal Robert Monroe was cheating, and when everything went awry, they saw him kill his wife. They thought the mistress was dead, too, but Robert saved her, somehow."

Caleb's eyes bug out. "That's all in there?"

I nod frantically. "There's also a song in my mom's handwriting. It literally says, 'a love for a love.' Plus they mention something about a legend? But I haven't heard anything like that, have you?"

"No, I haven't." A different kind of perplexed expression

creases his features. "Is this why you came into my room? Did my mom tell you it was in here? She gave it to me ages ago."

I exhale and the truth spills out. "I came to talk about last night and stumbled across it while I was waiting for you to come back."

"Since the crew was sent away, I've been helping down on the dock." His brow furrows. "I'd never waste my day locked in my room. You know that."

I do, so I say the only thing that comes to my mind. "Mateo said you were in here."

Caleb's head jerks back, his hands falling from my face. He bears the expression of a boy who's just been slapped.

"Sorry," I immediately say, not sure what I have to apologize for but feeling obliged to say it nonetheless.

Caleb's mouth opens and then shuts again. I can practically see the cogs of his mind searching for the right thing to say.

Did I do something wrong? Is he upset that I'm still socializing with his friend?

Finally, Caleb speaks. "There's no reason to apologize. It's just," his head shakes, "I was under the impression Mateo and I had an understanding when I invited him to join this summer."

"About what?"

"You."

I swallow hard, waiting for him to elaborate.

"Sky, for as long as Mateo has known me, he's heard about you." A different, unreadable expression mars his face. "He's been having a tough time recently, so I thought the lake house would help take his mind off things."

I'm curious about what's dampening Mateo's world, but before I can pry, Caleb keeps talking.

"Mateo's a good friend, but he has the habit of making everything feel like it's a competition. From our grades to who skates the fastest at practice to—"

Caleb trails off, his eyes meeting mine. He pauses long enough for me to shiver under the intensity of his gaze before finally uttering, "I trusted him to not make a move on you."

My eyes blink rapidly as I digest this information. Is this where I confess just how big of a move Mateo made?

The impulse is quickly squashed when I register Caleb told his friends from home about me. That realization—validation—shoots a wave of warmth through my body. Maybe this crush wasn't as one-sided as I always presumed. How long has Caleb returned my feelings? How much time did we waste?

Caleb nudges my nose with his. "Stop smiling like that."

"I can't." I giggle helplessly.

This time, when we kiss, I have the confidence to take control. I'm the one pulling him closer. Setting our rhythm.

"Be careful," Caleb whispers against my lips.

I pull back immediately. "About what?"

"Mateo. He's a good guy—and he means well—but it's easy for him to get caught up in a game. You don't deserve to be treated like a prize."

"Thank you for looking out for me. Mateo is sweet—"

Caleb offers me a pained expression, so I hurriedly add, "But it's always been you, Caleb. You know that."

It's his turn to fight off a grin. "I do. It's always been you, too. You're impossible to resist, Sky. You're stunning inside and out. Even your voice is beautiful." He breathes out a helpless laugh with a shake of his head. "I love how you always sound like you sincerely mean every single world that crosses your lips. You're a walking temptation. It was only a matter of time before I cracked."

Finally, the question I desperately need answered escapes. "But why now?"

He blinks at me thoughtfully—like it's the silliest question he's heard all day. "Sky," he indulges me, "it's like I told you last night. I never felt worthy of you. My life—my family—is carefully-crafted chaos. Before making a move, I needed to know you understood what you were getting yourself into. My family is a lot to handle, but after you stuck around for all these years, I knew it was only a matter of time before one of us finally caved."

"I adore the Quinn-family chaos. You know that."

"I know you do, Sky. You're one of us. This is where you belong."

"I thought you considered me family," I chide him for his statement earlier this week.

He rolls his eyes, petting my cheek again. "Family doesn't mean blood, Sky. You know that. It means the people you care for most. Love the most."

Our gaze connects at this. I don't want to press my luck and push him to elaborate on what he just said. Though, I'm not sure I could articulate a single word if I tried. Not after the colony of butterflies migrated from my stomach to the back of my throat.

So, I kiss him instead.

Then it's his turn to pull back, wincing like he's just remembered something. "I forgot the reason I came up here. I was sent upstairs to find you."

"For what?"

"The kids need something to get their mind off things. They've decided a supervised field trip will do the trick."

I gawk at him like he just suggested we drain the lake. "We're leaving?"

"Only for a little," he says comfortingly. "We'll have security with us the entire time."

This sounds like a terrible idea. If the lake house is the safest place for us, we shouldn't be testing our luck by leaving its borders. But I know my place in this household. If the Quinns want to leave, and Samuel signed off on it, they're going to get what they want. I can either accept the chaos or lose it altogether. And I always know what I'll pick.

After a long pause, I finally nod my head. "When do we leave?"

"Five minutes ago."

With a sheepish grin, I guiltily back away from Caleb. "Sorry for making us late."

"I'm certainly not," he says, laughing.

My lips part when Caleb offers me the notebook before we depart.

"You don't want it?"

He insists, "What's mine is yours, and we both know you're the better detective."

My heart swelling all over again, I eagerly accept the little book from his hands. I know the answers lie somewhere between these pages.

The truth is waiting for me, and as I peck Caleb's lips one last time, I'm thankful that I don't have to find it alone.

"Where are we going anyways?"

"Your mom hasn't reached out yet?" he asks with amusement. "You're hosting, Sky."

My eyebrows raise as I fight to keep the disappointment from showing on my face. I've never told the Quinns about my rocky relationship with my mother; although, I'm sure if they cared to look closely enough, it would be obvious.

And then it hits me.

"We're going into town," I say slowly, my mind whirring as I formulate a plan.

Caleb catches on quickly, taking an eager step toward me. "What are you thinking?"

"I think it's about time we pay this famed mistress a visit."

17

EVEN WITH THE promise of answers, I still hate heading into town with the Quinns.

There's nothing worse than escaping to my safe haven for the summer, only to have to return home for an unexpected excursion and be reminded of the lackluster reality that awaits me come fall.

Part of me wishes I could've pulled the same stunt as Mateo and stayed back at the lodge. When a few spare guys from Samuel's team pulled up the front drive in a sprinter van, Mateo was nowhere to be found.

"He probably needs some space," Caleb whispered before we followed the others into the vehicle.

Although it made sense, it didn't make me feel any better. I don't like knowing I'm the reason Mateo doesn't want to be around the rest of the group. But if space is what he wants, I'll respect his wishes.

The small town of Casper is about a thirty-minute drive from the lake house, and with every passing mile marker, my mood worsens.

It's not that I'm displeased with my hometown. Casper is a fine place to grow up. The area is quaint, with mostly small businesses and a decent school system. The people are generally kind.

No—my issue is visiting with the Quinns.

It's only natural for the locals to be curious about the uber-rich family that summers at the abandoned camp on the outskirts of the city limits. My boldest classmates attempted to drag tidbits of information out of me; I always remained totally loyal and tight-lipped. After a while, my peers got the hint and gave up.

However, as soon as someone catches sight of their dark sprinter van, I know the inquisition will resume. It always piques everyone's interest all over again.

What do the Quinns do all day long? Does being their friend come with a salary? Can you introduce me to the oldest one?

I push the thoughts from my mind. Now is the time to focus on finding answers—from the mistress and my mother. If I know more about Lacy and this supposed Camp Casper legend, maybe I can connect the dots as to who this "secret admirer" is and why they are targeting me.

"Let's pull over and grab cupcakes at Coco's," Caleb suggests, putting our plan into motion.

While the others happily chatter in agreement, the security guard at the wheel parallel parks outside of the bustling bakery. While delicious, the pastries are merely a cover for our true pit stop: Mystics by Miriam, the shadowy trinket shop next door.

"Thanks, Beau," Caleb addresses the driver before helping myself and his siblings out of the vehicle. Allowing the others to go ahead, he quietly asks me, "You ready?"

I nod, sucking in a nervous breath.

Coco's is located at the heart of town, so we're already attracting all sorts of attention. Weekend shoppers slow to ogle the mysterious family who rarely show their faces. One brazen woman even snaps a photo on her cellphone.

"Good ol' Casper." Caleb chuckles under his breath.

"You're lucky," I huff, walking through the door he holds open for me. "You don't have to evade everyone's nosy questions all year long."

The inside of the bakery is pristine and white. Coco relies on her beautifully iced pastries to be the establishment's sole splash of color. If I weren't so on edge, I know my appetite would be hankering for one of her lemon-raspberry cupcakes. Instead, the smell of sickly-sweet buttercream wafting through the air makes my stomach twist uncomfortably. For all I know, one of these patrons is the admirer. Despite the security guard standing beside me, my eyes dance over everyone in the store, but no one's attention is on me. Everyone is too busy ogling the Quinns.

"Poor you." Caleb mockingly pouts at me while Amelie orders two dozen cupcakes to-go. I recognize the girl behind the counter from school—a fellow junior named Hope—and offer her a wave. The girl blinks at me with shock, and I already know she'll be messaging me a dozen questions while on break.

"I'm being serious!"

"I know you are," he says, a wry grin stretching his face, "which is why I'd like to apologize in advance."

I frown. "For what?"

"For what's going to happen after I do this."

With no further warning, he leans down to peck my lips in the middle of the bakery. Behind me, I hear Hope gasp, but her reaction is nothing compared to that of the other Quinn siblings and Diego.

Zane whistles while Cricket giggles. "About time."

Immediately, I search for Amelie's face, exhaling with relief when I find she looks pleased. Once she gives me an approving nod, I turn back to Caleb. I'm confident my pink cheeks match the frosting atop a strawberry cupcake.

"You're evil."

"And all yours," he whispers in my ear, enjoying every second of my squirming.

Gossip-mongers be damned. Those three words have me practically levitating as Caleb approaches the counter. "We'll take a dozen banana nut muffins, too. They're Ms. Sue's favorite."

"Trying to get on Ms. Sue's good side?" Amelie asks coyly, and when her brother shoots her an unamused look, she innocently blinks back at him.

"They'll be out of the oven in ten minutes," poor Hope stammers from behind the counter. "Do you all mind waiting a moment?"

Caleb's lips twist into a knowing smirk. There is *always* a wait for Coco's popular banana nut muffins. "Sounds perfect to us."

Metal chairs screech against the tile floor as our group settles into a small, round table in the corner. We wouldn't look all that abnormal if it weren't for the two looming security guards sporting matching *don't-mess-with-us-we-mean-business* expressions.

I shoot Caleb a glance. Getting away from his guards is his responsibility.

Right on cue, he frowns at me. "Did you leave your phone in the car?"

"Yes," I groan, immediately playing along, "and I'm supposed to tell Mom when we're close."

"Let's go get it," he suggests, and when one of the guards moves to accompany us, Caleb politely waves him off. "Don't worry. We're just ducking outside for a moment. I'll keep a close eye on her."

"Bet you will," Zane snarks as we exit out the front door unchaperoned.

"Good work," I compliment Caleb as soon as we're back outside. "Let's keep this quick."

Caleb nods in agreement, grabbing my hand and pulling me toward the darkened shop next door.

The only indication that Mystics by Miriam is actually open is a single sign on the front door that knowingly reads, "Yes, we are open."

"Can't imagine why she needs that," Caleb mutters under his breath. Heavy maroon curtains hang over the windows, blocking any shoppers from peeking at what awaits within.

Before we can even reach for the handle, the door flies open and a boy storms out. One with copper hair and a glinting stud in his ear.

My pulse quickens when I realize it's *him*.

"Logan Lewis?" I ask before I can think better of it.

The boy stops in his tracks, turning on his heel to look at me. His face is unreadable, but that doesn't stop me from scrutinizing his expression for any sign that he's secretly harboring a dangerous crush on me.

If he is, he doesn't show it.

"Do I know you?" Logan asks, his eyes narrowing.

Caleb instinctively takes a step nearer to me.

"We ran into each other at the lake house on the outskirts of town," I say.

Logan shrugs. "Okay?"

"Do you make deliveries there often?"

His posture turns defensive. "Does it matter to you?"

I shrug, trying to keep my cool. "I was just curious."

"Don't be," Logan snaps before whipping back around and stomping down the street.

We watch him leave with baffled expressions on our faces.

"Did that sound suspicious to you?" I whisper as soon as Logan is out of earshot.

Caleb shrugs helplessly. "I dunno, but I'll message security about his whereabouts."

"What happens when they realize we aren't at the car?"

"I don't want to find out, so we better be quick."

I force my mind to focus on the task at hand and not the strange boy who seemed unusually agitated with me.

A bell jingles as Caleb pulls open the front door and guides me inside.

Rapidly blinking my eyes so they adjust, I finally take in the store that has eluded me all my life. Mom never permitted me to enter, and now that I'm here, I truly have no idea why. Nothing inside of Mystics by Miriam screams authenticity. I bet the shopkeeper wouldn't recognize the presence of an actual spirit if it spun her around and kissed her on the mouth.

The store is nothing but shelves upon shelves of hokey knickknacks. Decks of pop culture-branded tarot cards that look like they were bought in bulk online, crystals shaped like cats, little ghost statues that allegedly whisper whenever the dead are nearby. A sign behind the dusty counter boasts of the most accurate palm reading in town, which is a hilarious claim, because she's the only palm reader in town. The whole place smells strongly of incense, making my nose wrinkle.

There's not a soul in sight. The only time I've ever seen someone walk in here is on a dare. Otherwise, the sleepy town of Casper does not subscribe to this way of life. For most people around here, spooky is purely a season, not a state of mind. It's one of the many reasons Mom ensures we keep our secret to ourselves.

What was Logan doing in here? Making another delivery? Or picking up his next freaky prop for tormenting me?

"How can a place this empty stay in business?" Caleb whispers as he takes in the vacant store. It's his first time here, too. Even a haunt-loving family like the Quinns knows better than to waste their money on parlor tricks.

"She must have a very motivated investor."

Caleb catches on. "Someone who wants to keep her busy and quiet."

Robert Monroe.

Both Caleb and I startle at the sound of a croaking voice coming from a back room behind the register. "Come for a palm reading?"

A woman in her early seventies limps toward us. She has pale skin that sags down her face and a helmet of curly hair colored in a vibrant shade of maroon that can only come from a bottle. She carries herself like a snake charmer, ready to coax whatever cash she can out of my bag with her whistling lies.

But I know better than to fall for the likes of Miriam Davis. She's the sort to keep her secrets close, too.

The woman's beady eyes dance between us, studying our clasped hands before offering, "I can tell you how long you'll last."

Caleb bites back a laugh before nodding for me to take charge. We don't have much time, so it's best to hop right into things.

"My name is Skyler," I introduce myself, "and this is Caleb. We're here because we're hoping you can answer some of our questions about Camp Casper."

Miriam's eager-to-please act drops at once as her face twists with disgust. "I don't know anything about Camp Casper."

"Except you do because you were spotted there on multiple occasions the summer it closed down."

"Spotted by who?" Miriam challenges as her eyes narrow.

"Doesn't matter," Caleb cuts in. With his free hand that isn't protectively wrapped around mine, he rifles through his pocket and pulls out a hundred-dollar bill.

"You think you can pay me off?" Miriam barks out a laugh. "I am not so easily bought, boy."

Caleb's eyes dart around the shop. "Aren't you?"

We don't have time for this old lady to dance around the topic. I need to know what happened the night Winifred Monroe died and just how closely Miriam Davis evaded death. Was it a close encounter or did Miriam actually—

"Did Winifred kill you?" I hear myself ask.

What little air exists in the stuffy shop stands still as both Caleb and Miriam gawk at me. I shrug at Caleb innocently. We don't have the luxury of beating around the bush.

The woman finally finds her voice. "You should know the answer to that, child."

My brow furrows. "How?"

"Because you reek of the dead," she hisses, her lips curling at my shocked expression. "What? Did you think I was an old fraud?" The woman sniffs at me with disdain. "If you are incapable of sensing when you're in the presence of a fellow seer, you have not been honing your skills."

"You don't reek of the dead," I retort. Neither does Mateo or my mother.

My mother. She's going to kill me if she learns I all-but-confirmed my sight to Miriam.

Miriam cocks her head to the side. "Well, unlike you, I am not continuously graced by the presence of the dearly departed."

"Why not?" It's not like a ghost to be picky on who they interact with when their options are already so slim.

"They don't like me very much."

"And why would that be?"

"Jealousy." Her thin lips quirk with the satisfaction of a woman who cheated death, and I realize, that's because she did. But how narrowly did she escape?

Miriam reads my mind. "I'm never going to answer the question you long to ask. Don't waste our time."

Caleb squeezes my hand, silently encouraging me to pivot.

"Fine, we don't have to talk about your death," I say, scrutinizing her reaction to my choice of words. Miriam remains stone-faced. "Let's talk about Lacy's."

"Don't say her name in here," Miriam snarls, slamming her palms down on the counter so forcefully that Caleb puts himself in front of me.

"Why not?" He urges the woman. "Because your lover killed her?"

"No," Miriam croons, "because your mother did."

If my bold questions made the air grow still, this statement sucks it out of the room.

"My mother would never," Caleb bites back. I don't think he realizes just how tightly he's squeezing my hand, but I have no intentions of fighting his grip. Not after the life-altering accusation he just heard.

It worked.

Gianna Quinn's statement blares in my mind.

A counselor died. Robert told them to *use* Lacy.

A love for a love.

"Are you suggesting it's possible to come back from the dead?" I ask, side-stepping Caleb, whose tortured expression has returned. My heart sinks. I thought we'd moved past whatever ails his thoughts.

"Am I?" Miriam cackles, reaching into her cash register and withdrawing a silver handgun. "Shall we find out right now?"

Fear slices through me like a bullet. I have absolutely no intention of discovering what a *real* bullet feels like today.

"Skyler, run!" Caleb shouts, pushing me toward the door.

"Don't you dare cause a scene in my store!" Miriam screeches, making us freeze. We might be fast, but neither of us can outrace a short-range gunshot. Slowly, we turn to face her, and when we do, we're greeted with a mad, toothy smile.

"I warned you to stop snooping," Miriam hisses, waving the gun between us. "Some questions should not be answered."

"But someone is coming after me," I plead with her to understand. "I think they're going to kill me!"

"Then they must love you very, very much." Miriam's grin turns sour as her expression clouds over. I wonder if she's recalling the love she shared with Robert Monroe. Whatever she's thinking, she shakes it from her head before snapping her attention back to me. "A word of advice, Skyler?"

My blood turns cold at the knowing expression on her face.

"Be careful who you gift with your love."

"What's that supposed to mean?" I ask her helplessly. Must she only talk in cryptic statements and veiled threats? Or maybe I'm incapable of thinking straight in the presence of a weapon.

"Get out of my store," Miriam mutters, waving the gun at the door. "You're only welcome to return if you're dead."

18

At the same time we escape into the sunlight, our crew exits the bakery next door. The security guards' shoulders sag at the sight of us.

I'm disappointed to see both of them standing there. The feeling only grows after one mumbles to Caleb, "Target got away."

Great. Logan is MIA once more.

"Where have you two been?" Zane drawls, making it apparent everyone else might have been concerned, but not him.

"Sky thought she saw a friend, so we popped in to say hello." Caleb's excuse sounds effortless, but I'm sure his siblings don't miss the pained expression that's returned to haunt his features.

I long to assure him that Miriam very well could be lying about his mom, but even I'm beginning to have my doubts. Hopefully, my mother will offer clearer insight.

Neither of us mentions the incident with the gun to the guards. Miriam isn't a real threat, and it'll only draw focus to the wrong suspect.

Amelie scrutinizes the shop behind us, and as we climb back into the van, she whispers, "Outsourcing for insight?"

"A total bust."

My friend waits for me to say more, but I pretend to busy myself with buckling my seatbelt. I'm not going to be the one to share Miriam's accusation with Amelie. That sort of information is a burden no one deserves to bear.

Realizing I have nothing more to say, Amelie leans over to whisper in my ear. "You're ten times better than any *seer* who needs a neon sign. We'll figure this situation out without consulting old frauds."

Despite feeling further from the truth than ever, I shoot her an appreciative smile across the backseat. I'll never know what I did to deserve an encouraging friend like Amelie.

<hr>

I can count on one hand how many times the Quinn siblings have visited my house.

Why bother when they have every form of entertainment imaginable at theirs? A majority of their visits occurred when Gianna was hosting an important board meeting at the lodge and needed her rowdy children kept as far away from it as possible.

It always felt jarring to see the most important people in my life gathered inside my childhood home. I never felt insecure about the size of it, nor our outdated furniture. Obviously, the Quinns were going to have a nicer place than me. The oddity stemmed from how real it made them feel. Like they weren't just a figment of my imagination that my lonely mind manifested every summer.

Our home appears exactly how I left it a few days ago. A little brick house at the end of a cul-de-sac. Mom's front garden bed is blooming with irises and indigo. She's always had a green thumb. Anything she touches grows well.

It sounds like she took the afternoon off to welcome her second family, which says a lot about our bleak situation because Sue Pierce never likes to take a day off work.

The woman waits on the front stoop, earning wide grins from her honorary children. It's the first time I've seen many of them smile all day long.

I look very little like my mother. Where I'm short and blonde, she is tall and brunette. Apparently, I got my coloring from the man who got her pregnant and skipped town. Amelie once asked me his name, and when she realized I didn't know it, we spent the rest of the day suggesting odd possibilities between fits of hysterical giggles.

"These can't be my kids!" Mom cries as Cricket runs into her arms. "You're far too old."

"I've started using retinol under my eyes," Amelie offers, earning the desired reaction from my mother.

She clicks her tongue. "Then you better hurry inside before the sun wrinkles your skin."

Amelie skips through the door, Cricket, Zane, and Diego at her heels. Caleb stops to give my mother a tight hug.

"It's great to see you, Ms. Sue."

Mom pats his cheek. "I heard you're spending plenty of time with my daughter."

"Where'd you hear that?" Caleb responds coyly. He'd never lie to my mother, but the boy will never miss an opportunity to pull her leg.

"Do you not think I hear what goes on in that house?"

"Thanks, Mackenzie," he groans playfully, despite both of us knowing it very well could have been his own mother who told mine.

I'm dying to ask Mom about her secret history as a camp counselor with Gianna Quinn and the meaning behind the song lyrics she wrote, but now is not the time. It's best to wait until I can get her alone to press her about the contents of the journal tucked into the bottom of my tote bag.

Once it's only Mom and I on the front step, her charm evaporates as she sets me with a stern expression. "Why didn't you tell me the moment you received the first note?"

There she is. My mother excels at mothering anyone who's not her biological kid. It's a reality I've never shared with the Quinns, because all it does is make me feel unlovable. If my own mother doesn't really like me, why should anyone else?

Unfortunately, Mom has every right to be frustrated with me right now. However, in light of recent developments regarding the boy I've loved all my life, I'm not giving her any further reason to keep me from returning to the lake house. She can't know I'm terrified.

"Technically, I didn't know the first note was for me."

"Skyler Marie Pierce," she says in a warning tone, and I know it's time for a slightly different approach.

"Samuel is confident this 'admirer' doesn't even know me," I explain as calmly as possible, "but is just another fanatic trying to capture the Quinn's attention."

Unless there's some kind of sacrificial legend I can't wrap my head around...

"I don't care who it is. I want them to leave you out of it."

"Me too," I murmur. "But the Quinns will keep me safe."

"You're here to get your mind off things," she mutters, more as a reminder for herself than me, before turning her attention to the two security guards. "One of you is stationed at the front door while the other is at the back?"

"Yes, ma'am."

"Good. You think Samuel is scary, just wait. Don't you let anyone or anything get near these kids, understood? Not at my house. Not anywhere."

To their credit, the men don't appear frazzled. "Yes, ma'am."

Stepping inside the quaint house, my eyes skim over the familiar eggshell walls and framed landscape paintings my mom likes to make in her free time. Every corner hosts a potted houseplant with thick stems and large leaves. Following her into the living room, my brow furrows at the sight of the new flatscreen television and mounted speakers for surround sound. At the base of each piece of the entertainment system is the TeQ logo. The open space inside the letter "Q" is filled with a futuristic-looking globe.

I shoot my mother a puzzled look. "Uh, when did you get that?"

My mother repels technology. The woman's been using the same hand-me-down box television from my late grandmother for as long as I can remember. Mom refuses to pay for any subscription services, not that the old television could handle it. Hell, she'd still be working with a flip phone if Gianna Quinn hadn't insisted she have an up-to-date device available while caring for the children.

My mother blinks at the upgrade like this is not a groundbreaking development. "The house is quiet with you gone."

I squint at the poor excuse. "*You're* rarely home."

"What are we playing first?" Zane asks, easily capturing my mother's attention. The crew has settled themselves onto cushions around the low coffee table.

"Cricket gets to pick," Mom says, sliding past me and into the room.

Perplexed, I stare after her. There's no way my frugal mother decided to buy a fancy entertainment set-up from TeQ.

So, who gifted it to her? And why do I feel like it was Gianna?

Just what I needed. More questions surrounding the adults in my life.

Mom has the coffee table set up for a cozy afternoon with board games and lemonade. A patented Sue Pierce strategy to cheer anyone up. She's been using it since we were kids. The siblings were disappointed Gianna skipped a family barbecue for a surprise meeting? Board games and lemonade. Cricket lost her favorite doll in the lake? Board games and lemonade. Zane had a frustrating guitar lesson? Board games and lemonade.

So, that's exactly what we do to clear our heads now. We don't talk about the lake house or the unimaginable loss of Phoebe. No one dares admit we are all absolutely terrified. All we do is play.

"The rules are not up for interpretation," Amelie snips when Zane starts to negotiate with Diego about trading game pieces.

"How very closed-minded of you, sister."

"We're screwed if Mom decides you should be the one to take over TeQ."

"If you want to inherit the family business," Caleb quips, "can you decide sooner rather than later? My window to go pro hasn't closed yet."

"Tough life, bro," Zane retorts with a patronizing pout. "Can't decide if you want to be the heir to an empire or play ice hockey. Whatever will you do?"

When Mom excuses herself to the kitchen to refill her pitcher with more lemonade, I trail after her.

"It's nice of you to take the afternoon off," I say, helping her pull a new jug from the fridge. Though no one would ever dare say it aloud, we all know she likes to pass her store-bought lemonade as homemade by transferring the gallon into a glass pitcher.

"You all are welcome over whenever you need to escape," she says, unscrewing the lid and pouring. "You know I'd do anything for you kids."

Those kids, I silently amend for her.

Keeping my bitterness in check, I try to guide the conversation in the direction I need it to go. "The lake house used to be where we all went to escape."

"Even our happy places can succumb to the occasional cloudy day."

"Right now feels more like a hurricane than a cloudy day."

This earns her full attention. "Is there something else I should know about?" she asks, scrutinizing my face.

"Is there something I should know?" I ask her back, and before she can pretend she doesn't know what I'm talking about, I reach into my bag on the counter and pull out the counselor's log.

Her face pales at the sight of it. "Where did you find that?"

"Caleb gave it to me," I answer honestly, hoping it'll encourage her to do the same. "Why did you never tell me you were a counselor at Camp Casper with Gianna?"

"Because there are some parts of the past that don't need to be dug up." Her expression darkens as she stares at the leather-bound book.

"And yet you chose to accept a job at the very same spot over twenty years later?"

"Gianna Quinn has always had my back," Mom explains matter-of-factly. "It was only right of me to accept when she asked me to come care for her kids."

"I don't understand why you two kept your history with the camp a secret. I thought only out-of-towners were granted access at Camp Casper."

"I once thought it was a blessing to be the sole exception to Robert and Winifred Monroe's elitist rule, but I was sorely mistaken," she snaps. "Gianna's and my time as counselors was not a happy one. We don't like to talk about it, just like you won't ever want to talk about Phoebe."

Without saying as much, she's referencing Lacy's death. Like Miriam, I can tell my mother isn't going to be an easy nut to crack.

"I saw her, Mom." My voice softens as I recall the girl who visited my bedroom last name. "I saw Phoebe. After she died."

Mom sucks in a breath before nodding like this makes perfect sense. "Poor girl. With how she went, I wondered if she would be trapped in between. She'll find peace eventually."

I read between the lines. Phoebe is on her own when it comes to passing on. My mother has no intention of intervening. Maybe Mateo and I can figure it out on our own; that is, if he still wants to talk to me.

In the living room, the Quinns' bickering increases in volume. Knowing my mother will want to break it up soon, I hurry to reach my point.

"It's not just Phoebe, Mom." My voice is barely louder than a whisper as her eyes widen. "There's someone else, too. A young woman. I think she's Lacy."

Mother's eyes darken. "You must be mistaken. I never once felt her presence during my tenure with the Quinns. Have you ever seen her during the day?"

"Well, no, but—"

"Don't you think there's a possibility your current situation is giving you more vivid night terrors? It's never real, Skyler. You know that."

"This isn't a night terror, Mom! Her grave was disturbed, which reminds me." I hold up the journal. "This song you wrote."

"I didn't write it by myself."

"Semantics," I groan. "You mention 'a love for a love.' What does that mean? And what's this about a legend?"

She shrugs, fiddling with a strand of her hair. "I don't remember. That song was written years ago. Half the stuff in that book is utter nonsense."

"What about the other half?" I ask, meeting her eyes. "You don't know anything about a camp legend? Something to do with holes?"

"They're just words in a song. Meant to keep counselors from getting into trouble after the kids went to bed."

"What kind of trouble?"

"Like don't leave a mess in the tool shed or break a bunch of hearts!"

"But what's this about a legend, Mom?" I hold up the

journal, politely reminding her of what she wrote. "They found Phoebe in a hole."

"You're so keen on finding meaning behind what's happening right now, and that's natural and understandable, but sometimes, scary things happen without explanation. That's what makes them so jarring."

I'm close to pulling out my hair. Nothing about this conversation is going as anticipated. Why does it feel like she's holding out on me when it matters most?

"What about Miriam Davis?"

Mom stares at me blankly. "What about her?"

"Did she actually die that night?"

"And rise from the dead to run a junk store?" She scoffs. "Skyler, you're allowing yourself to spiral. This isn't one of your books. Get a hold of yourself."

I blink away my frustrated tears. No one who is supposed to be helping me is doing so.

"All these questions, Skyler," Mom murmurs after seeing the emotions cross my face. "You don't sound like you feel safe. Are you sure you want to go back?"

Despite the horrors we've endured in less than a week, I cannot ignore the fact that I'm finally experiencing the summer I always wanted with Caleb.

"Yes," I respond coolly. "I can't imagine a summer without the Quinns."

The alternative isn't an option. How am I supposed to feel safer here when my own mother isn't giving me the whole truth?

"I figured," she remarks with a sigh before meeting my eyes. "Is there anything else you want to tell me?"

Visions of the strange figure I saw running around Old Camp from the boat cross my mind, and before I can think better of it, I ask, "You haven't stopped by the lake house at all this summer, right?"

"And not seen you? Never." Mom laughs, tucking her hair behind her ears.

"Yeah, duh. Sorry. Dumb question."

Mom awkwardly pats my arm before heading back into the living room, leaving me to spiral with a confusing bout of new fears. Because my mother has the very same tell as I do when she lies. She tucks her hair behind her ears.

19

When we finally return to the lake house, I find Mateo sitting on the edge of my bed.

His lips purse when I don't shut the door after me. We both know privacy only leads to distraction, and considering the muddy situation I've dragged us into, we need to focus. That feat is easier said than done, considering his very scent still tempts me to draw nearer.

My feet remain firmly planted in the center of the room. I imagine ropes of binding ivy growing over my sneakers, trapping me in place. I cannot keep toying with him. It's not right.

"Hi," I say, careful to keep my voice low. I might not want to cave, but I don't want anyone interrupting us either.

He matches my volume. "Hi."

"We missed you today," I say, and I mean it. Mateo would've known how to handle Miriam.

His throat bobs as he swallows. "I wish I could've gone."

"Why didn't you?" I ask, fearing I already know the answer.

When those midnight eyes gloss over in confirmation, my stomach sinks with guilt.

"I'm so sorry," I whisper. "I've made a total mess of every-

150

thing. You don't deserve to be put in such an uncomfortable position with your friend."

He rises from my bed, daring to take a step toward me. The imaginary ivy keeps my feet tethered in place. "So, that's it then?"

"What do you mean?"

He draws another step nearer, and I swear that intoxicating scent of spearmint and forest foliage grows stronger. For the first time, I detect a new smell intermingling with the others. The indescribable musk of lake water. He must've taken a dip while we were gone.

"You're choosing him?"

My breath hitches. "I—"

Not caring that the door is wide open, Mateo closes the space between us, gently resting his hands on either side of my face. My pulse spikes at the contact as I fight to maintain control of my beating heart. I must remain focused. He deserves an unwavering response.

As if seeing this resolve etch itself across my face, Mateo shakes his head in denial with a groan. "Come on, Skyler. I know you two have known each other forever, but he is not the guy for you."

My weak heart gains control of my voice. "Why not?"

"Because he doesn't see you the way I do. He only sees a prize to be won. You started to move on and he did everything in his power to reel you back in."

"But—"

"You're not this dumb, Skyler. Stop letting your silly little heart lead you down this path."

"So it can walk straight to you instead?"

"Anyone that's not him."

My brow creases with confusion. "I thought you two were friends."

"We are," Mateo murmurs with a low laugh. "That's how I know he's not good enough for you."

My head is spinning like water swirling down a drain. These boys have the most baffling friendship. Both claim to care about the other, but as soon as one isn't around, they're flinging a knife straight into the other's back.

"Skyler," his voice softens as he trails his thumb over my bottom lip, "you owe it to yourself to explore your options."

I helplessly blink up at the boy, pleading with him to have mercy on me. *Exploring my options* is eating me alive. It is impossible to venture down two paths at once. If I keep trying, it'll only rip me in two.

"I can't," I hear myself whisper.

The pained expression on his face has me immediately questioning those two words. I don't want to hurt him. He doesn't deserve this.

Then, somehow, those nighttime eyes find a way to darken even more. He shakes his head at me in disgust.

"You're going to regret that choice, Skyler."

20

I KNOW this impossibly long night is about to get even longer as soon as I spy the Ouija board.

"I told you we didn't need a batty old fraud to find our answers." Amelie dares me to argue with a quirk of her eyebrow.

I'm tempted to reveal Miriam Davis isn't as much of a fraud as we once assumed, but I keep my mouth shut.

Amelie's room is the only one in the lodge where it's easy to forget we're in the middle of the woods. She went full glamping with her choice of decor. There's not a speck of green in sight. Instead, everything is in shades of pink, from her bubblegum bedspread to the rosy walls. A plush baby pink rug covers most of the floor, but Amelie wisely pushed it aside so she could ring the board with every candle from her bathroom. Her favorite scents are inspired by baked goods, so the space smells strongly of cinnamon rolls, vanilla frosting, and blueberry muffins.

I'm immediately reminded of the kiss Caleb gave me in the middle of the cupcake shop. I was right to predict I'd receive a nosy message from the cashier, Hope. And if she knows me as well as she thinks she does, she'll correctly predict being left on read.

Caleb comes up behind me in the doorway, peering into his sister's room with a sigh. I don't miss one of his hands curling around my waist. "Put that away."

She blinks at his audacity. "No? You said yourself Phoebe visited you and Sky last night."

"I don't think Phoebe wants to talk," I warily say, remembering the agonizing expression on the girl's face.

"Then we'll reach out to Lacy!"

"Lacy has ignored us for years," Caleb reminds her. "What makes you think tonight will be any different?"

"Because now she has a reason to answer. We want to get her buried back where she belongs."

Amelie directs that second sentence straight to the board, as if Lacy Monroe is trapped inside the wood. When it doesn't start trembling on the floor, my friend pouts.

"My point exactly," her brother quips.

"It'll sound better when Skyler asks," Amelie bites back, her eyes cutting to his hand on my waist. I'm waiting for her to broach the topic of whatever's blossoming between me and Caleb. Not that I'm worried with how it'll go, but what exactly does one say when they start dating their best friend's brother? I highly doubt Amelie wants the juicy details.

Caleb gives my side a quick squeeze before sliding his hand away. "You're not making Skyler talk to ghosts because you're nosy. She's been through too much already."

Amelie barks out a laugh. "You speak for Skyler now?"

I was worried it would come to this. The last thing I want is to be the source of bickering between the siblings. I'm not the only one who's experienced a traumatic few days. We all should be taking it easy.

Or maybe, we'd be better off if we found the answers we needed so we can all move on.

"I'm fine," I speak up. "Let's put this mystery to bed."

Caleb sighs again, offering me a concerned expression. "Sky—"

"I mean it," I insist. "Lacy clearly wants to make her presence known and we need answers. We can't leave any stone unturned."

Not when this is a matter of life or death, I mentally tack on. If no one else wants to help us find the truth, perhaps Lacy will oblige.

Jaw clamped shut, his firm gaze handles the arguing.

Whether he likes it or not, Amelie is right. We need peace —and that doesn't come without answers.

"What are we doing?" Mateo asks, attempting to peer around us and into the room. Over my shoulder, I catch his eyes widening at the sight of the Ouija board. "Never mind. I'm out."

I can't say I blame Mateo for not wanting to get roped into all this. Even as an untrained seer, I know these boards are bad news. They're known for attracting dark spirits—when they work, that is. But desperate times call for desperate risks.

Still, I don't miss Caleb muttering something indistinguishable under his breath as Mateo departs back down the hall toward his bedroom.

"You don't have to stay if you don't want to," I softly suggest to Caleb.

The boy spares me a stubborn look as he pushes past me into the room. "Please. Someone needs to keep you and my sister from becoming possessed."

Amelie sniffs with disgust. "Don't talk about Lacy like that. You'll make her ignore us."

It's not like Caleb to disrespect the dead. He's a Quinn, after all. He was raised to revere the other side, not shirk away from it. Amelie's right to call out his attitude. If Lacy catches wind that we fear her, she won't come anywhere near us.

"Are you sure you want to be here?" I ask again.

His eyes firmly lock onto mine. "If you're staying, so am I."

The protectiveness in his voice makes my heart skip a beat.

The wooden floorboards creak as we join Amelie, each of us taking a side of the board to sit alongside. One of the four spots is empty—but hopefully not for long. It would be the first time a spirit ever actually graced us with their presence.

"Okay," I say, getting comfortable as I take control of the situation. "I know I don't need to remind you both about how this is going to go down, but I'm gonna do it anyway. Keep your hands on the planchette and your mouths shut. If we make contact with Lacy, I'll handle the talking. Are we clear?"

The Quinn siblings nod obediently. I can't deny that the power shift is sort of satisfying. Finally, I'm in charge.

"Good." I reach to gently rest a few fingers on the heart-shaped wooden tool used for communicating with spirits. "Let's begin."

The others reach for the planchette, as well. Ever her mother's daughter, Amelie's eyes glisten eagerly. Caleb remains stoic and unreadable.

Breathing deeply, I calmly close my eyes and focus my energy on the board. The wooden planchette feels cool beneath my fingertips, but deep within, there's no denying the static hum. The others won't feel it. Without me, this is just a piece of wood, and the board is no better than any of the other games in the closet downstairs. Only someone truly tied to the other side can bring this board to life. Anyone who pretends otherwise is a fraud.

After a never-ending string of failures, I know it's best to take my time and become well-acquainted with the board. Spirits can sense if you're rushing. No one—on our side or otherwise—is keen to respond to a demanding invitation.

I allow the wood to warm under my fingers, syncing my pulse with its internal rhythm. Slower. Slower. Like I'm meditating. There's nothing more soothing for my head than becoming one with both sides of the world.

Then, as if a sheer curtain is torn away, I feel the connection spark.

"Let's begin." My voice is low, commanding, and completely comfortable.

Is this it? Will we finally make a connection with the other side in this hauntless house?

The others shiver with anticipation. Even Caleb, who I was worried would ward off any activity with his attitude, is back to the boy I know as well as I know myself. I'm not so egotistical to think our new relationship is helping his disposition, but I don't think it's hurting, either. He's processing the news about his mother well enough, and I have no intentions of spoiling his mood by bringing it up. Not with him at least.

There's a curious glint in his eye as he observes me at work. It makes my insides flip happily. All I've ever wanted was to be on the receiving end of that look from Caleb Quinn.

Focus. You can ruminate on that look when you're alone. Lacy won't come anywhere near us if she senses I'm distracted.

It takes all my willpower to break eye contact with Caleb and return my attention to the board. Adjusting my posture, I channel my energy into the heart-shaped piece, willing my first question to be answered.

"Is anyone with us?"

The silence is charged as we wait for any sort of sign. Glancing around the room, I search for a clue that we aren't alone. A knock on the wall. The flicker of a light. A faint tickle at the back of my neck.

But there's nothing.

What's worse is the planchette no longer tingles beneath my fingertips. Was it even there in the first place? I'm beginning to question everything.

I genuinely thought someone—Lacy or Phoebe—would make themself known.

Please, I beg the board, the room, and anything else that wants to pity me. *Please, show yourself. We want to help you.*

Suddenly, goosebumps prickle up and down my arms.

Heart pounding, my eyes shoot open as the wooden piece beneath my fingertips begins to drift. Amelie's jaw drops as Caleb breathes out a curse. The planchette is moving.

"Now is not the time for jokes." Amelie's voice shakes slightly.

We've all been guilty of messing with one another over the years. The Quinns have wanted their home to be haunted for so long. Who could resist giving the others a quick scare by faking a moving planchette?

But that's not happening now, I'm sure of it.

"This isn't a joke," I whisper back, noticing the peculiar dance of the candlelight. It's like an invisible being is twirling a finger around the flame, making it bob in a rotation. "We're not alone."

Confirming my assertion, the planchette comes to rest on a single word.

Yes.

My pulse pounds in my throat. This is really happening.

"Will you please tell us your name?"

I can't outright ask if Lacy is among us, lest it not be her and I offend our present visitor with my assumptions or give a dark spirit a name to hide behind. Whoever is with us—I want them to know they're enough. We crave nothing more than to hear them out.

Amelie gasps as the wooden piece begins to move on its own accord. Meanwhile, Caleb's gaze darts up to me in disbelief and... is that fear?

I offer him an encouraging nod. We have nothing to be afraid of tonight. As long as we remain cordial, so will our unknown guest.

The planchette moves to the center of the board, where an alphabet awaits. With bated breath, we allow the piece to spell.

L

A

C

"Oh shit, it's her," Amelie gasps.

Y

But the piece isn't finished moving.

"Wait, what?" Caleb wonders aloud as our fingers drift toward the left side of the board, away from the letter M. "Isn't Monroe her last name?"

His sister responds, "Maybe she's sharing her middle name? It isn't on her tombstone."

A

The piece scrapes back across the board at an agonizingly slow pace.

N

Back it goes to the left.

D

Then it pauses.

"A-N-D?" Caleb spells aloud. "Did she forget how to spell her own name?"

The question is barely beyond his lips before the lights flicker angrily.

"Don't disrespect her," Amelie snaps.

"I'm trying to understand her!"

"It's not A-N-D," I breathe out. "She's saying *and*."

"What?" Caleb blinks at me, that glint of fear growing more noticeable.

I swallow hard. "Lacy isn't alone."

The planchette dramatically bolts across the board in response, zigzagging back-and-forth. Our bodies jerk uncontrollably, fighting to keep a hold of the wooden piece as it darts around the board. Amelie uses her free hand to muffle her scream when the surrounding candles are snuffed out, leaving us in darkness, aside from a panel of moonlight shining through the window.

Blinking rapidly, I fight for my eyes to adjust so I can make out the board.

We all gasp as the planchette flies up and slams into Amelie's closed door with a heavy *smack*. Immediately, I jump to my feet.

Amelie's voice tremors as she untucks her legs to rise, too. "What's going on?"

"Wait," I say firmly, throwing my arm out. "Stay where you are. Both of you."

"Sky," Caleb whispers, "what is it?"

But I'm rendered speechless as goosebumps prickle every inch of my body. An unnatural chill seeps its way up my spine until it swims precariously close to my heart, which beats out of control. The others don't know she's here, but I do.

When I finally find her name on my tongue, my voice is barely audible.

"It's good to see you again, Lacy."

<h1 style="text-align:center">21</h1>

SHE LOOMS NEAR THE DOOR, one leg on either side of the planchette. Her eyes might seem unseeing and empty, but it's clear she knows I can see her. Alabaster skin glints in the pale moonlight and her blue-tinted lips remain agape. Like her other midnight visits, Lacy must be incapable of speaking. But she's here for a reason.

One way or another, I'm figuring out what it is.

"Sky," Caleb says my name under his breath, like Lacy won't hear him, "are you sure about this?"

Still, he doesn't make any movements to tug me away from Lacy Monroe.

"I'm sure," I respond calmly, not taking my eyes off our guest. "After all, we invited her here."

"She's with us now?" Amelie gasps, blinking wildly. From her perspective, I likely appear to be staring at the empty space before her bedroom door.

"Will you two let me focus?"

The Quinns fall quiet as I shrug apologetically at Lacy.

"Thank you for coming," I say to the spirit. "I'm sure this takes a considerable deal of effort."

Lacy stares blankly at me.

"Is anyone with you, Lacy?"

I spy her eyes dancing around the room, causing me to follow her gaze. The Quinns nervously mimic my movements, frantically searching the room. For once, we all see the same thing. Neither Phoebe nor any other spirit makes their presence known. Turning back to Lacy, I find her gaze set firmly on me. It's clear whoever was here earlier is no longer present.

Though it is impressive and brave of Lacy to fully manifest herself before me, it would be considerably easier to communicate if we were still using the board. But there's no going back now. We must make do.

"That's okay," I assure her, letting Lacy know her presence is more than enough. "I was hoping to speak with you."

Taking a deep breath, I hesitantly ask, "Are you comfortable with me asking about your time at Camp Casper?"

There's a faint clattering sound as hairbrushes and tubes of makeup begin to vibrate.

Lacy stares at me, mouth still stuck open wide. The insides are dusty-blue and impossibly dry. A pleading expression tortures her face. It's clear formulating any words is a significant challenge for the poor soul.

Still, it's obvious the mention of Camp Casper didn't bring happy memories.

Of course it doesn't. Camp Casper is where she died. If Lacy wants peace—eternal rest—we have no choice but to uncover the truth about her gruesome end.

Hesitantly, I glance back at Caleb, silently asking for permission to broach the lead we learned earlier today in Miriam's store. When he cautiously moves to stand behind me, I take that as my signal to proceed how I see fit.

"Do you remember how you died?"

Eyes pale as moonstones dart to her right, lingering a moment, before returning to me. The room continues to vibrate with emotion.

Immediately, I jerk my head toward the spot. Amelie's

nightstand. Like the rest of Amelie's room, it's thoroughly decorated with a white wicker lamp with a frilly shade, an expensive water bottle, a stack of journals, and... a framed picture of the Quinn family.

I suck in a breath. *It's true.*

"Did Gianna Quinn have anything to do with your death?"

The room rumbles even harder in response. None of us say it, but judging by our concerned expressions, we all take that as a resounding "yes."

Caleb swears under his breath at the confirmation. For once in her life, Amelie is too stunned silent, her lips parting in horror.

"Why would Gianna want you dead?"

My question is too complex for Lacy as her face twists with anguish.

"Was my mother involved?" I pivot, needing to find some connection.

Somehow, the shaking intensifies even harder, so much so that Amelie jumps onto her bed to have something firm to hold onto. A strong arm curls around my waist. Leaning against Caleb, I fight to keep upright. It's a miracle the whole house hasn't woken up.

Returning my attention to Lacy, I watch as her lips fight to form a word.

"Please," I say, "I know it's hard, but we need answers."

The girl before me strains, using all her energy to mold her mouth into the correct shape. I spy her tongue fighting against her front teeth.

L-

Her mouth drops open.

O-

The movements grow too difficult for her as her shoulders heave, like she's lost the breath she didn't have in the first place.

"You can do it, Lacy," I encourage her. "Don't give up."

Her eyes jump between Caleb and me. If he could sense her chilling gaze, the attention would probably make him squirm.

L-O-?

"Love?" I finish for her.

Then it hits me.

"A love for a love?"

An earthquake rattles the contents of the room in confirmation. As Caleb tightens his hold on me, I blink at Lacy in shock. I didn't want it to be true, but there's no denying it now. My mother, Gianna, and Lacy. The pair still living are trying to cover up a sinister secret surrounding Lacy's death.

"Am I in danger?"

But I've lost Lacy's attention. She frantically glances around the room as the rumbling intensifies.

"What's happening?" Amelie bellows from beneath the covers.

Caleb cries, "We have to stop!"

"Lacy!" I plead with the lost girl before more. "Please, stay. I can help you!"

I startle as her focus snaps back to me, eyes hardening as they bore into mine. And then, she does the last thing I thought possible.

"Go!"

Even Amelie and Caleb must've heard the departed girl's command, because both of them start screaming. But they have no reason to be afraid. Not when I'm the one she's speaking to.

"I can't!" I beg the girl to understand, but Lacy vanishes before my eyes, making the room fall still in her wake. "No! Please, come back!"

Frantically flying from Caleb's arms, I dash for the planchette. I have to help her return. Nothing makes sense. She can't leave me with so many questions.

"Sky!" Caleb pulls me away from the piece. "Stop!"

"We need answers!"

He twists me so I'm facing him, hands coming to rest on either side of my face. "Not like this!"

Lacy's right. I shouldn't have required a séance to know what's good for me. Leaving is out of the question, but if love is the poison at the center of all this, I have no business fraternizing with a boy who means the world to me.

Caleb must read my mind. "Don't you dare, Skyler."

"You two need to get out of my room right now!" Amelie cuts in, poking her head out from under the bedspread. "I'm on the verge of a mental breakdown and I cannot handle your drama."

Not needing any further encouragement to escape, I yank open her bedroom door. I do my best to forget Lacy stood in this very spot a moment ago, prophesying my doom before disappearing. Caleb charges after me as I hurry toward my bedroom.

"Don't let her leave," I hear Amelie call after him.

"I won't," he promises under his breath.

They don't have to worry about me escaping. I know the lake house is the safest place for me. Whoever is taunting me hasn't made contact in a full day, and I can only hope that means Samuel's security efforts are working.

As long as they'll have me, I have no intentions of leaving. But I am not walking right into this "love for a love" nonsense. Not with Caleb. Not with Mateo.

From here on out, my heart is under lock and key.

22

As I FLING OPEN my bedroom door, a new voice calls my name from outside his room at the end of the hall.

"Sky, what's wrong?"

"Stay out of this, Mateo," Caleb snaps, slamming the door after him.

Crossing my arms, I turn around to find Caleb brooding in the middle of my bedroom. "Was that really necessary?"

"Would you rather have him in here than me?"

My hands frustratedly drag down my face. Now is not the time for jealousy. "I don't think it's a good idea for either of you to be here."

He takes a devastated step toward me. "You don't mean that, Skyler."

"Stop saying my name like that."

"Like what?"

"Like I'm breaking your heart."

"But you are!" he roars helplessly.

I turn to him in disbelief, finding those cornflower eyes glistening. "That's not fair, Caleb Quinn. I've wanted you for years—you know that. I've been dealing with heartbreak for as long as I've known you. It's only now that you started wanting me. I know it can't hurt that bad."

He huffs incredulously. "You don't know anything, Skyler Pierce."

"I know that love is at the root of every single one of our problems. So, until they're put to rest, you and I cannot be together."

"Please," he whispers, taking another hesitant step forward. It chills me straight to my bones. Caleb is never nervous. "Sky, we were finally figuring ourselves out."

With every word, he inches closer, until the back of my knees rest against the bed and we're toe-to-toe. A warm hand comes and supports the side of my face, his calloused thumb gently rubbing my cheekbone. "We deserve to fight for this."

I swallow hard, forcing myself to refocus despite him being so close. Between the intensity of his stare and the smell of his citrus shampoo, this proves to be an impossible feat. All I want is to allow him to wrap me in his arms and hide me from the horror story unfolding.

But it's too late to hide. The story will keep writing itself unless I slam the book shut.

"This secret admirer has made it abundantly clear I have to choose. Until we have a better understanding of who is behind this, I'm not choosing anyone. I can't put you at risk."

"Don't give this monster what they want. They think they love you most, but they have no idea what kind of love you're deserving of, Skyler."

I suck in a breath as Caleb grapples with his next words. Tucking a strand of hair behind my ears, he finally utters, "I can't say that I blame anyone for being captivated by you, but when I find out who they are..."

The fierceness in his voice makes me shudder.

"Sky," he says my name with such sincerity that my lips part, "please, don't end us. I'm not allowing anyone near you.

Hell, I won't let you out of my sight if that means you'll feel safe. Just please, don't let them win."

I want nothing more than to believe him.

"You promise?"

"I swear it."

Unable to resist any longer, I pull him down to me. Caleb responds immediately, eagerly closing the gap between our lips.

At that moment, while breathing him in, I wonder how I ever thought I could relinquish this. Him. When he shifts us onto the bed and draws me nearer, it occurs to me that I'm wholly and totally incapable of giving up on us.

I could never abandon Caleb Quinn. Not after I finally have him.

I truly am a girl possessed by love.

"Us," he promises against my lips.

"Us," I recant back.

"Good." He nudges my nose with his. "This is where you belong."

Believing him is easy after he locates an air mattress so he can respectfully sleep on the ground near my bed. But once he's sound asleep, I'm left to reconcile with my choices.

Lacy doesn't think I'm safe here.

Caleb is confident I am.

I want to trust the latter. I've known Caleb most of my life. The boy bleeds responsibility and good decisions.

But it's that glint of fear—and genuine concern—in Lacy's eyes that keeps me wide awake for the remainder of the night. Am I making a huge mistake? One that'll cost me everything?

As I lay there, lips still tingling, I will that to not be the case.

23

ONCE DAWN BREAKS, I accept defeat. Sleep simply wasn't an option after the sky awakened with pale-blue light. It's better to cut my losses and salvage the day the best I can, starting with a steaming cup of tea.

I'm relieved Caleb sleeps like a rock as I slip from my bed and toe around him. Too tired to pick out an outfit, I silently grab the first thing I see in my closet, which happens to be a white sundress. Ducking into the conjoined bathroom to slip it on and brush my teeth, I try not to miss Caleb's close proximity to me. However, I can't ignore the reality that my mind is sharper with a little space between us. Caleb Quinn makes it hard to focus on anything that isn't him.

But if I'm going to have any shot of hunting down Phoebe's killer—and my supposed secret admirer—I'll need a clear head. Despite his valiant promise to not let me out of his sight, a little space is precisely what I require.

Thankfully, I've never been the sort to suffer horribly after a sleepless night. It comes with the territory of being on the receiving end of a lifetime of night terrors. The school bell doesn't care if you have a sleep paralysis demon. There's no choice but figuring out a way to make it work.

My mother loves to remind me it's an unhealthy habit, but I cannot ignore how my finest thinking occurs after a long night. My best essays are written hours before they are due. I've yet to fail a test after pulling an all-nighter.

So now, while faced with the most-dangerous puzzle of my life before me, it's time to take advantage of my exhausted state. I'm going to discover *who* is targeting me.

Pulling my bedroom door open, I jump at the sight of a shadowy figure looming on the other side.

Cursing, I almost slam the door shut in Amelie's face.

"Uh, you good?"

I slowly blink at her, trying to steady my heart. "I thought you were sleeping in Cricket's room."

She shrugs. "Sleeping is generous. When I heard creaks coming from your room, I figured you were also in need of some fresh air."

Bless this old lodge and its ancient floorboards. Clearing one's head is useful, but there's nothing better than doing so in the company of your best friend. Even one who is suspiciously glancing around me at the dozing figure on the floor of my bedroom.

Sheepishly, I carefully close the door, ensuring the latch doesn't loudly click into place.

"Don't worry," she assures me. "I absolutely do not want to know. But I'm glad you two worked it out."

"Me too."

We make quick work of padding down the grand wooden stairwell that winds to the first floor. A surprise to no one, Mackenzie is already in the kitchen. She's always in early to prep the day's meals.

Spying us, she knowingly fills two cups with boiling water, dropping a strong-smelling tea bag into each, before screwing on the lids. The beverages, along with fresh lemon-poppyseed muffins, are placed in our hands before she shoos us from her domain.

Murmuring our gratitude, we leave the sweet woman be, not daring to utter another word until we're in the already-too-warm outdoors. The silence continues as we descend from the back deck and into the dewy grass below.

The sun rises on the opposite side of the house, so most of the grounds are cast in cool shadows. The lake is perfectly still, mirroring the light sky.

"Are you okay after last night?" Amelie finally asks, cutting left toward the forest.

That's a good sign. I'm glad we're on the same page with the kind of conversation we're having. Casual chats occur at the water's edge. Only the serious stuff is discussed deep in the woods, where no one can overhear.

It takes all my willpower to not glance over my shoulder every few paces and ensure we aren't being followed, but I'm choosing to have a little faith in the ample security cameras strapped onto trees. As long as we don't veer off the beaten path, security will have eyes on us.

I take a long sip, allowing the hot tea to burn down my throat. It does nothing for the chill that refuses to abandon my forearms. Maybe I'll have goosebumps forever. A punishment for ignoring Lacy Monroe's advice to abandon ship while I still had the chance.

"I guess," I finally answer. "You?"

"Uh, no?" Amelie scoffs, furrowing her brow at me. "You had a full conversation with a freaking ghost in my bedroom. I'm not exactly sleeping like a baby after that, Sky. How did you?"

"I didn't."

Her nose wrinkles. "Stay up all night with my brother?"

"I know you did not just ask that." I breathe out a laugh, side-eying her.

"All I care about is our sisterhood becoming more imminent by the day." She nudges me with her hip, but in a matter of seconds, her knowing grin fades away. "Do we really think my mom is mixed up with all this?"

I can't lie to her, so I don't. "I believe your mom was involved with Lacy Monroe's death, but she's not the one targeting me now."

Gianna Quinn has no reason to pose as a tortured lover or kill Phoebe. This isn't her doing. I've also crossed out Logan Lewis' name from my list of potential culprits—not that he was much of a suspect from the start. He had his chance to capture my attention yesterday but did nothing of the sort.

After clearing my throat uncomfortably, I continue. "Caleb and Samuel both think our culprit is someone who's fascinated with me romantically. Or someone attempting to capture your family's attention."

But not because there's some ominous legend, I think darkly. *No one wants to consider anything of the sort remotely possible.*

Probably because it's not, and even thinking otherwise is a sign I'm losing my mind. The more I consider yesterday's events, the more I believe Miriam Davis played me. What's worse—she did it free of charge.

For a long while, all that can be heard are the creaking tree branches overhead and the eerily cheery tune of songbirds.

Finally, Amelie asks the obvious question. "But who?"

I shrug helplessly, thinking of my subpar love life. Up until lately, I wasn't aware of any suitor taking notice of me. Now, I have more attention than I know what to do with. Although, I guess it's not completely unexpected. Caleb and I were a long time coming. Sure, it took him a while to make a move, but we've always flirted. My feelings were nurtured summer after summer. My prior plans to "move on" were a foolish hope. I was never, ever going to fully get over Caleb Quinn.

Then there's Mateo. The boy who wanted to remain an option until it was completely off the table. The one who I can't seem to shake from my brain, no matter how hard I kiss his best friend. It's a shame the pair have a history of wanting the same things. It only makes the guilty pit in my stomach grow.

I don't mention my confusing situation with Mateo to Amelie. The last thing I want is her judging me for fraternizing with not only her brother, but also his friend.

"Then we need to figure out who has feelings for you. Other than my brother."

"Yeah, other than him," I echo her, my words trailing off as I grow lost in thought.

Whether I want to accept it or not, the reality of this "secret admirer" situation is this individual is either a perfect stranger or... one of the two boys who recently admitted their feelings for me.

I stop dead in my tracks as the gruesome possibility hits me like a train.

It can't be. They would never. Right?

Surely, it's not Caleb or Mateo behind all this.

It would be easy to leave a note at my door with access to the house...

Reading my mind, Amelie crosses her arms, her forehead creasing with exasperation. "Please, don't make me speak highly of my brother, Sky. You and I both know he's too good of a guy to be some freak with a taste for blood."

"I didn't say he was."

"You were thinking it!"

Unable to deny it, I shrug again. "If you were okay with us suspecting your mother—"

"You don't think my mother partook in some shady shit on her way to becoming a powerhouse in the tech industry?" Amelie scoffs. "But my brother? That boy wouldn't hurt a fly!"

"He's a hockey player."

"That's a *game*!" She shakes her head with disgust. "I don't get it. He finally returns your affections, and you think that makes him a murderer?"

"I don't!" I plead, my voice cracking. "But you can't deny there's something different about him this summer. He's always moody, constantly picking fights—"

"Can you blame him? His spring was a freaking nightmare, and while he tries to recover, his safe haven has turned into the set of a horror movie."

I frown. "What happened last spring?"

Even the birds stop singing to eavesdrop.

Amelie blinks her dark eyes at me. "He didn't tell you?"

"Tell me what?"

Her pink lips part with surprise, and I can practically see the wheels turning in her sharp mind.

"It's okay," I urge her, already knowing the loyal girl is questioning how much she should reveal. "Whatever it is, I won't bring it up with him."

Her throat bobs, but I know she'll surrender the truth when she starts trekking deeper into the woods.

"Brackenridge Hockey were having a record-breaking season. They made it deep into their division playoffs, which meant they were balancing extra practices and school, plus traveling farther for games. The boys were exhausted by February."

Both hands cradling her cup, Amelie recites this, as if in a trance. Her gaze doesn't raise from her feet, though we both know she doesn't need to watch her step in these woods.

"Caleb was on cloud nine. He was the captain of a team that refused to lose. What more could he want for his senior year?" She shakes her head. "Coach saw how much the guys respected Caleb, so he was given more responsibility during away games."

"Like what?"

"Mostly making sure the boys stayed in their hotel rooms and behaved."

My lips purse because I already know where this is going. Someone didn't comply.

"It's worse than you think," Amelie says, her eyes flitting up to me for a brief moment before returning to her shoes.

The pit in my stomach becomes firmer, and my voice is barely louder than a whisper when I ask, "What happened?"

"That's the thing—no one really knows what exactly went down. But the night before the championship game, the boys were staying overnight at some crappy motel. Caleb swears everyone was in their assigned rooms, soundly asleep before the most important game of their lives. He stayed up late to make sure of it."

Oh no.

"But after Caleb fell asleep, I guess one of the guys snuck out."

Just like I did this morning...

"Where did he go?"

A tear glides down Amelie's round cheek, falling to the dirt below. "They don't know because he never came back."

"What do you mean he never came back? Like ever?"

"Geez, Sky, please don't make me repeat the horrible details. The point is that Caleb's teammate disappeared on his watch."

"Is he—"

"They don't know," Amelie answers. "They never found his body."

My stomach starts feeling so queasy that I'm worried I might need to empty it in a nearby shrub. Poor Caleb. No wonder he's been acting so differently this summer. That boy already has so much on his shoulders. Even though the horrible loss of his teammate is in no way his fault, I'm not shocked he still feels responsible. It's in his nature to bear the weight of the world.

It only makes sense for Mateo to accompany Caleb to the lake house this summer. I can't fault either of them for wanting to escape the horrible memory together.

And here I am, driving a wedge between them when they should be leaning on each other.

Amelie sniffles beside me. "So, please don't accuse my brother of anything so foul. He's wracked with enough guilt as it is."

"I'm sorry for even going there," I whisper, ashamed.

"You're desperate for answers." Amelie understandingly nudges my side with her hip. "I promise you're safe here. Especially with Caleb around. After this spring, he's not letting anything happen to the people he cares about most."

I nod with understanding. How could I have been so quick to assume the worst about the boy I've adored all my life?

But as we drain the last of our beverages, nibble at our muffins, and quietly make our way back home, my mind grows murky with the puzzle still before me.

The Quinns can promise me safety, but they can't keep every horror away. Bad people will always find a way to do bad things. With every creaking branch or unexplained snap of a twig, my body grows more tense. But no one jumps out and chases after us with a buzzsaw. It's only me, Amelie, and the trees.

That doesn't mean someone isn't out here, trying to get me. Someone who thinks they love me. And I'm no closer to finding them than I was before.

24

As soon as we return to the lodge, I rush to find Caleb.

Everyone but the boy I seek is at the breakfast table. Zane, Diego, and Cricket pick at parfaits piled with plump blueberries and Mackenzie's infamous pecan granola. No one wants to disappoint the chef by ignoring her food but, judging by the still-full bowls and glum faces, no one's appetite has returned.

"You aren't hungry?" Mackenzie's forehead creases with concern when I rush past the table.

"Don't worry. I'll be right back," I promise her, not wanting to hurt her feelings.

Amelie loyally stays so that I can go chase down her brother. He must've been worried sick when he woke up and I wasn't beside him in my bed.

I refuse to disappear on him like his teammate.

But when I reach my bedroom, Caleb is nowhere to be found. He's not in his own, either.

He must have gone for a morning run before the summertime heat can consume the day. I shoot him a text, and when he doesn't immediately read the message, I do my best to quell my anxiety.

Of course he's not checking his phone while working out. He likely didn't even bring it with him. Caleb Quinn is one of the few humans I know who prefers to run in silence, allowing the woods to be his motivational soundtrack.

How could I have thought either of these boys—Caleb or Mateo—would ever hurt me? They're here recovering from their own horror story, and here I am, blaming them for mine.

Before I can think better of it, my legs take me back down the hall, toward the one room I haven't dared step foot in since summer started. But guilt has me gently pushing open the slightly ajar door.

It used to be my mother's room.

Now, it belongs to Mateo.

Who isn't here, either.

Blinking around the familiar space, my first thought is how tidy Mateo is for a seventeen-year-old boy. Nothing is out of place—from the roller skates propped against the closet door to the neatly-made bed. It gives me pause. I can't help but find his cleanliness endearing. Then I remember the reason he accompanied Caleb to the lake house and my mouth grows dry.

Those poor boys. I haven't heard either of them mutter a word about the tragedy since the summer started. How have they held up so well? If I were in their shoes, I'd be distraught for months. I don't know what I would do if Amelie vanished.

With Mateo's room also vacant, I turn to leave, halting when something catches my eye.

Very few items rest upon the desk. A mug full of pens and a small stack of poetry books. I recognize almost all of the decor from when my mother occupied the room. These were her things. Items she left behind at the end of her last summer because she was expecting to be hired back. Everything is the same except for one new item.

A camera.

My mind immediately returns to the woods, where I was

blinded by the flash of a camera. I pride myself in knowing every inch of the Quinn's lodge and everything in it. Not once have I ever noticed such an old camera.

Is this Mateo's? Surely, this would have been a relevant piece of information to share after I was harassed by a similar camera in the woods.

Unless...

The thought barely has time to percolate as a new realization hits me. Other than the skates, there is no trace of Mateo anywhere. No duffle bag or suitcase. No glass of water on the bedside table.

Hurrying to the closet, I fling the door open, only to jump back with a gasp.

"Oh my gosh," I whisper in horror as I take it all in.

The closet is empty of all the expected personal effects. There is no clothing, or even hangers.

Instead, what's left in the tight space is something far worse.

It's a collage of *me*.

Tacked to the wall are photographs of me running in the woods, trying to dodge my assailant with a camera flash. Other pictures make it clear that I've been followed more than I was aware. There's some of me suntanning with Amelie and us eating breakfast on the porch. One startling image shows me asleep in bed.

Scratched into the center of the wall are those five damning words. A love for a love.

It's Mateo.

He's my secret admirer.

25

THIS CAN'T BE POSSIBLE. Not Mateo. The boy who understood me inside and out.

Maybe it was all for show.

Growing lightheaded, my thoughts shoot back to how eagerly I granted Mateo access to my orbit. I was so keen to prove I was over Caleb that I welcomed in the first boy who looked at me. Every single inch of me sizzles with agony as the truth washes over me.

He's a murderer.

Nothing makes sense, but how can I deny the evidence stuck to the wall of his abandoned bedroom closet?

Daring to inspect the monstrosity from a closer angle, I find far more than pictures of me.

A yet-to-be-delivered love letter also hangs on the wall.

ToNiGhT, MY LoVE

Fighting back a shiver, my eyes land on pages, which appear to be ripped out of a diary. My lips part with recognition. They're from the counselor's log. It appears I'm not the only one who paid a visit to Caleb's room this summer.

Ripping one page from the wall, I immediately begin to read.

A camper named Jonah Benn drowned in the lake. His sister, Maggie, is a counselor, and was hysterical. She refused to call her folks and admit what happened before she tried every way to revive him. Nothing worked. Not CPR or the defibrillator. Then we remembered how Ms. Winifred killed the red-haired-lady, but Mr. Rob saved her. Chris, another counselor and Maggie's boyfriend, nobly sacrificed himself in the hopes it would save the kid. Maggie buried their bodies together. Then her brother—

I nearly lose my skin when someone bursts into the room. The page flies from my hand as I swivel to face the intruder.

"Sky!" Caleb cries, rushing to me. "I've been looking everywhere for yo—what the hell?"

Slack-jawed, he stares at the disturbing sight inside his best friend's closet. Instinctively, his arms wrap around me, carefully pulling me away.

A few additional curses slip out of Caleb's mouth as he blinks with confusion. "I don't understand."

"Mateo left this," I whisper, still trembling with shock. "He's gone, Caleb."

The boy turns me to face him, his expression hardening as he asks, "What do you mean he's gone?"

"Look around! There's nothing else in here!" My pulse quickens as I spiral. "He thinks he's in love with me and now he's going to kill me."

"There must be some misunderstanding," Caleb says in disbelief. "Mateo would never. And why do you think he loves you?"

My eyes grow damp with guilt. "Because we—"

"Actually, I don't want to know." Caleb's expression becomes unreadable. "You think he's behind all this?"

"Even if we look past the physical evidence before us," I shriek, waving an arm at the closet, "how can we ignore the coincidence that the summer he joins us, everything goes wrong?"

The betrayal makes Caleb's eyes squeeze shut. Finally, he mutters, "You're confident he's gone?"

"I haven't seen him since last night. Have you?"

"No," he grunts, staring off into space. His expression darkens, like enormous clouds drifting into the sun's path. "This is all my fault."

"It's not!" My hand instinctively rises to cup his cheek. "You can't keep blaming yourself for the actions of others."

Caleb's eyes flash knowingly. "You know about last spring."

"Amelie told me about your teammate's disappearance. That wasn't your fault. And neither is this. You were trying to do the right thing by bringing Mateo here with you to heal. You couldn't have known."

"I don't know anything anymore." Caleb blinks around the room, searching for any sign of his friend's innocence. Finding none, he scowls before turning to leave.

"Wait, where are you going?"

"I'm sending Samuel after Mateo."

"I'm coming with you."

"Like hell you are!" he practically barks at my suggestion. "You're staying here at the lodge where it's safe."

"Safe?" It's my turn to scoff. "Mateo's been living here with us this entire time!"

"This isn't up for debate, Skyler. If anything happens to you—"

"Mateo can't hurt me anymore." My voice is raw, like I just swallowed a dozen hot coals.

I let him in. I sang his name. I allowed him to set the rhythm of my pulse. Now, what's left of it, achingly beats with betrayal.

You are a hopeless, foolish girl.

My eyes harden alongside my heart. "I dare him to try his worst."

26

Mateo didn't try.

In fact, according to security, there was no sign of him all day. In the early afternoon, Caleb returned from meeting with Samuel stoic as ever.

"Anything?" I dared to ask, despite already knowing my answer.

"I helped them comb the entire property. There's no sign of Mateo anywhere." Seeing my face fall, he tacked on, "That's a good thing, Sky. It's no wonder Samuel's team couldn't find anyone on the property. No one was looking for someone who was already here. With Mateo gone, they've tapped the local authorities to maintain the perimeter. He won't get anywhere near us now."

Still, Caleb dutifully kept his younger siblings occupied with activities inside the lodge. Between rounds of board games and puzzles, we helped Mackenzie make granola bars in the kitchen. The weather cooperated with his scheme, dousing the lake house with rain for the entire afternoon.

However, in true Quinn fashion, the whole household grows stir-crazy by the time supper concludes.

"If my feet don't touch the literal earth in the next ten

minutes, I'm gonna lose it," Zane groans, pushing away his plate of half-eaten cherry pie.

"The rain has finally stopped," Diego agrees, "and we have at least an hour before dark."

"I thought we wanted to play a round of charades," Caleb reminds the others. A valiant effort, but we both know it's in vain.

"Unless you want me to act out suffocating from lack of fresh air," Zane admonishes him, "I'm gonna need a rain check. Or a *it-finally-stopped-raining* check."

"Then how about we light a fire on the back deck and roast marshmallows?" I suggest, earning an appreciative grin from Caleb.

Immediately, my head rushes toward all sorts of fanciful ideas of the future, where we're parenting children of our own. In a perfect world, they'd have his eyes.

Before I can get lost in such lovely thoughts, Cricket brings me right back down to earth. "Please. I need to get my mind off everything. All who vote to play capture the flag, say aye!"

All but Caleb and I croon, "Aye!"

"The last time we went running around the woods at dusk, Skyler was harassed by a murderer!"

"Stop campaigning," Zane says, rising from his seat. "You were already outvoted. Besides, Mateo is nowhere to be found."

Caleb's eyes dart to me helplessly, but we both know there's no arguing with his siblings.

"We're back inside at sundown," he negotiates.

"Fine by me," Zane claps his hands on the backs of Diego and Cricket, "we'll beat you before the sun sets."

With teams clearly established, we all push in our chairs and regroup on the back deck. Heat clings to the air like a helpless lover, not budging for anything, least of all the competing breeze.

"Team Beauty challenges you to capture Diego's compass necklace," Cricket proclaims, grandly gesturing toward the chain around the boy's neck. A gold locket, which opens to reveal a compass, hangs to his collarbone on a long chain.

The term "flag" is used loosely when playing with the Quinns. The only requirement is that the hidden item must have value.

Caleb crosses his arms, his competitiveness returning despite his better judgment. "He can't be wearing it during the game."

"I won't be," Diego promises with a wink.

"Fine," Caleb grunts, "then Team Age challenges you to capture Amelie's bandana."

"Like hell we do!" Amelie protests. "This is designer."

"How about your walking stick?" I suggest, nodding toward the snapped hockey twig resting against the side of the deck.

Caleb complies with a nod, but I don't miss the way his eyes flash.

Immediately, I attempt to remedy the proposition. "Unless—"

"No," Caleb cuts me off, handing the stick to his sister, "I'd like to see them try to take this from me."

"Very well." Zane accepts the challenge. "We'll take the east side of the lake. West of the ropes course is yours."

"We steer clear of Lacy," I implore the others with a stern expression. "And if anyone sees anything funny, call Samuel right away."

Amelie wields Caleb's hockey stick like it's a heavy sword. "I dare Mateo to come at us."

Caleb wisely reclaims it from her grasp.

Zane grins wickedly at his older competitors. "Good luck, you lot. You'll need it."

"Don't forget, if no one makes a steal before sundown, the

game is over," I interject, unable to strike the concern from my heart.

"Paused," Zane counters. Capture the flag with the Quinns is known to last for hours. Between the enormous playing ground and few rules, very little is off-limits. Some hunts take so long that even the hiders forget where they've stashed their item, and we're left to stumble across someone's lost possession weeks—sometimes years—later.

"Deal," Caleb agrees, and the pair shakes hands. "Age before beauty?"

"Take all the head starts you need, brother. Your hiding spot will still be subpar."

Caleb doesn't take the bait, strutting down the steps of the back porch. After sharing a look, Amelie and I follow toward the west side of the property.

As soon as we're in the cover of the woods, Caleb turns to us, his face expressionless as he holds up his walking stick. "Any ideas where we stash this thing?"

I frown, realizing he has no intention of throwing the game with an obvious hiding spot. Who cares if Team Beauty sees right through us? The faster this game is done, the better. They can be mad at us after we're back inside the lodge. With Mateo no longer inside, it is actually the safest place for us.

"Sorry, why are we trying to win? I can't think of a worse time for us to be running around these woods."

"Don't you think we're safe out here?"

I gape at Amelie, starting to feel like I'm the only one who hasn't gone completely senseless. "You do?"

"We can't stay holed away inside forever, Skyler," she says quietly.

But I don't intend to let this slide so easily. "Do you think Phoebe's body even left the morgue yet?"

"Do you expect everyone to mourn forever?"

"What happened to you all?" I admonish them. "Our

friend is dead, but you're all ready to bounce back and get on with your summer vacation? Mat—"

"Maybe you should sit this game out," Caleb interjects.

I blink at him with shock. Am I missing something?

No one is reacting appropriately to the situation. They act like they're untouchable; meanwhile, not a single one of us is safe. And I no longer require the warning of a spirit to come to that conclusion.

Perhaps that's the problem with being the only person on the premises who doesn't have a millionaire mother, attend an elite boarding school, or have a privileged future awaiting them after graduation. When the summer ends, I go back to living in a nearly-always empty house, b-minusing my way through school, and praying I'll figure out what I want to do with my life.

Staring at the pair, I'm reminded of the cruel reality that I may be here, but I am not one of them. And as such, I have no say in what goes.

Is this what a relationship with Caleb entails? Will I ever be granted enough power to have my voice heard?

Caleb must notice this dawn upon my face because his expression softens. "It's going to be okay, Sky. As long as we stay on our property, we're safe."

"How can you be sure?" I ask in a hushed voice.

"Skyler," he locks eyes with me, "this is our family we're talking about. You're all that matters to me. We're only out here because it's safe and the kids need to find peace."

My cheeks burn at his use of *our family*.

This is my chance to prove I'm deserving of that inclusion. Being a Quinn isn't easy. They don't hide inside. A proper Quinn harnesses what scares them and uses it to their advantage.

Fear is fuel.

And so, I take the hockey stick from Caleb's hands.

"I'll hide it."

His expression warms with pride. "Atta girl."

"You two make some decoys. Upturn dirt and form piles of leaves." I hold up Caleb's prized walking stick. "I'll make sure they never find this."

"We regroup here in five," Caleb schemes, "and then we go after that locket."

The three of us share a nod of agreement.

As we all set to work, I forge my way deeper into the forest. An evening breeze rustles the branches above me, causing the dappled light to dance across the earth. Judging by its deep golden hue, we won't have long to play.

And thank goodness for that.

I believe Caleb's word when he says he wouldn't put any of us at risk, but I cannot completely reject the concerns that play at the back of my mind. The sooner we're all locked away inside the lodge, the better.

Attempting to shake the fearful thoughts from my mind, I force myself to focus on the task at hand.

A part of me is still tempted to stash the stick in an obvious hiding spot so the game is over soon. But the Quinns are far too clever for such a move. Caleb, especially, will see right through to my intentions. The last thing I want to do is upset him further. Today has been upsetting enough. The whole start to this summer, really.

Glancing around the woods, a dozen ideas dart through my head. I could bury the stick in the shadow of a shrub, but the upturned dirt would be a dead giveaway. In the end, I settle on scaling an enormous oak tree and masking the stick amongst the branches. High enough that it'll take time to reach.

Without wasting another second, I jump to the lowest branch, running my feet up the trunk to raise my body higher. The remainder of the climb is easy from here. Swiftly scaling the tree, I ascend until the branches bend beneath my weight.

Carefully lodging the snapped hockey stick on the upper

side of a branch so it doesn't appear when someone is prowling below, I slip back down before admiring my handiwork. It's a neat job, and I'd wager that Team Beauty won't find it for weeks.

Satisfied with my efforts, I turn on my heel, careful not to leave any incriminating footprints as I jog back to the meeting spot.

I'm surprised to find that I'm the first one to return.

Checking the time on my phone, I frown when I realize it's been nearly ten minutes since we were last together. Quinns are chronically punctual, so where are Caleb and Amelie?

Perking my ears, I listen for any sign of them nearby, but for once, the forest is as quiet as ever. The trees mock me by going perfectly still, highlighting that my friends are nowhere close. Which can only mean—

Did they leave me?

They would never.

All this quiet makes me feel like I'm losing my mind.

I want to call out, but a terrifying thought keeps my mouth clamped shut. Something is wrong here. They should be shouting for me. I'm the one who's late. But there's only silence.

They're gone, which means I'm out here alone.

Suddenly, the hairs on the back of my neck begin to prickle as an unnerving chill consumes the heat. Goosebumps rise all over my skin as I turn to find the source of my discomfort.

I was wrong. I'm not alone.

"I'm going to regret not listening to you, aren't I, Lacy?"

27

THE SPIRIT LOOMS between the shadowy trees, casting a pale, misty glow as the sun sets behind her.

Sunset? How long have I been out here? Why aren't the others looking for me?

I gawk at the girl before me. There's a reason she's here. Judging by the fury that manages to glint in her silver eyes, it's likely to tell me off for not leaving when I had the chance. Although, without the Ouija board, I worry we won't be able to communicate at all.

Apparently, that isn't a problem for Lacy. As soon as she captures my full attention, she turns to traverse deeper into the forest. The girl seems to know where she's going, which leads me to wonder how many times she's wandered these worn paths. Surely, never when I was around; otherwise, I would've detected her presence. Unless I'm not as in-tune with the other side as once presumed...

I usually am a tad distracted while on the premises. Plus, after I learned the lake house was anything but haunted, I allowed my mind to turn off while here.

Unable to resist, I follow Lacy through the trees. The forest grows darker with every footfall. The others will likely question my judgment to follow the lost soul of a dead girl we assume was killed by their mother.

Our mothers, I remind myself. My mom is acting just as suspicious as Gianna.

Lacy's attention snaps to her right, and I immediately follow suit. When I don't spot anything, a chill dances down my spine. The spirit only heightens my nerves by quickening her pace. If she's afraid of who or what is out here, I certainly don't want to meet them.

But what if it's one of the Quinns coming to find me?

Still searching the dense foliage, I stay put for a moment. Long enough to notice a tall shadow darting between the tree trunks a dozen feet away.

My mouth grows dry when I see his large frame. There are only two boys of that height and build here. One that I'm confident would call out to me. The other is a killer.

Mateo is out here.

I'm not going to wait around for him to kill me.

Sprinting to catch up with Lacy, I ignore the stitch at my side.

"He's here," I whisper to her, though I suspect she already knows. "We have to hide."

Lacy must agree because she shifts our path. At first, I worry she's taking me to her gravesite, but then she veers closer to the edge of Old Camp. Immediately, I know where we're going.

The cabins.

Picking up the pace, I sprint in the direction of the preserved structures, already plotting how I'll barricade the door with one of the bunks. Another will have to go against the window. Hopefully, the beds aren't terribly heavy, but thankfully, I have adrenaline on my side.

Fear is fuel.

I'll do whatever it takes to keep Mateo away. Today is not the day I die.

How an enormous hockey player is tracking me so silently is beyond me. But I know he's there from the way the back of my neck prickles. Mateo is gaining on me, and if I don't hurry up, these trees will witness another death.

Finally, the shadow of a cabin appears ahead. A piece of untouched history. The last thing I see before the sun sets are the faded words "Monarch Cabin" painted in orange over the front door. And then, they disappear into darkness.

I try to remember that's a good thing. Shadows are my friends right now.

Lacy beats me to the cabin, running straight through the front door. A breathless second later, I'm inside, too.

Goosebumps immediately prickle up and down my arms. It's freezing in here. Did the Quinns equip the old cabin with a new AC unit and then lower it to arctic temperatures?

It doesn't matter. Find a place to hide.

"Lacy?" I dare to whisper aloud, for the spirit is no longer to be found. "Don't leave me now!"

The familiar tug of her presence disappears as I realize I'm officially on my own.

She got me to safety. Now, it's my job to stay alive.

If I hadn't played inside these cabins a hundred times as a child, I would've likely fallen into a bunk by now. Despite the darkness, I know the layout like I know my own bedroom.

The bunk beds line the long walls, two sets on either side. A dusty, threadbare rug sits at the center of the room. Back in the day, I bet it was the perfect spot for cabin bonding sessions. I can only imagine the number of secrets that were shared upon it.

There's no lock, so I silently remove a lamp from atop a small table near the door and shove the furniture beneath the doorknob. It'll have to make do before I can properly barricade myself in. I'm not foolish enough to turn the lamp on.

Whipping out my phone, I frantically type a "SOS" text to the family group chat, along with my location. They'll send for Samuel. All I have to do is survive until they get here. Then, I turn on my device's flashlight as brightly as I dare and survey my surroundings.

Just as I remembered, sets of bunk beds stand tall against the two walls. I don't have to look to know the underside of each is carved with the names of former campers. One summer, Amelie and I spent an entire week on our backs, looking up at the girls' names and crafting stories about each one.

It's a wonder we never found our mothers' names. Did either of them spend their summer in this very cabin?

On the far wall, beneath the dusty square window, rests the old counselor's bed. It's the only one without a bunk, which will make it easiest to move and barricade against the door.

I place my phone face-down at the center of the floor so the flashlight illuminates only the outlines of furniture in the room. Just enough to see what I'm doing.

Darting toward the bed, I heave at the wooden frame until my muscles begin to burn.

"Come on," I groan under my breath. This thing is way heavier than I anticipated. Even while pulling at it with all my might, the bed barely scrapes an inch over the wooden floor.

Rising in defeat, I glance up at the window, and directly into the face of Mateo.

His posture straightens when we lock eyes, realizing he has me cornered. A moment later, the boy disappears from view, no doubt sprinting to the other side of the cabin toward the door.

Shrieking, I dash away from the window, looking for anything else I can successfully use as a barricade.

That's when I see it. A dark lump laying atop the sheets of the bottom bunk.

Praying it's something I can lift, I rush over, only to scream when I grab the edge of it.

What the—

Why the hell did that feel like a shoe?

Heart-pounding, I freeze, suddenly forgetting the outside threat. Is someone here with me?

Nabbing my phone, I shine the light on the lump, realizing it's a blanket-covered...

"Shit," I breathe out. Screwing my courage, I swiftly pull the blanket away.

A scream rips through my throat at the body lying before me.

The body of a boy with whom I shared my deepest secrets. A boy who saw the world like me. A boy who made me feel a glimmer of hope, and then immeasurable fear.

A boy who was just looking at me through the window.

This is impossible, and yet...

Here lies Mateo.

Dead.

28

I BLINK with horror at the boy's body, my mind humming with confusion. Nothing makes sense. Mateo. The boy who touched me. Fell for me. Fought for me.

The boy currently hunting me down.

How can he if he's *dead*?

My fears are foolishly thrust aside as I try to understand. The corpse's empty eyes stare past me, his lips chapped and parted. The tanned complexion I came to know has lost all its luster. The smell of rotted flesh hits my wrinkling nose, making me shudder.

I don't understand. Mateo was with us last night, but I know a body that's been sitting for a while when I see it.

A thousand possibilities whir through my head. Does Mateo have an identical twin? Or was that not who was chasing me through the woods? Or is the Mateo I know—

I jump as a figure bursts through the front door. Literally through.

Jaw agape, I take in the boy who just evaded the barricaded door like it was air.

Mateo freezes with apprehension, waiting for me to make the first move. My wide eyes dance over him, taking in the rich color in his cheeks and life in his eyes. How did I never notice the way his presence made me shiver?

You thought it was longing.

When the boy makes no sudden movements to kill me—if he even can—I accept that I don't understand anything at all.

"You've been dead this entire time?" I furiously whisper.

His throat bobs as he swallows. "I was waiting for the right time to tell you."

Like a video playing in double time, every one of our interactions thus far flashes through my mind. He always wore Brackenridge athleisure wear. I'm not sure I ever saw him open a single door, or even touch anything other than me, for that matter. I assumed his plates were always cleared because he'd finished eating before I arrived, not because he wasn't being served at all.

How could I have been so oblivious? I've been fraternizing with a ghost and had no freaking clue.

As soon as I accept that truth, his appearance shifts before my eyes. The hazy edges of his figure pulse with pale light. I was so naive for missing it before. Mateo is dead. He's *been* dead.

And I still fell for him.

"You think this is the best way for me to find out?" I cry, gesturing madly at his corpse. "What is going on, Mateo? You're dead? What is your body doing out here? How did you—"

Mateo cautiously crosses the room, closing the space between us in four long strides. Once he realizes I'm not going to run away screaming, he grips my arms, sending a chill through my body. It's not a threatening hold, but one that feels desperate. Protective.

I had it all wrong.

"How can you even touch me?" I wonder aloud, though it's the least consequential question.

Naturally, that's the one he tackles first. "I'm not sure, but please don't question it further, or the universe might decide to take this one blessing away."

"What happened?" I ask into glinting eyes.

"Skyler, I swear I will tell you everything as soon as you are far away from here. Please, you must—"

Before he can finish, another figure crashes into the cabin, this one actually opening the door. Wood screeches against wood as the bed is pushed aside.

For the first time in my life, the sight of Caleb Quinn brings me no comfort.

Breathing heavily, the newcomer's fearful eyes dance between Mateo, the corpse, and I.

A different kind of chill shoots through my system when it hits me. Mateo is dead, and yet, Caleb can see him. Caleb's always been able to see him. Talk to him.

Which means Caleb killed him.

Mateo is haunting Caleb.

I sway on my feet, struggling to accept the truth right in front of me.

Mateo immediately steps in front of me, shielding my body with his. Like Caleb's the threat.

And then, all at once, everything else connects.

Mateo is the teammate who disappeared. Only, he didn't just go missing. He was killed by his captain.

The shrine wasn't Mateo's. How could he have put a physical collage together in his current state? He's not deluding himself to believe he's in love with me.

Caleb is.

He's spent all summer giving me the attention I've always craved. And how eagerly I let him in, despite swearing I was over him. All it took was one kiss and I came undone. I fell for him, which is exactly what he wanted.

I shudder, making Caleb's eyes narrow. "What has he told you, Sky?"

Before I can answer, Mateo interjects. "Stay away from her. I'm not worth it."

A charged silence falls over the cabin as the final piece of the puzzle falls into place.

A love for a love.

It's real. After killing Mateo, Caleb convinced himself he was in love with me, to bring Mateo back to life.

Mateo isn't done threatening his friend, his voice laced with venom. "I mean it, Caleb. Don't go through with this. We were wrong."

We.

My heart plummets into my gut. This was *their* plan. To use me to save Mateo. They cooked up this idea together.

And now I'm trapped with both of them. A rabbit in the fox's den.

"This is not the time for cold feet," Caleb snaps. I didn't know he was capable of such a cruel tone. "It's too late to turn back."

Like hell it is.

"Stay behind me, Skyler!" Mateo shouts, but there's no way I'm listening to him. I don't trust the "cold feet" of a dead guy who once approved of my murder.

I sprint for the window in the back of the cabin, praying the glass isn't so thick that I can't break it open. I slam my elbow into the pane. The only cracking sound comes from me, causing me to cry out as pain surges up my arm.

Behind me, I hear the boys scramble. I risk a glance behind me, my eyes widening when Caleb runs directly through Mateo. Screaming, I throw myself against the glass even harder, but it's too late.

Caleb wrenches me from the bed, hauling me across the cabin as I fight against his impossible grip. Mateo grabs for me, too, nearly pulling my arm from its socket as he attempts to yank me free from his friend. I still don't understand how he can touch me, but my aching arm swiftly pushes the pointless question from my mind.

All that matters is escaping.

"Stop fighting this," Caleb grunts, trying and failing to get Mateo off me.

"This isn't right!" Mateo bellows back. "It's not too late to change our minds!"

But it is, and all three of us know it. There's no unlearning that the boy I've known all my life is responsible for Mateo's death, nor the lengths he's willing to go to cover it up.

Outmatching me, Caleb forces my hand into a fist, throwing it at Mateo's jaw.

"No!" I scream as Mateo winces, but the hit isn't strong enough to lessen his grip. If he can feel our kisses, he can certainly feel this.

"Let go of her!" Caleb orders, forcing my hand to do his bidding and hit Mateo again, now at his temple. This time, Caleb's strength possesses my fist, and the other boy winces in pain. Agony shoots up my arm as Caleb extends my elbow, making me cry out.

There's no fighting back. Mateo can't touch Caleb, and he won't stoop so low as to use me to fight on his behalf.

With my fist, Caleb lands another hit to the other boy's head, forcing him to stumble backward, his appearance growing hazy for a moment, before disappearing entirely.

"Mateo!" I scream as Caleb drags me from the cabin, but there's no calling the boy back.

Slipping down the stairs, Caleb pulls me into the trees I used to think were my safe haven. But apparently, every inch of this place is conspiring against me. Exposed roots steal my footing and shrubs scrape my legs. Backstabbing clouds drift before the moon, offering me no light to see my attacker.

"You love him, too?" Caleb barks a laugh, as I fight back with all my might. "Jeez, Sky, your taste."

Struggling to wrench myself free, I spit back, "He's a better man than you."

"Please," Caleb scoffs, like my movements are of no burden to him. "Mateo might pretend to have honor now, but days ago, he wanted you dead."

These words are enough to momentarily give me pause, and Caleb uses that to his advantage, pulling me further between the trees. And I know exactly where he's heading.

"Gonna toss me into Lacy's grave like you did Phoebe?"

"Shut up, Sky."

"What? I thought you loved the sound of my voice."

Before I can continue, he has me pressed against a tree so firmly that the sharp bark painfully pricks my back. With one swift move, both of my wrists are captured in one of his hands. I shudder as the other comes to stroke the side of my face. Desperate eyes dance between mine, and for one horrifying moment, I fear he'll kiss me. The very thought repulses me now.

"Do you think this is easy for me?" His hot breath warms my cheeks. "I *do* love you."

"You've deluded yourself into loving me," I spit back.

"Stop yelling, Sky, no one is coming. This is what they all want."

And there it is. The stunning, final blow that renders me completely immobile.

Heart pounding, I breathe out, "The others know?"

Caleb nods, his eyes glistening wildly. "I have to make things right after Mateo's accident. If anyone finds out I killed him, my family will be ruined. But everything's going to work out. Mom knows a way that'll bring him back."

"We have no proof this campsite actually brings people back from the dead," I hiss, willing him to return to the Caleb I know and see how heinous this all sounds.

"It's real, Skyler. Mom's done it before."

My soul drowns at the confirmation. He's known the truth all this time. Who else does?

My mother flashes in my mind. Surely, she'd never barter me away, right? Right?

Of course, she would. She's considered me a burden since I was born.

The raging waters flooding my soul begin to soak my brain, as well. This can't be happening. This isn't real.

I plead with myself to wake up from this night terror, but Caleb's tight grip on me reminds me this is very, very real.

And *deadly*.

"See?" Caleb implores me to see reason. "Now you understand why you have to die. We can save Mateo. He's my best friend."

"Your family values his life more than mine." The words come out in a snarled tone I never thought myself capable of using, especially while speaking with Caleb. "This is about reputation?"

"Don't think of it like that, Sky." His thumb trails over my bottom lip, but I'm too horrified to jerk away. "You're dying for me. Don't you love me enough to do so?"

I scream back, "Don't you love me enough to let me live?"

A pained expression crosses his face, and I'm forced to bite back a bitter, heartbroken laugh. How *difficult* this must be for him. Then his features twist with rage, giving me a glimmer of home. Maybe he doesn't actually want to go through with this.

"What are you doing here?" he suddenly roars into the trees, making me jump.

"Chill, brother," grunts Zane as he appears from the shadows, "it's just me."

Zane.

I practically melt with relief. This is a freaking prank. The real game of the night was seeing how hard they can scare me.

All hope dissipates when the boy doesn't even spare me a glance as he drags Mateo's body along the trail.

No, no, no.

The lightheadedness returns and I begin to sway where I stand. Caleb's grip on me tightens in an effort to keep me upright.

"I noticed you were getting, shall we say, lost in the moment, and forgot a key ingredient for this to work."

"Mateo will tell the world everything," I try to reason with them.

Zane actually laughs at this. "And say what? The Quinns killed him and then brought him back to life? I'd like to see him try."

"Go," Caleb demands, and with a bored shrug, Zane complies. We listen to him struggle with the body as he drags it away.

"You don't have to do this." Desperate tears slip down my cheeks. I'm not above begging.

"Get on with it," a new voice chirps from the shadowy tree branches above, making me freeze as the betrayal seeps through my body like poison.

"You're okay with this?" My chin rises, searching until I clap eyes on the girl I considered my dearest friend in the world.

Amelie merely blinks back at me, her face devoid of any emotion.

How could I let myself get so lost in this family? I thought they loved me, but in reality, I'm nothing more than a sacrifice. A means to an end. Is this why they kept me around for all those years? To ensure they had someone to slaughter if the need arose? Did any of them ever really love me?

I didn't think it was possible for my heart to hurt even more. But somehow, the shattered pieces grind down into dust. My heart has betrayed me. Dragged me straight to hell.

"I'm sorry it had to be this way," she replies instead, dropping something that Caleb catches in one swift motion.

The snapped hockey stick is so familiar in his grip that I recognize it immediately.

"Guess I should've hidden that better."

"Don't make this harder than it needs to be," Caleb begs, wrenching me from the tree and away from his sister.

Like a fish caught on a line, I attempt to free myself from my captor, but it's no use. Caleb Quinn has his hook firmly in me. No amount of kicking or hitting phases him as he tugs me toward the clearing we both know so well. It's obvious my screams are in vain. No one is here to save me. And even if they were, who would dare cross the Quinns?

My only chance of survival is myself.

The backstabbing clouds shift away from the moonlight, illuminating Lacy Monroe's grave. The freshly overturned earth has the audacity to smell sweet as my heels drag through the dirt.

Lacy's coffin waits for me, but it's not her body within. Mateo's corpse rests inside, slumped in an unnatural position. Caleb winces down at it, and I wish I didn't know him well enough to recognize he's internally cursing his brother's carelessness.

I wish I didn't know any of them.

I should've listened to Lacy when I had the chance. This whole time, she's been attempting to save me from this fate. She urged me to leave, and I ignored her because I thought I was *safe* with the Quinns. All because I'm such a lovesick fool.

I'm going to die because I yearned to be loved. I was so blinded by my eager heart that I never figured my steady Caleb could be my deranged secret admirer. He was the one leaving me notes. Taking my picture. Frightening me and then comforting me.

The idea strikes like a bolt of lightning. One last attempt to survive.

"Caleb!" I scream, as he dangles me over the hole. "Wait!"

And mercifully, he listens. Although, the wildness in his eyes tells me it won't last for long.

"You don't want to do this. I know you don't."

His lips part helplessly. "I have to, Sky."

"Those love notes. You were leaving me warnings." I plead with him to remember. "I know you don't want to do this because you were trying to scare me away."

His face twists with pain. "You should've run while you still had the chance."

"*We* can run away," I say earnestly, using what's left of my strength to angle my face closer to his. "Together. This doesn't have to be the end of us. They don't have to keep us apart. We love each other."

Proving my point, I press my lips to his, ignoring my internal screams of protest. My heart leaps with hope when he fervently kisses me back. His strength keeps us hovering over the open grave. I allow him to consume me, pleading with him to come to his senses.

Pulling back, his bright eyes glint with adoration before falling with sorrow. "I love you, Skyler Pierce."

In one swift motion, he slams his hockey stick over my head and releases me to fall into the cursed earth. Dropping into the casket with a painful thud, the last thing I see is the tearful face of the love of my life before everything goes dark.

29

My eyes crack open into darkness. Nothing but darkness.

I don't know how much time has passed. I cannot see anything.

Then, the murky shadows of low-hanging branches begin to take form.

Where am I?

The woods, clearly. But why am I here alone?

I suck in a long breath, but the air does little to quench the burning in my lungs.

Was I running?

I never run. But why am I breathless?

Kissing. You're breathless from kissing.

Then the memory electrocutes me like a snap of hissing lighting.

Mateo's body. Lacy's coffin.

Caleb.

A love for a love.

But something's wrong. I can't taste the air. It's not perfumed with the musty scent of a forest. There's no dewy grass or fresh soil. Like I'm breathing in nothing. How hard did I fall?

My throat is dry when I swallow at the realization. It didn't work. Something inside me aches at the implications. Caleb never truly loved me; otherwise, I wouldn't still be here.

That's when the sounds of sorrowful cries reach my ears. Surprisingly, my muscles don't pull as I sit up straight in the grass, trying to locate the source of the noise. The answer rests inside Lacy Monroe's grave.

Sitting inside her coffin, Caleb's sobs are uncontrollable as he cradles a body in his lap. I go to reach for him before it strikes me that he doesn't deserve my comfort. Not after he tried to—

My eyes fall to disheveled strands of white-blonde hair cascading from the lifeless frame in Caleb's arms.

At first, I think it's Lacy Monroe. Then Caleb shifts and I catch sight of a face.

My face.

30

I'm dead.

My shoulders heave with panic, but the motion is only for show. I'm not actually breathing heavily because I'm dead. Corpses can't freaking breathe.

But I'm not a corpse. That's my corpse in Caleb's arms. Those lifeless eyes are mine. The blood-matted hair is mine, too.

Is or was?

Can I still lay claim to that body?

I glance down at my new being. It looks almost identical to the one I left behind, except without the blood and bruises. No shadow trails behind me in the glowing moonlight.

If I could shudder, I would. I know what I am now. But just thinking the label makes me want to be sick.

Can I even get sick anymore?

Stop getting stuck on such trivial details. You're dead.

Before I can spiral over what this new existence entails, I startle at the sound of footsteps crunching through the brush.

Wait—why am I standing motionless, like a deer caught in the headlights? I'm dead, aren't I? Whoever's coming won't be able to see me.

The other three Quinn siblings appear through the trees. I don't have the energy to boil over the presence of the youngest. Of course, Cricket knows, too. The Quinns would never keep a secret from each other. Just me, apparently.

Their casual pace pisses me off. No one's concerned that their eldest brother is clutching the body of a lifelong friend. They all read ahead and saw the ending. To them, my death isn't a plot twist, because in their eyes, I'm disposable.

Tonight, I'm the only one truly mourning.

How humiliating.

Zane's bored drawl fills the forest. "Pull yourself together, brother."

"Don't be a dick," Cricket chastises him.

"What?" Zane bites back. "He didn't think killing Sky would mean she'd be *dead*? Please. We've had all spring to brace for this."

I wince. This has been on the agenda for a while. There was plenty of time to come up with an alternative solution to saving the family's reputation.

If I had a pulse, I know it would be pounding with hurt. I never expected any of them to be capable of such deep betrayal. Wetness begins to pool in my mouth, and I fear I'll give away my hiding spot by getting sick.

No—that's not possible. Surely, I can't get sick. Ghosts, or spirits, or whatever the hell I am are incapable of projectile vomiting. And even if I could, I highly doubt the others will be able to see.

The only one completely silent is Amelie. Face devoid of emotion, she stares down at my lifeless body. Is she wracked with regret? Or is she simply accepting the painful reality that her longest friend is dead?

Or maybe her face is blank because she doesn't care.

Screw this. Screw them.

I loved the Quinns with everything I had and this is how they love me back? By using me as a literal human sacrifice.

Something new takes a hold of me, and before I can think better of it, I'm marching into the clearing. Not a single head swivels in my direction, confirming my deepest fears. I really am gone. Eternally alone.

I halt in my tracks as a new pain blossoms within me. This time, death isn't the cause of my agony, but the loss of life. I'm too young for this stunted existence. There is so much I haven't yet experienced. Graduating high school. Figuring out what I want to do for the rest of my life. Buying a home. Adopting a pet. I'll never know what it's like to have my greatest love slip a ring on my finger or nurture children of my own.

I've lost a lifetime of firsts.

No, I correct myself. I didn't lose anything. It was stolen from me. By them.

My eyes narrow at the three siblings still peering into the earth. I'm so close to Amelie that I could run my fingers through her hair, but she is completely clueless to my proximity.

"Come on, bro," Zane is saying. "Leave her."

I pinch the soft skin at the back of the boy's neck; he has the audacity to rub the area, like I'm some itch.

"We have to find Mateo."

Mateo.

In the midst of my predicament as a newly deceased individual, I nearly forgot about him. The boy whose life was more valuable than mine.

What's worse is he played me, too. This whole time, he knew what the Quinns were planning. Add that to the long list of truths he hid from me.

So, where is he now? Shouldn't he be jumping for joy? Gulping in the fresh air? Gloating at how he cheated death at the expense of the girl he claimed to care about?

Another knife in my back. I guess it's a good thing I can no longer feel anything.

"Why'd he run off?" Cricket wonders aloud.

"It doesn't matter why," Zane snaps back. "We just need to talk some sense into him before he runs his mouth."

Finally, Amelie speaks. "Even if he spills the truth, no one will believe a word of it."

She's not wrong. The truth is incomprehensible.

"Still, we better hurry and track him down. Mom'll kill us if we lose him," Cricket murmurs.

There's a long silence, extenuated by blowing foliage that seems to chastise the children below.

"You have to leave her," Amelie says to her brother. The pained expression on her face makes my lips curl with disgust. How dare she look disappointed by my death.

"I'm coming," he sniffles.

The sight of my frail corpse in his arms makes me want to be sick again. Caleb pets the bloodied hair at the top of my head before pressing his lips to my forehead for a long moment.

I can't watch this anymore.

Stepping back from the hole, I plead with my head to stop spinning. I'm dead, for crying out loud. I shouldn't still be capable of feeling like I might pass out.

Crouching against a tree, I don't look up as I hear the others help Caleb out of the grave. He doesn't bother closing the coffin after him. Pulling my legs up to my chest, I press my face into my thighs, willing the screaming in my head to cease.

"Sam'll take care of the hole," I hear Cricket offer, as if that's supposed to ease anyone's pain.

Of course, he will. Everyone who's ever been graced by this family's payroll and knows the secret of Camp Casper likely knew my life had an expiration date the moment I stepped foot on property this summer.

My head remains between my legs.

"She was a good friend to all of us," Cricket continues sympathetically. "Right, Caleb?"

The best of friends—and look where it got me.

"Caleb?"

Something about Amelie's tone has me finally looking up. My back straightens when I realize Caleb's gaze is trained directly at me. Wiping the tears from his eyes, he stares at me with horror, like he can't believe I'm really here.

But I will be. Forever.

I will haunt the so-called-love-of-my-life until his very last breath. He killed me, and now he's condemned to see my face as a perpetual reminder of his betrayal.

Wagging my fingers at him, I make sure the jackass knows it too.

He gasps like a coward, before turning and running from the clearing with his siblings at his heels.

And then, it's just me and the whispering trees. I long for my heart to pound, but it'll never beat again. Not for a friend, or a boy, or myself.

Rising, I creep back toward the open coffin. I'm not sure I'm strong enough to gaze upon my body again, but a part of me craves to be near it.

I long suspected the final mourner at the wake was the deceased one themselves. Though, I'm not thrilled to make such a confirmation so soon.

I deserved so much more than this.

But before I can feel truly sorry for myself, a pair of hands wraps around my middle and yanks me away from my grave.

31

ALL AT ONCE, that woodsy-mint smell encompasses me.

The only scent to transcend the afterlife *would* be him. Just as I could touch him while in his spiritual state, he can reach for me now.

But long gone is my yearning for a set of strong arms wrapped around my waist.

"Get off of me," I grunt, shoving away from the boy. His hands drop immediately, and when I turn, I find that he's retreated a few paces.

My eyes rake over him, scrutinizing his frame for any difference between his spiritual state and this new form. There are few discernible differences. The color has yet to fully return to his cheeks. His skin isn't decaying anymore. Without being able to work out all these weeks, his biceps no longer protrude from his sleeves. But those glinting dark eyes still see right through me.

It's tempting to get lost in the relief that someone can finally see and hear me.

However, that temptation quickly subsides when I remember why I'm in this predicament in the first place.

My eyes narrow at the boy whose life was worth more than mine.

"What more could you possibly want from me?"

Mateo winces. "I just want to talk."

I actually laugh at his audacity. "Talk about what, Mateo? How you knew about their scheme this entire time? How you let them kill me? How you're going to go back to your old life like nothing happened while my body rots away in this godforsaken place forever?"

I find myself panting. Or miming panting. It's not like I'm actually breathing. This paralyzed state is worse than anything inflicted by a demon in my sleep.

I'm the nightmare now.

"Skyler," Mateo raises his hands in plea, "just give me the chance to explain."

"Nothing you say will be good enough."

"I know," he agrees sorrowfully, "but you deserve to know everything before we bring you back."

This gives me pause, and judging by the hopeful flash in his eyes, he knows it, too. Quickly masking my eagerness, I pointedly click my jaw with annoyance.

I resent how quickly this relative stranger learned me. If tonight has taught me anything, it's the dangers of opening up to a teenage boy.

Still, if this one plans to bring me back...

"Just hear me out," Mateo says again, his arms raised in the air, like that'll prove he isn't a threat. "I promise. I'm going to make this right."

My arms cross skeptically. "How?"

"There's more to this family than meets the eye. The lengths they're willing to go to stay on top."

"Trust me—I don't need a lecture on the Quinns," I spit back. "I've known them my whole life."

His head shakes. "You know what they want you to know, and darling, that couldn't be further from the truth."

Apparently, I'm still capable of feeling stunned without a working nervous system. Fantastic. "And you think you know the truth?"

"I'm alive again, aren't I?"

I scowl. "You're welcome for that."

He winces again, selecting his next words far more carefully. "This is bigger than damage control for Caleb's mistake. As far as I know, my parents don't even suspect the Quinns of foul play regarding my disappearance."

"Mistake?" I scoff at his word choice. "He killed you, Mateo."

"It was an accident," the boy insists. "We heard some rumor about an ODR—"

"ODR?"

"Outdoor rink," he explains. "Decided to celebrate the eve of our last night as teammates with a midnight skate."

I can practically see the memory play out in his mind. The two boys, not wearing nearly enough layers for a freezing February excursion, sneaking away after their teammates fell asleep.

"Did you fall through the ice?" I ask, before realizing this is a highly insensitive question. Then, I decide, I don't really care. I'm a ghost. What does it matter if I lack some manners?

Mateo shakes his head, his expression turning dark. "There was no ice. There wasn't even a pond. The rumor couldn't have been more wrong. There was, however, a nearby private airport and Ms. Quinn's pilot wasn't too far away."

My brow furrows, before I realize Mateo's ghost haunted the lake house, which means he must have—

"Why did you two fly here?"

Mateo shrugs helplessly. "Because we could? Because Caleb dared me to take a cold plunge in the lake?"

I blink at him like this is the most asinine idea I've ever heard... because it is. "You two *flew here in the middle of February* just cause?"

This is what happens when teenagers have access to unparalleled wealth. They don't know when to just call a day a bust and go back to bed.

"Ms. Quinn's pilot didn't seem to think anything of it. Guess he was used to spur-of-the-moment trips to the lake house."

"Naturally."

"It feels like a good time to note that I cannot swim."

I fight to keep my eyes from rolling. They could not have been dumber. Both of them. "Let me guess. Caleb didn't know?"

"I thought, how hard can it be to stay afloat in a lake?"

Really hard, if you don't know how to swim in this particular body of water.

A lake with a secret, lurkin' vines that can bound,

Heed our wise warning or you will be drowned.

The lyrics soberly ring through my mind like a funeral march.

Before, in my bedroom, Mateo had no right to claim he could see ghosts because of a recent "brush with death." The afterlife didn't graze him like a bullet to the side of his head. It struck home.

He can credit his new sight to a near-death experience now, I remind myself bitterly.

"He was only playing when he pushed—"

"I don't need to hear the rest." Fury punctuates every word. If these boys hadn't acted like they walk through life without consequence, I'd still be alive.

Mateo melts at my seething glower. "I'm sorry. If I had known—"

"You did know," I snap. He might not have when he decided to test fate by jumping in the lake, but he's had plenty of time to share the truth before now. I'm beginning to lose count of the number of people who could have spoken up and saved my life. "Where's this pilot now?"

"Beau? He recently took a job on Samuel's security team. Decided flying wasn't for him anymore." Mateo's tone makes it clear this career shift was determined for the man.

I remember him now. Beau was one of the security guards who escorted us into town. Why didn't he warn me?

Because everyone believes Mateo's life is worth more than mine.

"So, instead of accepting the tragic accident that happened on the coattails of a wildly foolish decision, the Quinns decided to kill me to bring you back."

"This isn't about valuing my life more than yours. Not at its core."

"Isn't it?" I bark a bitter laugh. "Then please, enlighten me."

"My death wasn't a tragedy to them. Neither was Phoebe's. And for that matter, neither is yours."

"What is it then?"

"An opportunity."

The forest seems to grow still, waiting to hear more. Not a single creaking branch risks drowning out whatever Mateo says next.

"I thought you knew the Quinns better than anyone?" There's no accusation in his voice. Only sadness. "What's the one thing Gianna Quinn loves more than her own children?"

"Her business," I answer immediately. Everyone—even her kids—knows that.

And then, the truth hits me harder than Caleb Quinn ever did.

"Don't tell me Gianna plans to monetize bringing people back from the dead," I say incredulously. As the notion leaves my lips, I know I'm a fool to be surprised.

Of course she does.

This revelation must display on my face, because Mateo relaxes a hair.

"So, what?" My eyelashes flutter rapidly as I attempt to piece it together. "We were her freaking guinea pigs?"

The nauseous sensation is back. I guess it's truly the one sense to not forsake me. How fortunate.

"Monetizing resurrecting the dead." I try the words on my tongue again, like they'll miraculously make more sense. When they don't, I can't help but scoff. "It's ridiculous. Gianna actually thinks she can get away with it?"

"Rich people think they can get away with anything," Mateo snips.

"Good point."

"We have my death to thank for her brilliant idea," Mateo says, his head shaking with disgust. "Here was a dead body on the doorstep of a cursed camp with the power to resurrect the dead. The body of a bright young man who was supposed to have his whole future ahead of him. How could Gianna not try to resurrect me?"

"Because it meant the death of another."

Mateo grits his teeth. "That's what they were trying to sort out."

"If they could bypass the 'love for a love' condition?"

"Yep."

I breathe out a laugh. "Shocking."

Because the only way Gianna's ridiculous business venture could work would be if people didn't have to sacrifice one love in exchange for another. No one in their right mind would go along with such a proposal.

"Apparently, this cursed campsite is stubborn. It won't resurrect just anyone. It must be someone you truly, wholly love."

The last thing I want to think about is Caleb truly, wholly loving me and Mateo.

"I guarantee you Gianna Quinn is more stubborn," I grumble instead. "She won't quit until she gets what she wants. Trust me."

"Unfortunately, I do." Mateo's dark eyes meet mine. "That's why we have to put a stop to her."

There's no need for clarification. I know exactly what Mateo is proposing. That doesn't excuse the fact that it isn't still completely ludicrous.

"We can't kill Gianna-freaking-Quinn and get away with it."

"We're not going to kill Gianna Quinn," he says in an incredulous tone. "We're going to convince one of her kids to do it."

I bark out a laugh. "That's even worse!"

"So, you want her to create a black market for zombies?"

"Obviously, I don't!"

"Then can you seriously think of any other alternative? We can't expose her plan to the world. No one will believe us."

"They won't even hear me," I grumble.

"Skyler, a girl like you could never be silenced."

But I can be. Since meeting them, I've let the Quinns dictate every summer of my life, down to the littlest detail. They decided each minute of my day. From what I did, to how I dressed, to what I ate. Hell, even when they weren't in town, my entire life revolved around them. I skipped school events if Amelie asked to talk on the phone. I turned down dates because my heart always belonged to Caleb. Every other friendship felt second-rate in comparison to what I shared with the Quinns, so why invest in anyone else?

The answer is I didn't.

And now I'm dead.

A new sensation washes over me. A sickly rage so unfamiliar I wonder if it can only be felt after one's life is stripped away. I feel like an inferno of fury, burning with betrayal. Nothing can extinguish these flames.

Well, nothing except vengeance.

My eyes lock with Mateo's. "Let's make them pay for playing god."

A wicked grin stretches his lips. "And pay they will."

32

Before we can plot our revenge, Mateo inquires as to how many horrors I can handle in one night.

"Do your worst," I say dryly. At this point, I'm not sure anything can phase me.

Mateo must disagree because he blows out a skeptical breath before offering me his hand. After blinking at him for a beat, I take it, silently making it clear that we're a team.

Mateo's made mistakes, but he isn't at the root of the problem at hand. And frankly, I'd be a fool to expect to exact revenge all on my own. When it comes to any sort of retaliation, I'm a total novice. I'll take any guidance I can get—especially from the newly-resurrected boy currently ushering me through the woods.

The forest feels lacking now that I've lost some of my senses. I still hear the whisper of the leaves overhead, but the sound is no longer accompanied by a cooling breeze that kisses my cheeks and tangles the wisps of my hair. Long gone is the smell of sweet earth and sappy tree bark. I fear my taste buds are shot as well. My tongue is impossibly dry.

Still, the warmth of Mateo's hand around mine breaks through the nothingness. It's no wonder he was hellbent on forming a relationship. What sparks between us transcends life and death.

I'm so busy worrying about my missing senses I don't even realize where Mateo is leading me.

"Why are we going back there?" I question when the cabin once concealing his corpse comes into view. I'm not keen on returning to the site where everything started to go downhill.

"You missed a few things the first time around."

My jaw clenches at the thought of what other horrors wait inside. "Nothing can be worse than finding your body."

Tensing, Mateo stops us, shifting so we're face-to-face. When he releases my hand, the warmth of his hold immediately fades from my system. "I should've told you the truth as soon as I realized you could see me."

"Why didn't you?

A helpless expression crosses his face. "I wish I had a good excuse, Sky, but I was just being cowardly. You loved the Quinns so much. What was I supposed to do if you didn't believe me?"

"I would've—"

The words get caught on my tongue. Mateo shrugs as if to say, "My point exactly."

We both know I'd want to hear the Quinns out, opening the door for them to spin some tale that paints them as innocents. I would have believed them, too. I always did. And look where it's gotten me.

"It was going to take more time for you to trust my word, and that time was difficult to find thanks to Caleb's constant hovering. Despite my attempts to convince him you didn't recognize me as a ghost, he didn't want to risk me getting anywhere near you."

My lips pinch at my obliviousness. "And what if I had immediately known you were a ghost? Caleb knows about my sight. He should've assumed I'd see you as such."

"We had an agreement that I wouldn't reveal myself to

you." Mateo explains. "Honestly, it took him a really long time to realize I had, but by that point, he decided to just play along with it and hover even more."

"Did you know my death date was drawing near?"

"Not until you found that shrine in my closet. That's what made Caleb reach his breaking point."

"Caleb made the shrine?"

Mateo frowns at his friend's name on my tongue. "I think Caleb was torn on what to do with you. After all, to make the curse work, he needed to genuinely fall for you. Despite still doing bad things, I don't think Caleb wants to be bad. Honestly, I think there's a part of him that sort of hoped you'd piece it all together and run for the hills."

I can't find it in myself to feel bad for Caleb. Regardless of his guilt, he still accepted the role of the predator, and unknowingly, I was his prey. Sure, his delusional feelings for me may have been genuine, but that thought no longer fills me with sweet joy.

I fear every time I hear his name, a wave of regret will wash over me.

I'm also beginning to wonder if only the horrible sensations stick around in the afterlife.

"If I had run, they would've just found someone else to sacrifice."

After we stare at each other in silent agreement, I nod for Mateo to keep walking. He offers me a relieved smile, and maybe I'm imagining it, but that smirk still manages to make something inside me flutter. I can't help but reach for his hand again.

You're hopeless.

For goodness sake, I shouldn't be swooning minutes after being killed. What is wrong with me?

But I've never been able to rein in these feelings. Nothing makes me feel more alive than my heart pounding for another —even if I don't technically have a heart that pounds.

So, despite my better judgment, I decide to indulge in the gleeful sensation. Who knows when—or if—I'll have this feeling again? If our plan doesn't work and Mateo returns to Boston with the Quinns, I'll be stuck here forever, feeling nothing at all.

The very thought makes me squeeze Mateo's hand.

He squeezes mine back as we near the cabin's front door. "Brace yourself, okay?"

I find myself miming a deep breath. The motion makes Mateo grin back at me.

"I did that, too," he says. "Living-isms. It makes you feel normal."

"As opposed to a ghost?"

He breathes out a laugh. "You're a pretty cute ghost."

The fluttering grows stronger, and I find myself hoping this boy never leaves. I'm not ready to give up this feeling, or any feeling, for that matter.

Maybe all this will work and I won't have to.

Offering me an encouraging nod, Mateo opens the door for the both of us, and we slip inside the dark cabin. I bet it feels amazing to open doors again. And breathe in fresh air. And smell the sweet earth below our feet.

I'm going to miss those little perks of being alive.

I instinctively reach for my phone's flashlight, before realizing I no longer have it in my possession, nor could I even operate the device.

Noticing the movement, Mateo nods with understanding. "I did the same thing for weeks. In retrospect, I wasn't so bothered by no one being able to see or hear me. It was being cut off from the whole world that did me in."

I huff out a sigh. "Guess I have that to look forward to."

"You won't be dead for long, Skyler. I swear it."

But I'm too busy blinking around the room to get swept away by the sincerity in his voice. I guess I don't need a flashlight. My eyes have never adjusted faster. Although now I find myself wishing my vision wasn't so sharp.

Mateo was right. There was so much I failed to notice the first time around.

Jaw agape, I stare in horror at the bunk beds, where every mattress hosts a blanketed lump the size of a body.

Suddenly, the freezing temperature makes sense. This cabin isn't just a relic of Camp Casper.

It's a morgue.

33

THERE AREN'T enough curse words in the world to properly articulate how I feel.

I swivel around to face Mateo and stammer, "You're telling me I was surrounded by dead bodies earlier?"

"Um," he says, having the audacity to crack an amused smile at my reaction, "I hate to break it to you, but you're kind of a dead body, too?"

"No! My body is still in the woods!" The argument isn't sound and we both know it.

"Who's here?" I whisper, my eyes darting around the blanketed figures, like I'm worried one might rise up and answer me themselves.

"They aren't listening to you," Mateo answers, reading my mind. He steps around me to draw us both deeper into the cabin. "Only their bodies are here, and if you stopped freaking out for a moment, I know you'd be able to tell that, too."

He's right, unfortunately. My ability to detect wayward spirits is likely stronger than ever. But I'm not exactly in the best headspace for such activities.

"Are you still okay to be in here?" he asks hesitantly. "I didn't realize you'd be so squeamish."

"I'm not!" I retort, tucking a strand of hair behind my ear. "But maybe we can speed it up through roll call."

"Heard." A knowing grin stretches his face as he gestures toward the bottom bunk nearest the door. "Well, you know Lacy."

Thankfully, Mateo does not lift the cover to reveal her corpse. If he had, I know we would've been met with a pile of bones.

I swallow at the shrouded figure of the woman who tried to save me. Where is she now? She probably wants nothing to do with me after I failed to follow her guidance.

Mateo nods at the bunk above. "Phoebe's up there."

My nose scrunches with disgust. "I thought they returned Phoebe's body to her parents to bury."

He scoffs. "You actually believed Samuel reported Phoebe's death after it was painfully obvious she didn't die by accident?"

My lips part when I realize it was all for show. The whole family had the audacity to *mourn* her. They put on quite the performance for their audience of one.

"Her death was for nothing. Why have Caleb kill her when he didn't lov—"

"Caleb didn't kill her," Mateo interjects darkly. "Cricket did."

This revelation is enough to make me feel again. Unfortunately, it manifests as stricken agony. Cricket's so young. Sure, she isn't without her quirks, but no part of her leads me to believe she's capable of killing her best friend. She couldn't have... unless her mother put her up to it.

A new wave of nausea rolls over me. Gianna Quinn will rot for this.

"Like I said," Mateo continues after allowing me a moment to process this new horror, "Gianna needed test subjects. Wanting to see if you had to love both parties involved, they had Cricket kill Phoebe in an attempt to raise me. When that didn't work, my body was swiftly returned to the cabin. They didn't have time to stash hers before you discovered it."

Eyes wide, I glance at the other figures. "Who else is in here, Mateo?"

"That's Camila over there." He points toward the bottom bunk near the back wall.

My jaw drops. "Amelie killed her girlfriend? But they've been video-chatting whenever Camila has cell service."

"This family is sick, Skyler. Every last one of them."

I'm beginning to accept I didn't really know the people I considered to be my closest companions. The Quinns I grew up with were morbid, but I never thought them to be murderous. It's not like any of them were killing rabbits in the woods or dancing in circles around Lacy's grave.

But I sensed something was different that first night back at the lake house. If only I'd questioned that odd tug at my gut. So many of us might still be alive.

"And Diego?" I ask, not wanting to know the answer.

"Not yet." Mateo responds, before tacking on, "I overheard Zane tell his mother he doesn't love Diego enough yet for them to try."

My eyebrows quirk sardonically. "Zane must really love him then."

"Agreed."

I didn't realize the boy had it in him, but he's the only one strong enough to not sacrifice his dearest love for his mother's will.

Swallowing hard, I glance at the two other figures.

Before I have to ask, Mateo explains, "The one across from Camila is someone from school. Eve." He guiltily eyes the blanketed body. "I didn't know her name until they brought her here a week or two after I arrived. You'll meet her spirit eventually, but she prefers to keep to herself."

I don't recall the Quinns ever mentioning an Eve. "How did she get mixed up in this?"

"She says her parents made some sort of deal with Gianna."

My lips curl with disgust.

"And now you're familiar with Beau, the pilot who joined Samuel's team. He was getting cold feet and I guess they figured him to be a liability. Obviously, no one here loved him, so his death was totally in vain."

Immediately, I feel guilty about my initial disgust for the pilot. He was just as disposable as me. Neither of us deserved to meet this fate.

I wish it didn't make sense. The Quinns would need the aid of their security team to keep things hush hush. The more I witness, the more I'm beginning to realize every single one of them was in on it. Still, I can't help but ask—

"Does Mackenzie know?"

"I'm sorry, Sky," is Mateo's answer.

Damn.

Everyone put on the performance of a lifetime just for me.

No one is more guilty than my own mother. I know she always resented me, but enough to send me away for slaughter? Was she that desperate to sever ties with her only flesh and blood to start anew? I hope whatever Gianna offered her was worth it.

And it better not have just been a new television with freaking surround sound.

My head spinning painfully, I mentally curse the spiritual world for still allowing the manifestation of such an agonizing sensation. It's like I'm on the brink of passing out, but I suspect I'm incapable of doing so. So, lucky for me, I'm stuck here in this dizzying limbo. Left to wonder when my life, or my existence, or whatever this is now, will stop feeling like I'm being gut-punched on repeat.

I fear it never will. Not after every single person I loved with my whole heart betrayed me.

How the hell am I supposed to beat them when I fell right into their trap? I'm not clever enough to stay alive, let alone come back to life and put a stop to their horrible scheme.

"We're screwed," I whisper, backing away from the bodies.

"No, we're not."

But I'm already flying through the wooden door and back into the forest that used to be my safe space. Now, these trees mock me, but I'll take anything over the bodies slain by my supposed second family.

"We are!" I cry over my shoulder. "The Quinns are one of the most powerful families in the country. Everyone is loyal to them. *Everyone*."

Mateo grabs my shoulders and turns me around. For a moment, I still at the contact.

"Skyler, we can do this."

"You don't understand," I stammer, trembling beneath his grip. "For most of my life, I've been at this family's mercy. They get whatever they want from everyone, but especially from me. I always bend to their will. I can't help it. How am I supposed to be their downfall when I've spent my whole life doing everything I can to please them?"

"They freaking killed you, Skyler!" Mateo's eyes bug out. "Do you seriously still love him after that?"

"No, but—"

"But what? He. Killed. You."

"I know that," I assert back, suddenly feeling unbelievably spineless. I shouldn't burden an ounce of guilt for seeking revenge. For doing what's right. Gianna Quinn cannot continue with her monstrous, murderous business venture. She's already ruined her children. We can't allow her to corrupt anyone else.

But if I know this, why am I hesitating? What am I so afraid of?

Surely, I should not fear disappointing the family who falsely filled my heart and then ripped it from my chest.

"I don't love him," I choke out, the truth raw on my throat. And it is the truth. Caleb Quinn can no longer have his hand around my heart. He played me. Pretended to love me so I would swiftly fall for him in return... all so he could use me.

I could never still love a boy like that. And yet, I ache. I'm mourning the loss of him—and the only family I've ever truly known—when I should be mourning myself. All I ever wanted from this life has been stolen from me. Every night before bed, I dreamed of one day becoming a Quinn. I'd marry Caleb. Amelie would be my sister. We'd spend most of our time in Boston and then summer at the lake house where it all started. The place I call home would finally be mine.

And now, because I loved them, I have no future at all.

"My heart is so weak," I finally whisper. "I wish I could forget them—*him*—but the Quinns are a hard habit to break. My head knows they're wrong, but my heart wants nothing more than for this to be one of my nightmares. I need to forget the dream life they teased me with and wake up."

Staring up at Mateo with desperation, I find my gaze stuck on his lips. He's all I have left. I might not have known him all my life, but I'm coming to realize that loyalty doesn't require years to develop. A second chance at life was dropped in his lap, but for some reason, he's still here with me.

"I need to move on for good." My voice is firmer as my eyes dance around the rest of his face. From his impossibly dark eyes to the square of his jaw. I may be gone to the rest of the world, but not to him.

There's a new glint in Mateo's eye as he catches on.

"I can help with that," comes his confident response, before hastily adding, "if that's what you want."

Nodding once, I reply, "It is."

"You sure, Skyler?" A wry grin plays at his lips. "I thought my previous efforts successfully made you forget about him, and, boy, was I wrong about that."

"It's different now," I assure Mateo and myself.

I'm no longer swirling with feelings for the boy who broke my heart. The memories may sting, but Caleb Quinn couldn't be farther from the kind of person destined to be my forever. I knew this coming into the summer. I knew it the moment I met Mateo. I may have wavered, but the universe continues to find a way to set me back on track.

Tilting my chin upward, I swear, "Mateo, neither life nor death can figure a way to keep us apart."

"I'd like to see it try," he murmurs, bending so our lips can reunite.

The gentleness of his kiss takes me by surprise. Like he's waiting for me to take the initiative and prove this is what I really want. So, when I raise on my toes to curl my fingers into those shaggy, black locks, he happily wraps his arms around my waist to draw me closer.

I may no longer have a future to write, but I have now. A present that very well could last an eternity. And if this is my new normal, perhaps the afterlife won't be so bad after all.

Kissing him harder, I attempt to wash away every tainted memory of people who claimed to love me, so that all that is left is Mateo.

Mateo.

Mateo?

Why does kissing him feel different now?

Because you finally know what it's like to kiss his friend.

I banish the horrible thought from my mind. I'm done with Caleb. I have to be. He no longer can stake a claim to my heart.

Unaware of my internal turmoil, Mateo pulls back to grin at me. "We can do this, Sky. Your heart isn't what makes you weak." His bright eyes dance between mine. "It's what makes you still alive."

I blink up at him, realizing he's correct. Despite my stubborn heart, I've never felt more alive than I do at this very moment. Hope is not yet lost. My future still rests in my ghostly hands.

And with that clarity, a plan pops into my mind.

"I know how we kill the queen bee."

"Go on," he encourages me.

I smirk. "We cut her off from her hive."

His eyes glow with pride. "Let's go haunting, Skyler Pierce."

34

MATEO'S vengeful grin falls the moment he realizes whose bedroom door we're outside.

"This isn't the direction I thought we were going." He glowers at the door, like he can still see right through it. Maybe he can. I've yet to learn what side effects come with returning from the dead, but if all goes according to plan, I'll find out soon enough.

"Now it's your heart getting in the way," I chide, bracing myself for what lies on the other side. "And don't try to convince me this isn't exactly where we start."

Nothing Mateo can say will dissuade me from going into Caleb's room. If the boy truly did love me—and all evidence points to that being true—then this is exactly the worker bee we target first. Ideally wracked with guilt, Caleb will be the easiest to crack. If he's anything but, our plan could very well deviate toward ending a different life first. I'm open to exploring my options.

"This is a terrible idea."

"He's the only other one who can see me."

"Because he killed you!"

"Something I hope he feels tremendously guilty about!"

My head shakes frustratedly. "Don't empower me and then take issue with how I use said power. If that murderer on the other side of the door is my way back to life, you better believe I'm going in there and haunting the shit out of him. So, are you going to open that door for me like a gentleman or make me walk through it myself?"

I could get used to this newfound rage. *So long, sweet Skyler.* They may have stripped me of my beating heart, but from the ashes, a broken-hearted bitch arose.

Mateo blows out a hot breath but doesn't argue any further. He knows this is the right move, and his hand coming to rest on the doorknob confirms it.

"I'm with you, Skyler."

With those words comes a shift between us. Our fates cementing together. If I could sigh in relief, I would, because finally, a boy who cares about me is on my side. I'm not an unknowing means to an end. On the contrary, I know exactly what Mateo wants from me. To dismantle this dangerous evil from the inside out. Together.

After setting me with a stare that says *I'm-following-your-lead*, Mateo waits for my signal before twisting the knob.

Caleb's room is pitch black, which in all fairness, makes sense because it's the wee hours of the morning. But that doesn't stop my nose from wrinkling with disgust at his ability to simply *fall asleep* after murdering me. That loathsome, self-pitying bastard.

The darkened space is no match for my new-and-improved eyesight, so I observe the blanketed boy with contempt. If I have it my way, he'll never rest easy again. He's going to pay for how he used me.

This new-found fury is unfamiliar. Startling, even. But now that it's here, I might as well use it to my advantage. The daunting challenge of destroying one of the wealthiest families in the country would be nearly impossible with-out it.

We freeze as our target suddenly sits upright. Mateo immediately places himself in front of me.

"Mateo? Is that you?" Caleb groans while rubbing his eyes, and I internally swear to never again compare them to something as beautiful as the ocean. When he spies his teammate, he scrambles from under the covers to stand. "Is this real, bro? Are you actually back?"

"Does this feel real to you?" Mateo asks, pulling his fist back.

I frantically grab his hand before he can sock Caleb in the jaw. "Don't make him cry. He'll wake the whole house."

Shifting to make my presence known, I relish the gasp that escapes Caleb's lips.

He should fear me.

Or maybe you still like making his gasp.

Stop thinking like that. This is the boy who took everything from you.

"Sky," he whispers. His palms immediately return to rubbing his eyes. "I knew you'd come."

"Hey, Caleb," I say, low and menacing. "Miss me?"

He stumbles backward, and when the back of his knees knock into his bed, he clumsily falls onto the mattress.

I prowl around Mateo until I'm toe-to-toe with the boy who killed me. "What's wrong? You look like you've seen a ghost."

Mateo exhales a low laugh behind me. "You're enjoying this too much."

"Don't worry," I say to Caleb. "I'm just here to talk. Couldn't lay a finger on you if I tried." To prove my point, I shove my fist through his chest, close enough to his heart that he shivers from my frigid touch. My hand is granted an immediate blast of furnace-like warmth that disappears as soon as I withdraw it.

Good. I can't allow any part of this boy to linger on my being.

Caleb stares at his unmarred chest in horror before blinking up at me. "Sky, I-I'm so sorry," he croaks out.

"For what?" I coax him, bending so we're eye level. "Murdering me?"

"It was my mom, Sky," he stammers.

"It was your mother who cracked my head open with a hockey stick?" I pretend to recall the earlier events of the evening. "Wait—that's not right! It was you, Caleb. You're the one who killed me."

"I didn't want to!"

"What didn't you want to do? Waste your summer convincing yourself you loved me? Stay up all those nights with me and lie about what a future together would look like? Get your hands dirty while you murdered me?"

"Stop, please—" he chokes out.

But I have no intention of doing what this boy wants ever again. "Do you find comfort in feeling bad for what you did to me, Caleb Quinn? Is your remorse the reason you can still crawl into bed after you left my body in the woods?"

"I haven't—"

"Stop talking," I order, and to my surprise, he immediately complies. An unfamiliar feeling surges through me.

It's power, I realize.

I've never had any ounce of power in this house. Not until now.

"You think you feel bad, Caleb Quinn? Anguished?" I purr, allowing my voice to caress him in place of my fingers. "You cannot begin to fathom the agony I promise you will experience."

The threats sound foreign on my tongue, but boy do they feel good.

"This can't be real," Caleb says, more to himself than anyone else. He uses the heels of his palms to rub his eyes again, as if trying to wake himself up from a dream.

"Shut up," I snap, but Caleb is staring around the room madly and scrambling away from his bed and toward Mateo.

"Are you real?" Caleb shakes the boy.

As quickly as I felt it, that sense of power is gone. He can't mark my words if he believes I'm a figment of his conscience coming to haunt him.

"She's as real as you and I." Mateo shoves him away. "You better start listening to her."

But Caleb seems to have officially snapped. He's rampaging around the room, frequently glancing back at us while he flails for the door.

"Don't!" I command, but it's too late. Caleb is already sprinting into the hall.

Mateo and I share a shocked glance before charging after him.

"Help!" Caleb's cries echo throughout the lodge. "She's gonna get me! Help!"

Is he joking? This six-foot-one hockey player is scared of me?

Mateo charges down the stairs, hot on Caleb's heels. I startle as the door directly to my right flings open, revealing Zane. His frown indicates he is less than thrilled to be woken up.

"Get a hold of yourself. It's the middle of the night," he groans.

I freeze when his sharp eyes bore straight into me.

Wait—no. Right through me. Zane Quinn cannot see me because I'm dead.

Taking full advantage of the situation, I sprint past the boy and after the other two barreling through the lodge.

I dodge armchairs and end tables in the living room before racing through the kitchen and out onto the back porch. Instantly, I'm hit with another cruel reminder of my lack of mortality. No midnight chill tickles the hair on my arms. My heart no longer pounds with exertion.

But despite where I may be lacking, I realize I've come into the possession of a new talent because I've never run faster in my life. Using my heightened vision in the dark, I quickly spot Mateo chasing Caleb over the vast yard before disappearing into the trees.

Pumping my legs, I charge after them. The grass may no longer tickle my ankles, but I'll gladly accept this newfound speed as consolation. I traverse the long lawn in a matter of seconds, hurtling into the trees. My thighs feel no exertion as I trail the boys, and sooner than any of us expect, I'm on their heels.

Maybe I'm not running at all, but rather, manifesting my spirit into a new location.

"Damn, Sky," Mateo puffs as he fights to keep up with our limber prey. "Impressive."

I grin, knowing he hasn't even begun to see what I am capable of. I don't know the extent of my abilities, but if the power surging through me is any indication?

Well, Caleb Quinn better watch his back.

The target in question must sense something is afoot, because after glancing over his shoulder, his eyes widen before he quickens his pace.

Like a jungle cat hunting her prey, I'm silent in my pursuit. No twigs or dry leaves crack beneath my footfalls. Not a single pant of exhaustion escapes my lips. It's more than I can say for the others.

"Still think you're dreaming?" I croon at Caleb's heels.

He's too out of breath to answer.

We careen through the trees so swiftly that I lose myself to the motion. Our whereabouts are meaningless. All that matters is stopping Caleb.

He's only a few feet ahead of me. Another few paces and I'll be able to cut in front of him.

I don't exactly have a plan for when I catch him, but I'm quite enjoying my chase without wasting any thoughts on it.

I'm confident future Sky will handle her role as enforcer just fine.

"Sky!"

My name accompanies a warning tone on Mateo's tongue, but the last thing I'm going to do is halt my pursuit now. Not when I'm so close. If only I could reach out and grab this coward myself.

"Sky!" he cries again, "Stop!"

The fear in his voice has me scrutinizing my surroundings, but nothing stands out to me as any cause for concern. We're near the metal fence at the edge of the property. What's Mateo so freaked out about? If I don't hurry, Caleb will climb the fence and escape.

An instant later, I find my answer by way of electric shock.

Suddenly, I feel everything all over again. The agonizing pounding in my head as I died. The sticky trickle of blood streaming down my cheeks from the gaping wound left behind by Caleb's walking stick. The veil of consciousness between life and whatever-the-hell-this-state-is grows fuzzy as I fight to maintain control of my being.

My knees press into the dirt as I collapse, and immediately, Mateo is by my side. His arms tuck around me as he pulls my writhing frame onto his lap.

"I'm so sorry," he says over and over. "I should've warned you about the boundary."

And that's when it hits me. A pain far worse than any death. No—this cruel reality might actually be what does me in.

I can never leave. For as long as I'm trapped in this state, I'm stuck here. At the place that gave me the world and then stripped it away.

With my heart heavier than ever, I think I die for good.

35

But I don't.

When I regain consciousness, I'm back in the Quinn's makeshift mausoleum. Mateo must've brought me here and laid me in one of the empty beds. Though I should feel anything but comfortable in a place like this, I must admit I'd take a morgue over the lodge any day. The further away from the Quinns, the better.

Though, I guess I better get used to their proximity if I don't find a way to come back to life.

Just the thought of spending an eternity here makes my mouth taste of dust. I can't watch them carry on with life like they didn't strip me from mine. Watch Amelie make new friends and invite them over to sleep in my room. Witness Caleb find someone he loves—truly loves—and brings home to his family. I bet he never mentions the ghost of his former love still hanging around. To have and to haunt. Forever and ever.

Geez, I need to get a grip. This is the last thing my sick brain should be romanticizing.

Mateo might not think it's a weakness, but I know better than to allow my heart to wander as far as it wants. That's what got me into this mess in the first place. I was given every hint and warning sign in the world and still wound up dumped in a shallow grave.

No—I've learned my heart isn't the most trustworthy of guides. Best to give it a short leash, unless I want to live out this horror story forever.

And that's the last thing I'm going to do.

Seeing me rustle, Mateo appears at my side. Running his hands down my face, he checks for any unseen injuries, despite both of us knowing there are none. It may have felt like I died a second time, but the fact of the matter is I don't actually feel anything at all. It's all in my head.

"Welcome back," he murmurs, a grim look on his face.

"Thanks, I guess."

"You came to faster than most."

"Am I supposed to take that as a compliment?"

"I'm not sure," he responds, the corners of his lips quirking upward. "How ya feeling?"

"Like I just died again."

"You're not gonna like to hear it, but that's actually sort of what's supposed to happen. I'd be concerned if you felt any different."

"Awesome."

"I really am sorry for not warning you earlier about the boundary."

"It's okay. I would've likely tested it anyway."

His lips pinch with understanding, and I immediately wonder if he did the same after Lacy warned him, or perhaps he was left to make the painful discovery on his own.

I sit up, resting against my elbows as I survey the room. "Still just the two of us, huh?"

"It would appear so."

"Why does it feel like the others are avoiding me?"

Mateo is quiet for a long minute. "Everyone wants to fight their way back to life," he finally murmurs. "But unlike the rest of them, you actually have a decent shot at it."

My brow furrows. "What do you mean?"

"Sky," he explains slowly, "a Quinn loved you enough to raise me from the dead. It didn't work out so well for any of the others."

I swallow hard at the senseless loss that surrounds me. Their deaths were in vain. Despite knowing the outcome wouldn't be favorable, the Quinns tested the cursed camp and experimented anyway.

What I still fail to comprehend is how the four siblings I've known all my life could go down such a dark path. They're always the first to disparage their mother's greed. Why comply now?

Glancing around the dim room, I take in the blanketed bodies of my new companions. No longer does the sight of them fill me with fear. Only sadness. They may not want to face me yet, but I vow to destroy the Quinns for them. Their deaths will not be without retribution.

Out of the corner of my eye, I catch Mateo yawning. That's when it hits me that I have yet to feel tired, despite it being the middle of the night. On the contrary, I'm more awake than ever.

I guess that makes sense. It's not like the dead need to recharge their mortal bodies. I cannot say the same about Mateo.

"You should get some sleep."

"I'm fine," he immediately responds, attempting to shake the sleep deprivation from his face. "We need to come up with another plan before sunup."

My eyebrows raise. "You don't think Caleb is still our main target? He seemed pretty close to snapping."

"I'd say he's already snapped. A boy that far gone won't be of any help to us now."

"I wouldn't be so sure. There are few people better at

thriving under pressure than Caleb Quinn. He might be freaking out now, but I wouldn't be surprised if he pulls it together. He always does."

"I'm not so sure about this time," Mateo mutters before finally meeting my eyes. "He really cared for you, Sky. I don't know if he'll ever be able to forgive himself for what he did."

It's clear these aren't easy words for Mateo to admit.

Reaching out to grab his hand, I give it a careful squeeze so he knows there is nothing to worry about. I can't allow myself to forgive Caleb. Not for as long as I live.

"We won't be able to enact any plan in the morning if you don't sleep a few hours." I bring my other hand to his face, stroking the curve of his jaw. "I'll brainstorm some ideas and we can determine which is the best course of action when the sun rises."

Mateo's mouth betrays him with another yawn. "Fine, fine. But only a few hours."

"Fine," I agree, knowing full well I am not waking him until it's absolutely necessary.

We shift so that he can lay on the bed beside me. Snuggling until his body is curved around mine, Mateo buries his face into the crook of my neck, peppering it with sleepy kisses.

"I've wanted to do this since I met you," he whispers against my skin. "Ever since you could see me—touch me— I've wanted us to find ourselves here."

My insides twist with guilt. We're finally united, but I can't ignore how empty it feels for me. I know my heart is capable of more.

Figure it out. Mateo deserves as much.

Maybe my hollowness is because I'm dead.

Or maybe, it's because your heart only beats for a monster.

If that's the case, what does that make me? I don't like any of the answers I come up with.

Turning to gently kiss both of Mateo's closed eyelids, I wish him a good first night of sleep. He's had months to think about this moment, and despite everything going on, I hope he rests well. We have no clue what new disasters await us in the morning. A boy like him deserves to escape his thoughts while he can.

"I kind of forgot what it was like to feel tired," he admits sheepishly, and in that moment, despite my life being traded for his, I'm filled with an ounce of contentment. He deserves dreams as sweet as him. He deserves life.

No matter what it takes, I'm going to claw my way back to it as well.

I lay still beside him, counting his slowing heartbeats. But I'm moving out from under him as soon as his breathing shifts. Careful not to jostle the boy, I extract myself from his arms and slip from the bed.

Immediately, a chill washes through my body. Not one caused by the cool, nighttime air. No—it's because I'm no longer against Mateo.

Forcing my eyes to stop drifting to the other corpses in the cabin, I hurry out the door and into the dark woods. For some maniacal reason, I still yearn to feel at peace between these trees, but I'm not sure any inch of this camp is on my side.

I find myself miming breathing in the fresh air, filling my lungs with nothing but the comforting act of being alive. I pretend I can still smell the pine-scented breeze. All sap-sweet-ened and woodsy. If I squeeze my eyes shut and try hard enough, I can actually feel the cool wind toy with the hairs on the back of my neck.

My eyes shoot open when I realize the sensation isn't only in my imagination. Running a hand over the back of my neck, I flatten the hairs that stand on end.

"Hello, Skyler," comes a low voice behind me. "At long last, it's my turn to greet you."

I whip around despite already knowing the face that accompanies this mysterious voice.

"It's good to finally hear you, Lacy," I say, gazing upon the face of the girl who has haunted me all summer.

She looks different now that we're on the same side of the universe. There's more color in her cheeks and her eyes are less hollow. Still, I don't miss that her soul is trapped at the age of nineteen. She never had the chance to grow old, like my mother, Gianna, and Samuel.

"You may hear me, but I wonder if you'll finally listen."

I wince, knowing I deserve such a remark.

"I'm listening now."

Lacy snorts before turning to drift deeper into the woods. Neither of us makes a sound as we traverse through the trees.

"You've really been here this whole time?" I ask, shattering the silence, but only for us. To the rest of the world, we're nothing more than an unidentifiable chill. "I've come to Camp Casper every single summer since I was a child and never once felt your presence. Not until now."

"I made myself known only when it was necessary," Lacy says over her shoulder, setting me with a firm stare. "I thought my old friend, Gianna, had outgrown her fascination for this property's peculiarities. It wasn't until she proved me wrong that I knew it was time to reach out to you."

"But you could've had years of company," I push, "and yet, you chose to remain alone."

"I'm not in the habit of keeping the company of my killer and her children."

I click my tongue. "Fair enough."

We're quiet again for a long while, the only sounds around us from the rustling trees themselves and a hooting owl in the distance. But when the path bends toward a particular grave, I'm forced to speak again.

"Wait—I don't want to go anywhere near my body."

Lacy doesn't stop moving. "I thought you wanted to speak with the others."

"Why are the *others* gathered at my gravesite?"

"*Our* gravesite," she snaps back.

"Fair enough," I mutter again. "Still seems rather morbid, don't you think?"

"Our existence is morbid."

And that shuts me right up.

Trailing after Lacy, I focus all my energy on bracing myself to see my dead body again. But when the trees open into the clearing, I realize no amount of mental preparation is going to suffice.

Every part of me aches when I spy them grouped together. Phoebe, Camila, Eve, and Beau. I might not have known all of them in life, but we are forever bonded in the beyond. On the freshly overturned dirt, they sit in a circle, their feet dangling into the grave. When Lacy and I near, they all glance up to me with bleak expressions.

"Welcome to your funeral," Lacy says.

"Happy to be here."

Phoebe jumps to her feet, hurrying to wrap her arms around me. "I'm so sorry, Sky. You didn't deserve this."

"None of us did," I murmur into her lavender hair.

Pulling back to study my face, the girl catches me looking over her head at the hole in the ground hosting my body. "It's not so bad."

I release a shaky laugh. "Isn't it?"

"No," she says thoughtfully, "you'd be surprised how easy it is to forget that body is yours." She squeezes my middle. "This is you now."

"For now."

Phoebe offers me a sad grin. "If you think this campsite is going to work in your favor, you're as bad as Gianna Quinn."

"You don't want to come back?"

"What makes you think I can convince someone to start loving me now? They can't even see me!"

I frown at the girl. "Someone will be able to."

"You don't have to lie to me," she says softly. "It's okay.

I've accepted my fate. Now, all I care about is finding enough peace to pass on for good."

We're quiet for a long moment before I finally concede with a nod. "I'll help you."

She offers me a small, sad smile. "I know."

Leading me to the grave, Phoebe gestures for me to sit beside her. I slowly place myself upon the dirt, careful not to look down. I'm not ready yet.

Instead, I study the others, wondering if they all share the same goal as Phoebe. Not craving to come back, but rather, to find peace and pass on.

Camila's the first to meet my eyes. Her brunette pixie cut has grown out from the last time I saw her, which was last summer. She came to visit for a week.

"It took my ex-girlfriend a while to buck up the courage to kill me," Camila explains after noticing my lingering stare. "So, they kept me captive here until she could."

My nose wrinkles with disgust. "I hope you haunt the hell out of her."

"Please, it's bad enough we're trapped on this cursed property until we find peace." Camila scoffs. "She doesn't deserve to be graced by my presence."

"None of them do," Beau remarks, his voice low and husky. I look at him now, really look, before I grow embarrassed for not paying him this much attention while he was alive. He appears to be in his mid-thirties, with a short, stocky stature. He died because he worked for the Quinns. He had a moral compass and they considered that a liability.

His light eyes meet mine. "Did Mateo delude you into thinking you can come back yet?"

"You don't think I can?"

Beau cocks his head to the side. "I think if any of us had a decent shot, it would be you. But no. I don't think you can."

Beside him, Eve says nothing. I scrutinize her freckled face and auburn curls for any sign of familiarity but find none.

This girl really is a total stranger who was brought here to die. She simply stares at me blankly before returning her attention to the casket below.

I'm still unable to manage a look downward. Maybe that makes me a coward.

It's only been a few hours, I remind myself. *That's barely any time to process.*

"Is it bad if I try?" I hear myself whisper.

"Never," comes Phoebe's immediate response.

But I'm looking to Lacy for her answer. Out of the lot, she has the most experience with this state.

Lacy considers her words. "You should probably try. For your mother."

I blink with surprise. The last person I expected Lacy to be concerned with is my mother. Not after she played a role in Lacy's death or my own.

"My body may be a sack of bones, Skyler," Lacy chides, "but I still like to pretend I have a heart."

"But my mom—"

"Do you know why she accepted a job to work for Gianna Quinn here in the first place?"

My shoulders shrug. "To rekindle with an old friend?"

Lacy's eyebrows raise. "And you think that's Gianna?"

"Seeing as I didn't know you two were friends until a few days ago... yeah."

Lacy humphs. "You would think the woman I died for would have enough couth to mention me to her daughter."

I balk at her. "Excuse me?"

The others have tuned in, as well. Apparently, tales of Lacy's past life are not usual topics around the gravesite.

"Sue Pierce drowned while we counselors were rehearsing a synchronized swimming performance for the campers."

Only the rustling trees know what to say to that. The rest of us are stunned silent.

This was my mother's brush with death. The reason I

grew up with ghosts. It wasn't a "close call" as she led me to believe. She was the counselor who died.

Mr. Rob told us to use Lacy to revive her.

"Your father sacrificed you to save my mom?

"He knew I stopped loving him the moment I learned of his betrayal." Lacy's eyes harden. "So, yes, it was his idea, but Gianna Quinn was the one bold enough to go through with it.

"We counselors swore to never tell a soul about Camp Casper's dangerous ability to bring back the dead. We took an oath to only revive someone in desperate need of a second chance and then agreed this camp's secret would die with us. Apparently, Gianna considered your mother to be worth it."

The very notion makes my tongue feel numb, which leads to my unintelligent response. "Did Gianna love you and my mother?"

"Platonic love is just as strong as romantic, sweet girl. Anyone with a large heart like yours should know that. You also saw that Quinn boy raise Mateo."

She sets me with a stern look that begs me to keep up before continuing.

"The three of us were the best of friends. Practically sisters. But Gianna Quinn has always had a proclivity for bold moves. She chose your mother, just like she is choosing her bottom line now."

"It worked" rings in my ears. I never did get the chance to read the rest of that ripped page from the counselor's log, not that I think it would've helped me much. I was always going to walk right into the grave the Quinns dug for me.

My mother knew it too, and yet, she did nothing to try to stop me. She let me walk out of our family home and probably turned on her new TeQ television.

Mom probably felt like she *owed* Gianna for saving her life.

Without any blood to get in the way, betrayal burns through my veins.

Every single one of them decided I was not worthy of this world. They stole everything from me.

"You have more faith in my mother than you should," I say through gritted teeth. "I can never go home to her."

Lacy Monroe sets me with a scorching stare. "You misinterpret me, Skyler. I don't have a heart for the woman I died to save. Sue Pierce is a hypocritical coward. She sneaks onto the property to clean my grave before sending her own daughter to be buried in it. Humans like her are why I have a heart for revenge, and out of all of us, you have the best shot at it."

My lips quirk at the thought.

"So, yes, I do think you should try," Lacy says. "If you should succeed, I trust you'll give them hell on our behalf."

"It would be my honor," I swear, looking every single one of them in the eyes. Seeing them the way they deserve.

Finally, I glance downward at the husk of a girl who was stripped from this world. Fighting the churning in my stomach, I force myself to gaze upon my blank face. My stringy hair is matted with dried blood. Brownish-red streaks trail down my cheek like tears.

Whether I stay dead or come back to life, I guarantee every single one of my betrayers will spend the rest of their pathetic existences regretting what they did to me.

36

Once the sun graces us with its presence, I rustle Mateo awake. His eyes shoot open immediately.

"You have a plan."

"I have pieces of a plan," I respond honestly. "You hungry for some breakfast?"

"I haven't had a meal in months."

"Perfect, let's get some food in you."

Fifteen minutes later, I'm trailing Mateo into the lodge. The family must be taking breakfast indoors today because the porch is empty.

"Too afraid of what skeletons lurk outside?" I snark under my breath.

We find the Quinns soon enough. Sounds of clinking silverware and the passing of dishes come from the formal dining room. It's obvious this morning's meal is also serving as a family meeting. I attempt to ignore the fact that I can no longer smell the warm maple syrup, freshly brewed coffee, or smoky bacon.

If all goes according to plan, it will only be a temporary lapse of senses.

Peering through the glass dining room doors, I search for any sign of Caleb.

"He's not here," Mateo mutters under his breath before flinging the door open.

Perfect. The last thing we need is that buffoon causing a scene after seeing me.

Invisible behind him, I follow Mateo through the double doors in time to hear the others gasp at his presence. No one's eyes appear to flit to me as I peer around him, so I take the time to relish the shocked looks on their faces.

Almost everyone appears to be present at the family meeting. At the wooden, rectangular table, Amelie and Cricket sit across from Zane. The only house guest missing is Diego.

My pulse might be nonexistent, but something inside me lurches. Where is he? Surely, I would've known if they killed him, too.

"Ah, Mateo!" Gianna Quinn croons from the head of the table. "How lovely to see you up and about. It's more than I can say for others."

"Diego wanted to sleep in," Zane attempts to excuse his missing partner, and immediately, I swell with relief. Zane is miles better than the rest of them. At this rate, Diego might actually survive the summer.

Gianna waves off her son. "I'm far more concerned by the absence of my eldest."

"He's upset, Mom," Amelie says meekly.

"He's a coward."

This shuts down any further discussion of the matter. Not that there was much else the siblings could say in further defense of their brother. Instead, they return their attention to pushing scrambled eggs around their plates.

Good. I hope their stomachs are churning after last night's events.

Mateo fills the seat beside Zane, and on cue, Mackenzie

appears to place a plate before him filled with French toast, eggs, and bacon.

Now, it's my turn to feel sick to my stomach. How could Mackenzie go along with their cruel plans? Though she cannot see me, I scowl at her as she retreats into the kitchen. Mateo and I are going to make sure every single one of them face lifelong consequences for their actions.

As soon as Mateo takes his first bite, Pamela frantically begins scribbling notes from a corner in the room.

Gianna takes a gleeful sip of coffee, studying Mateo over the rim of her mug. To his credit, he doesn't glare back. Instead, he enthusiastically tucks into his breakfast.

"Fascinating," the woman whispers, shaking her head. "Tell me, how do you feel?"

"Like I haven't eaten in a few months," Mateo responds with his mouth full of bacon.

Gianna laughs. "You must be hungry. What else?"

"I feel like I was dead and now I'm not."

The woman remains unfazed by his tone. "Darling, please spare no detail. You are a scientific marvel! We want to understand everything." She nods toward her associate, who jots this down, too.

"Do you feel any pain?" Pamela asks matter-of-factly.

"No."

"Nausea?"

"No."

"Depression?

Mateo shoots her a look. "I find this terribly depressing, yes."

"No need to write that down," Gianna snaps at Pamela before returning her attention to her test subject. "Let's try to keep our wits about us. After all, you were provided with a second chance at life."

"At the expense of who?"

"Science doesn't come without its sacrifices."

"This isn't science." Mateo raises his voice. "It's murder."

"When a piece of one's heart is ripped away, they'd pay anything to have it back."

Mateo scoffs. "Except the price is the death of another loved one and a hefty service charge from TeQ."

"I can think of many who find the price reasonable. Your parents sure did, as well as Skyler Pierce's mother."

"Excuse me?" Mateo roars, his jaw agape with horror.

But Gianna Quinn doesn't need to explain any further. Not when the truth couldn't be clearer. Mateo's parents knew he was dead all along. Like my mother, they played right into Gianna Quinn's hand and paid the price.

Did they even know my name? That I would be the girl sacrificed to bring their son back?

Tears in his eyes, Mateo vows, "You'll all rot for what you've done. First in prison, and then in hell. You, your children, your employees, my parents, and any other twisted fool who fell for the horror story you sold them. This isn't innovation; it's inhumane. Against the laws of fate and nature."

Gianna's eyes glint brazenly, but all she says is, "Your poor parents."

"I do not regard those who condone murder as my family," Mateo bites back.

"That's very well then," the woman responds cooly, revealing a gun from a concealed holster and firing it without warning.

"Mateo!" I scream, but no one hears me as the bullet pierces his heart. Blood drenches the front of Mateo's gray t-shirt as he gurgles and slumps in his seat. Rushing to him, I find myself completely helpless in resuscitating him. He's dying. Again.

"Mom!" Amelie cries in horror as she rises from her chair. Her eyes dart around the room to measure her siblings' reactions. For a split second, I feel like her eyes dance over me.

Then I realize she's staring through me as she watches Mateo die.

"What the hell, Mom?" Cricket bellows, covering her eyes so she doesn't have to witness the boy bleeding out over his breakfast.

Zane simply gags as he runs out of the room.

You'd think the Quinn children would be used to death by now.

Gianna must think the same thing because she says, "Steel yourselves, young ones. Death is a fact of life."

"I thought you wanted to study him!" Amelie protests.

"We've learned all that we can from this one. Hopefully, our next subject will be more grateful for the second chance we offer them."

"Your plan was to bring him back to life just to kill him?"

"Get a grip, Amelie Quinn," her mother booms. "Science doesn't come without it's sacr—"

"Shut up!" Amelie screams back before running out of the room. Cricket follows closely at her heels.

Gianna clicks her tongue, before shaking her head helplessly at Pamela. "They'll understand when they're older and this pays for their grandchildren's college fund."

Having had enough of her, I return all my attention back to the boy dying in my arms. He gasps for breath, struggling to suck air into his lungs.

"Please, don't die. Please, don't die," I whisper over him, knowing it's no use.

I cling to Mateo as he takes his final breath before going motionless.

"Damn," I hear his warm voice behind me. I turn to find the ghost of the boy, looking precisely how he lived, though anything but alive. "Well, now we're screwed."

37

THE SOUND of Gianna rising from her seat earns both of our attention. She crosses to Mateo's body, peering down to inspect the still-bleeding corpse.

"It's incredible, isn't it?" she says, using the end of her revolver to push the hair out of his eyes. "There were no immediate side effects after he came back."

Mateo snarls at the woman's comfortable proximity to his dead body. "Not even hell will know what to do with her."

"If she makes it that far," I add wryly. "Unfortunately, I see a long and arduous afterlife ahead of her. People like her don't pass on quietly. Why can't she see you after being your cause of death?"

"The living only see us if we make a conscious effort to be seen. She's technically your cause of death, too. Do you want her to see you?"

"Absolutely not."

Mateo nods. "Your soul can sense that and is working in your favor right now."

Not having heard us, Gianna Quinn continues to study the corpse. "We'll need to be more selective with our next subject, however. Someone who won't turn their nose up at the rare opportunity presented to them. Please remember to send a note to his parents explaining that, due to unforeseen complications, their son won't be returning home after all. We'll provide them with a partial refund."

Mateo is officially fuming as he stalks angrily toward Gianna, only to pause when the eclectic chandelier begins to flicker.

Everyone in the room—living and dead—stops to observe the scene overhead.

"Ah," Gianna Quinn says thoughtfully, "does that mean you're still among us, poor boy?"

My lips part with shock. Did Mateo cause the lights to flicker? I think back to all the times I've noticed the presence of a lonesome spirit and realize they must share a connection with the energy in a room.

So I must be able to make my presence known too. Flexing my fingertips, I reach out into the air, trying to feel something. Anything.

And then the air pushes back, like it was simply waiting all along for me to try to capture it. I feel the crackling fizzle of energy snake through my empty veins, suddenly understanding why so many spirits spend their days sending a draft through a warm room and toying with the lights. It's a relief to finally feel again.

Waving a hand through the air, I rattle the silverware on the tabletop, grinning maniacally when the living souls in the room jump with surprise. Mateo and I share a stunned look before immediately causing a cacophony of noise. As glasses of orange juice topple over, forks and knives clamber on the table. The lights flicker on and off.

This is way more fun than manifesting ourselves before her.

Pamela screams while running from the room. To her credit, Gianna stays put.

"Are you both here?" she calls, spinning wildly, as if she

might catch a glimpse of us. She won't. I never want this woman to lay eyes on me again.

I swirl a cooling breeze around her in response. It's a shame it doesn't knock her off her feet.

"Skyler," she says knowingly. "How fitting of you to haunt this property after your mother nearly did the same. Do you think she's bothering to mourn or has she already redirected her energy to entirely focus on her new family?"

"Witch," I hiss under my breath. It's a term that suits both of them.

Mateo reaches for my hand before I find a way to drop the chandelier on her. Unfortunately, Gianna Quinn can't die. Not yet.

"If it helps you rest easier, my dear, please know that it took a fair amount of convincing to get my children on board."

Not a single one of them should've gotten "on board" with murdering me.

"In life, some people are simply more expendable than others. It's a harsh truth many prefer to ignore for the sake of niceties, but it's a truth, nonetheless. Besides, how could we not capitalize on your little crush on my eldest son?"

Shaking with fury, I release Mateo's hand to throw both of mine in the air. I channel all my energy on flinging the knives from the table skyward. Finally, this silences Gianna, forcing her to flee. Like lethal little birds, they follow her across the dining room. Some even make it through the doorway into the kitchen, where a harsh scream rings out.

Without hesitation, Mateo and I sprint to identify the source.

"No!" I exclaim when I find one of my knives sheathed in the center of Mackenzie's back. Face-down, her blood slickens the checkered kitchen tile. It stains her golden-blonde hair that's splayed out around her empty face. "No, no, no, no."

I kneel beside the woman, trying to feel for a pulse, but my fingers keep slipping right through her corpse.

"She's dead, Sky," Mateo murmurs, as if this is meant to comfort me.

"I killed her." My voice shakes. "I can't believe I killed her."

He reminds me, "She knew they were going to kill you."

He might be right, but that doesn't mean I want to be responsible for her death in return. Up until the end, Mackenzie was always an angel to me. She continuously went out of her way to make sure I felt seen in a house where I was easily drowned out. She might have known what the Quinns were planning, but I refuse to believe Mackenzie wanted me to die. Now, she's no better off than me. I'm beginning to fear that, one way or another, anyone who devoted their time and energy to the Quinns may be susceptible to the same fate.

"We have to go," I whisper as I rise. "I cannot bear to look her spirit in the eye."

Mateo numbly pulls me back into the dining room.

Once we're utterly alone, the severity of our situation sinks in.

"Fantastic," Mateo mutters under his breath. "We're worse off than when we started!"

"Technically, yes."

"I'm such a fool. She was always going to kill me."

I've never seen him spiral quite like this. He's pacing around and around the dining room table, madly tugging at the ends of his hair.

"I can't believe I didn't see it coming. I marched right into my own execution."

Guilt washes over me. I should've anticipated this outcome and warned Mateo of the risk.

But it's too late for regrets, so I attempt to settle him down instead. "We're going to figure this out."

Mateo keeps talking like he doesn't hear me. "Now no one

can see either of us. We have no way of convincing anyone to join our side. Bringing one of us back was already a tremendous crime. But two of us? We can't be responsible for the deaths of two more people. Not that we'll be able to convince anyone to go along with it or even love us enough for it to work! What were we thinking? This was our genius plan?"

"Hey—"

"We are totally and royally fu—"

"Mateo!" I interject loud enough to finally gain his attention. "We're going to be fine."

"But—"

"Trust me. This is only a setback," I say as calmly as possible. "I already have a new plan."

I have no intentions of succumbing to the dirt and earthworms just yet.

I find Mateo's intense gaze locked on me. "What plan?"

"Follow me."

And he does. It's nice to be listened to for once. To have someone trust me enough to trail after me upstairs. I vow to not make him regret placing his faith in me.

I do have a plan. It has a similar composition as my original scheme. Just a slightly different route. We'll both come back to life and put an end to the Quinn's regime.

Lacy's words from the night before still ring in my ear. *Platonic love is just as strong as romantic.* I pray we're both correct when I walk through the bedroom door at the end of the hall.

38

Amelie Quinn's tear-streaked face startles upward. She locks eyes with me for a split second before realizing what she's done and averting her gaze.

"Don't act like you can't see me!"

She winces at the harshness in my voice, though this movement is all I needed to confirm Amelie really does love me. My death has haunted her as much as it haunts her brother, and because she is technically equally as responsible for my death as him, she can see me, too. Because I want her to know I'm here.

I've never felt more relieved to have been betrayed by my best friend. It might be our key to everything.

Amelie whispers in disbelief, "Is this real?"

I can't keep the bite from my voice. "You always wanted this house to be haunted."

She emits a horrified gasp, and for a brief moment, I allow it to satisfy my rage. Unfortunately, now is not the time to be a terror. That's not how I'm going to get my way.

"Amelie," I say cautiously, crossing the room to stand before her bed. The last thing I want is to scare her off like I did her brother. She frantically pushes herself back as far as she can, but when she presses against the twisted gold headboard, she's trapped. "I'm not here for revenge against you."

"Why not?" she moans. "I deserve it."

"You do, but I know that, deep down, you didn't want me to die. Just like you didn't want Camila, Phoebe, Mateo, or any of the others to die."

Her eyes glisten at the mention of her ex-girlfriend. Too fearful to utter a word, she frantically nods.

I continue to speak slowly, hypnotizing some sense into her. "You didn't want any of it. It was your mother. She burrowed into your mind and tricked you into believing you had no choice but to go along with her."

No confirmation is necessary to know this to be true. Gianna Quinn has been holding her children's privilege over their heads for as long as I've known them. They can only afford to attend the best private boarding school because Gianna worked tirelessly until TeQ took off. The food on their plates was a result of her launching a new product. Their mother may have missed a dozen games and art shows, but it was always so she could hear an inventor's pitch or sit in a board meeting. After all, how else would they pay for all those lessons and equipment?

I guess I'm no better than Gianna Quinn now. But I'll gladly guilt Amelie into betraying her mother. The fate of humanity may rest on it. No one can have access to this camp-site. Not the Quinns or anyone.

And so, with that motivation, I put on my kindest, most innocent smile as I lean over the bottom of the bed frame. "What you and your family have done is wrong, but there's still time to make it right."

Amelie blinks those big eyes at me, clearly not believing there's any hope of doing so. I already know she's going to hate what I'm about to propose; however, maybe there's enough remorse and anger in her heart to want to make amends. She's already killed once, after all. I'm sure she can stomach it once more.

"You don't want your mother getting into the zombie business, right?"

"Zombie?" Mateo chirps from the corner of the room. "Is that what I looked like to you?"

I go to wave him off before realizing Amelie cannot see or hear him, so this gesture will only freak her out more.

"I know you, Amelie. You never agree with your mother, least of all on this."

The girl offers me another petrified nod, and in that moment, I can't decide who she fears more. Her mother or myself.

Hopefully, it's me.

"You know this is dangerous territory," I continue. "If your mother continues to test the laws of life—"

"I know," Amelie finally whispers.

"Then you know she needs to be stopped."

"How?"

Here it comes. The moment where I sink to their level.

"Kill her." The words slip out easier than I expected.

The girl's eyes widen at the thought.

Before she can argue, I tack on, "I know how it sounds but—"

"You just asked me to murder my own mother." She stares at me like I've grown a second head. "Is this so you can come back to life?"

"Who do you think deserves to live more? Me or a murderer?"

"You just asked me to *murder my mother*. Pretty sure that makes you murder-complicit."

"Amelie," I move to grab her hands before realizing I cannot touch her, "I didn't deserve to die, but right now, that's beside the point. If your mother lives, so many others will lose their lives."

"We could convince her to stop."

"She won't," I say firmly.

I'm careful not to tuck a strand of hair behind my ears and give myself away. Gianna Quinn will always choose her own life over her business. But I'm not about to value the life of my murderer more than mine.

The Quinns have spent all their lives running around this summer camp, playing axe murderer. Now, it's my turn to don the mask.

"It's normal to not want to kill your mom," I say, drenching my voice with pity. "Honestly, I'd be concerned if you weren't pushing back. But this is the correct course of action, Amelie. Your mother must die."

"But—"

"There's no time for hesitation."

I allow the spirit that I am to command the energy of the room. I enlist every particle of air onto my side, coaxing a soft breeze to caress a strand of Amelie's dark hair. Reminding her I'm real and deserving of a second chance at life. All I need is a little justice.

"With your mother gone, you'll finally get to live a normal life. You can choose if you want to be online or never seen again. There won't be anyone to tell you that 'content creation isn't a real job' or that you won't ever outshine your eldest brother."

I pause to discern if my words are having any impact at all. My friend's face is completely blank, and for a moment, I fear she's shut her mind off completely in an attempt to fully disassociate from the situation. Once she goes down that road, there'll be no reasoning with her whatsoever.

But before I can attempt to usher her back into reality, Amelie finally speaks in a broken whisper. "I don't know if I can kill someone again."

If I had a beating heart, it would be racing. This is precisely what I needed her to admit. I'm so close to returning to life that I can practically taste the sweet air on my tongue.

"Camila's still here, you know."

This earns me Amelie's full attention. "She is?"

I nod. "I spoke with her last night."

"How is she?"

"I wouldn't say your ex is thrilled with her current predicament," I begin, before I start to weave a tale of my own, "but she understands your mother put you up to it. However—"

Amelie sucks in a breath.

I wince, making it clear I don't want to deliver the bad news but have no choice in the matter. "Camila's vowed to make what's left of your life a living hell before your soul is damned forever."

"What's left of it?" Amelie squeaks. "Damned forever?"

I shrug helplessly. "She says there's only one way to make it right."

"Camila wants me to kill my mother too."

I nod again. "She says it would be a fair trade for killing her and not loving her enough for it to mean anything."

It's blunt—not to mention a blatant lie—but I watch with satisfaction as the words hit home.

"You don't think I can resurrect Camila?"

A cruel laugh escapes my throat. "You don't love her enough for it to work."

This assertion is a complete stab in the dark, but when Amelie's shoulders slump, I know I've hit my mark.

"And if I kill Mom, it'll bring you back?" Amelie asks quietly.

"The only reason you can see me now is because you love me."

"Okay," Amelie says almost like she's convincing herself rather than me. "I'll do it."

We both startle when Caleb Quinn barges through the door.

It's my turn to gasp like I've seen a ghost. How can I not when the boy is *drenched* in scarlet blood. It seeps into his t-shirt and coats his skin. The worst part? I don't think it's his.

I compose myself long enough to demand, "What did you do?"

Falling to his knees before me, he presents himself, blood and all. "My mother is already dead, Sky. I killed her for you."

39

You have got to be freaking kidding me.

I gaze down at him in horror. Caleb Quinn cannot have killed his mother for me. This wasn't the plan.

Still on his knees, he beams up at me with a twisted grin. Why couldn't he let me do this my way?

Because Caleb always has to be in control. He may have lost himself to grief last night, but I know this boy as well as I know myself. When Caleb does wrong, he vigorously course-corrects. If he's back, that means he's come with a vengeance of his own.

My spirit betrays me by fizzling at his pleased smirk.

For crying out loud, this is the boy who killed me! I don't have a pulse to quicken because of him.

My lips purse with frustration. Even in death, Caleb Quinn finds a way to get under my skin.

Behind me, I hear Amelie begin to cry. "You're lying," she wails at her brother. "You couldn't have killed Mom."

As if she herself hadn't agreed to do the very same moments ago. It goes to show that you cannot trust anyone in this family. Not really.

Caleb doesn't break eye contact with me. "It's the truth. Mother needed to die. I killed her for Sky."

"Show me," I demand, needing to see proof of Gianna Quinn's death. For all I know, this is another one of her manipulative tricks.

At once, Caleb rises to his feet and gestures for me to walk ahead of him out of the room. I meet Mateo's unreadable gaze before giving him a helpless shrug. We have no choice but to improvise.

Though his jaw clenches skeptically, he still brings up the rear of our group as we depart Amelie's bedroom, down the hall, and begin descending the stairs.

Suddenly, the stairwell begins to fiercely shake, as if Camp Casper exists at the intersection of two tectonic plates. My ears begin to ring fiercely, burning a hole in my head. Falling to their knees, the siblings cling to the banister in an attempt to not topple down the wooden stairs. Mateo and I remain unaffected by the jostling ground, but the shrieking in our ears proves to be just as debilitating. As he holds his head, mouth agape with agony, I fight to stay conscious. If this sound continues for much longer, I fear I will lose control of my remaining senses altogether.

And then, as quick as it came, the home settles and the hissing in my head disappears.

Frozen in place, we all blink at each other in shock. Everyone is too stunned to speak.

"What was that?" Cricket's head pokes out of her bedroom.

"Stay in your room!" Caleb bellows up at her. "You, too, Zane! I know you can hear me! Go hide in your closets and stay there until we come get you!"

Long gone is the crazed boy from the night before. It's clear Caleb is in full control of his faculties once more.

"Was that an earthquake?" Amelie cries. She still has no

clue Mateo is behind her. If Caleb is still aware of his friend's presence, he doesn't let on.

"No," I answer, "I think that was your mother."

It's the only explanation for such a furious surge of energy throughout the house. I no longer need to see Gianna's corpse to know she is now on my side of the universe.

Amelie sniffs. "But I thought Caleb—"

"Your mother's ghost," I elaborate as a corpse at the bottom of the stairs captures my attention.

Pamela's.

Amelie squeaks at the sight of it.

"She tried to keep me from Mom," is Caleb's only excuse as his eyes bore into mine, silently making it clear that anyone who stands between me and life is as good as dead.

"Where is Gianna's body?" I ask him.

Those piercing blue eyes bore into mine. "In the woods. All I need is your permission to bury your body with hers."

I swallow before realizing the movement is purely theatrical. A mundane action for those still alive. "Let's go."

Not needing any further encouragement, nor wanting the angry spirit to immobilize us again, we fly down the stairs and through the house. It's when we reach the back porch that the shaking returns with another bout of sharp ringing in my ears.

Amelie shrieks, falling to hug the deck. "She's trying to stop us!"

"She's only going to grow more powerful as she learns to control her energy!" I cry, slamming my palms over my ears. "You need to get the others out of here!"

Caleb agrees. "Sky is right. Amelie, grab the kids and run."

Her pink lips part with horror as she shouts, "Run where?"

There's only one person who understands their present predicament. "Go to my mother. She'll take care of you."

"But your mother—"

"—will always put your family first!" I interject.

Legs wobbling, Amelie fights to rise to her feet and return inside.

"Wait!" I hear myself scream, stopping the girl. "Tell her she's dead to me."

Setting me with an understanding stare, Amelie turns and bolts back into the lodge.

As soon as she's inside, Caleb calls, "Let's go!"

The three of us turn on our heels and sprint into the woods.

"You gonna acknowledge me at some point?" Mateo calls over to his friend.

I cannot even begin to comprehend how Caleb can still see Mateo. There must be some cosmic rule about still being haunted by whoever you killed, regardless of if they come back to life and then die again.

Or perhaps it's so unheard of that even the universe doesn't know what to do with their current predicament.

"Hang around as long as you'd like," Caleb says, not sparing Mateo a glance. "I already gave you a second chance at life."

"At her expense."

"Pass all the judgement you want for my sins. I'm just trying to make things right."

"You really think you can bring her back?" Mateo scoffs.

I hold my metaphorical breath while waiting to hear his response.

"I know I can." Caleb's eyes find mine and he spares me a long, meaningful look that begs me to read between the lines. And of course I do.

He still loves me.

I wish that realization didn't make my insides flip.

"You're going to let him bring you back?" Mateo snaps after watching me process Caleb's words.

"How is Caleb bringing me back any different from his sister doing so?"

Mateo barks out a laugh. "Spare me, Skyler."

I want to scream at him to trust me but that would spoil my newly crafted plan. I resolve to set him with my sternest stare, willing him to discern the truth.

Instead, Mateo huffs before masking himself out of view like a candle being snuffed out. Jealous fool. If any of the boys in this house would take five seconds to truly understand me and my intentions, we might not be in this convoluted, romantic mess.

Caleb remains totally unbothered. "It's hard to accept our history," he says simply.

"A bloody one," I remind him.

"I'm trying to make it right, Sky."

I know he is, but that doesn't mean I have to forgive him to reclaim my life. In fact, remaining as apathetic as possible toward the boy seems to be my safest route.

We run the rest of the way through the woods in silence. The tickle at the back of my neck tells me Mateo is still keeping a close eye on the situation, which grants me the confidence to hurry. I cannot have hope of bringing him back if I do not return first.

When we reach the clearing, Caleb bends over to pant from exertion. Realizing I am completely composed, he gapes up at me.

"Don't say death suits me."

He breathes out a shaky laugh. "Never. Only a coward could think otherwise."

"And you're not a coward?"

"Not anymore."

I spy the body of Gianna Quinn slumped against a tree. My nose wrinkles as I count the knife wounds in her chest. Blood mats her hair as her blue eyes stare blankly at nothing.

"You're a killer, not a coward," I murmur, just loud

enough to ensure Caleb hears me. "And I worry you're a little too good at it."

"Me too," he responds darkly.

My attention shifts back to the grave when Lacy Monroe appears. Caleb follows my gaze, squinting when he cannot see who I'm staring at.

"You're still here," I remark.

She smiles up at me. "I won't be for long."

I nod, pleased. The death of her murderer was bound to bring eternal peace. Now, after all these years, Lacy can pass on.

"Who are you talking to?"

I ignore Caleb to address Lacy. "How long do you have?"

"Enough to make sure her bloodshed is worth every last drop."

"Why isn't Gianna here now to stop him?"

The grin that stretches Lacy's lips is truly terrifying. "My old friend knows it's no use to convince her son to reconsider his agenda. She's back at the house, attempting to gain the attention of her fleeing children."

The woman is a hopeless fool. In her quest to conquer death, she manipulated every single one of her children so greatly that they all turned against her. I doubt any of them will glance back at the lodge during their escape.

"But the boy is right," Lacy prompts, bringing us back on track. "This camp is impatient and neither of us has much time."

"Thank you," I say hurriedly. "For being the woman to look after me."

Lacy nods. "This gruesome world is so bleak and dark. I hope there's more light in the beyond."

"I look forward to finding you there."

"It's not a race, Skyler. You deserve to live a long life surrounded by people deserving of your love."

"I promise to help the others pass on."

A content breeze whispers through the trees, and I realize the others are with me now, too. If this all works, I will help every last one of them find the peace they deserve.

I offer Lacy one final smile before returning my attention to a dumbfounded Caleb. "Let's get on with it."

"Were you just talking to another ghost?"

"Caleb, we need to focus."

Shivering, he nods at me, making it clear he's focused. "You're really going to allow me bring you back?"

"Don't let it make you feel special. You're the reason I'm dead in the first place."

"You don't have to love me back, Sky. It's my love for you that matters."

"Do you actually think it's real love or a temporary delusion in order to meet an end?" I hear myself ask before I can think better of it.

"It's real." His steely eyes meet mine. "But you don't have to take my word for it. I can think of a few ways for you to uncover the truth for yourself. All I need is time."

A fizzling energy crackles through the forest, fiercely swaying the branches until they threaten to snap. Mateo may not like Caleb's words, but he still doesn't make himself seen. Whatever is about to go down, it's clear Mateo wants it to unfold without outside influence.

"Let's see if I can return first," I bite back.

Nodding once, Caleb continues with the task of dragging his mother's body toward the grave. Not a single tear drips down his cheeks and I realize we've all grown too comfortable in the presence of death.

He has the good sense to guiltily droop his chin as he heaves her into the grave; he waits for me to approach before carefully placing his mother's body beside my abandoned frame. I realize he's doing this more for my benefit than his mother's. If I return, I won't have to climb out from under her.

As soon as the earth envelops her body, it begins.

Losing control of my corporeal spirit, everything goes dark as I disappear into a vast nothingness.

40

HERE, in this inky atmosphere, I find my senses nonexistent.

Spinning for anything, I freeze when I see a pinprick of white light in the distance. It pulls at me with the promise of warmth and peace. Immediately, I take a few steps toward it before I feel a tug from the opposite direction.

Whipping around, I find nothing but darkness. And yet, that midnight appears to have the power to compete with the light.

Each side picks one of my arms, attempting to pull me in opposite directions. I realize it's up to me to decide which way to go. I should've asked Mateo more about his transition back to life when I had the chance.

As soon as the boy pops into my mind, he appears. The two directions seem to not have an impact on him as he walks through the shadows. With every step he nears, I feel an inviting warmth, not unlike that from the white light in the distance. His hand curls around mine. The one closest to the light.

The darkness tightens its grip on my other hand, attempting to yank me closer. Mateo grimaces at the sight. "You have to let him take you."

"Him?"

Lacy's final message enters my mind. *This gruesome world is so bleak and dark. I hope there's more light in the beyond.*

In order to come back, I have to embrace the murky mess that comes with life. I must accept Caleb and the darkness that resides in him.

And so, I pull myself away from Mateo and the warmth.

Instantly, the shadowy cold victoriously embraces me. With one last look at Mateo, I turn into the shadows and jump into the gloomy nothingness.

As soon as my feet leave the ground, I feel the breath knock back into me.

"For what it's worth," I hear Caleb's raspy voice in the distance, "I'll never forgive myself for what I did to you, Sky."

"Neither will I," I retort, climbing out of the grave.

41

I SUCK IN A DEEP BREATH, relishing the sweet morning air as it fills my lungs.

I'm alive.

All at once, I feel everything again. The rapid beating of my heart and a cool breeze that kisses my cheeks. The grass is soft beneath my hands as I drag myself the rest of the way out of the hole.

After clearing my throat, I test my voice. "It worked."

"Did you doubt me?"

A hand appears before me. Glancing up, I find Caleb grinning with relief. Accepting his hand, he pulls me to my feet.

I use the momentum to pounce on him.

Caleb grunts when his back slams against the ground. Immediately, my hands wrap around his throat, and I squeeze with all my might. He gasps for breath beneath me, but his hands don't attempt to overtake mine.

"What are you doing?" I groan down at him.

He says nothing as his eyes dance over my face, like he's committing my features to memory.

Pressing my thumbs into his Adam's apple, I watch as his

bloodied face turns even redder. And yet, he does nothing to fend me off.

"Come on," I say through a grimace. "Fight back."

"No," he wheezes.

My hands loosen but remain clasped around his throat. "Why not?"

"Because I don't deserve to live in the same world as you. Not after everything I've done."

"Oh, please, we both know you don't believe that."

"I do." His hand reaches to caress my cheek, making me flinch away. He winces at my reaction. "And that's why."

Staring down at him helplessly, I try to muster all my strength to keep my plan in motion. In order for Mateo to come back, I have to kill Caleb. It's the only way.

He offers me a bleak smile. "It's enough for me to know you still love me."

I hate that he's right. That after everything this boy has put me through, he still owns a piece of my heart. It's been his for so long. Maybe it's impossible to completely banish the first boy you've ever loved. The very thought makes me furious with myself.

Still, if the boy who stopped my heart can continue to stake a claim to it, it seems only fair that I get to return the favor.

"It's okay, Sky," he whispers. "I knew this is how it would happen."

"No, you didn't," I argue, for no reason other than I don't want him in control of this situation, too. This time, I don't flinch when he wipes a tear from streaking down my cheek.

"When I found Mateo's body in the kitchen, I realized how my mom completely used me. I'm done being a pawn in her perfect life, so I killed her, and when I golf carted her body out here, I made sure to bring Mateo's, too. He's on the other side of that tree, waiting for you to bury him with me."

This information only makes me cry harder.

Because this is why a part of me will always love this boy. For his ability to see right through me. No one's ever predicted my every move quite like Caleb Quinn.

"You can choose him right now," he murmurs, "but we both know nothing in life or death lasts forever."

My grip loosens. "I'm not sure I can go through with it."

He blinks the tears out of his ocean eyes. "You can, Sky. It's the only way we can forgive each other."

I sniff. "You really believe it's meant to be us in the end?"

"Sky, falling in love with you was easy. Too easy. I only wish I hadn't needed such prodding to start pursuing you, but we can add that to the long list of regrets I'll take to my grave."

"You're doing it again," I point out. He's softening my heart toward him and giving Mateo a fighting chance at coming back.

"It only works if you truly love me." Caleb offers me a sheepish expression. "I like to believe your feelings for me are still in there, but I figured you could use a little help coaxing them back to the surface. I don't want to die for nothing."

"But you'd die for him?"

"Mateo is a good guy—even if he did swoop in and steal my girl."

My girl. Those two words make my insides ache. For so long, that's all I've ever wanted to be. His girl.

Now, I'm the reason he's going to die.

Maybe he's right about us needing to destroy each other in order to forgive, because right now, I'm no better than him.

I need to get this over with. Drawing it out is only making it hurt more.

So, before I do something dumb like kiss him, I fix my grip.

"It's not forever," he reassures me.

"How can you be so sure?" I whisper through the tears.

"Because it was always meant to be us, and I trust in time, you'll remember that. I lost my way. It's only fair you get to do the same. But I know, Skyler Pierce, that I'll be seeing you soon."

With one last look at me, his eyes close as he grants me the peace of not watching the light leave them when I squeeze his throat.

My hands tighten as every spirit in the forest possesses me, loaning me their strength. All who were damned by the Quinns—Camila, Phoebe, Eve, Beau, and Mateo—manifest in my hands. Though the boy we are strangling isn't the real criminal here.

Choking on sobs, I slam my own eyes shut as he starts to tremble.

And then, the boy I loved all my life, stills beneath me.

Even in death, he's so beautiful. Tanned skin and pink lips. I refuse to allow my brain to wonder what the earth will do to him.

Petting his cooling cheek, I place a soft kiss on his forehead. This is the boy who ruined my life, but he saved it, too.

For as long as I live, I will never forget Caleb Quinn.

As gently as possible, I pull him to the grave. His mother's body is still inside but I know the camp will understand my intentions. It knows who I love.

Mateo is right where Caleb promised. Sat against a tree near the tombstone. I'm unable to meet the corpse's unseeing eyes as I shamefully join the boys in the grave. My entire system screams that this is wrong. I shouldn't be picking who lives and dies. This doesn't feel like righting wrongs. Instead, it feels like I'm simply making new ones.

"You'll forgive yourself one day," Mateo promises, climbing out of the grave.

My vision is too blurry to properly make him out as he hesitantly approaches to wrap his arms around me in a cloud of spearmint, musk, and coppery blood from his wound.

"I'm so sorry, Skyler," he murmurs into my ear as I sob against his chest.

I know I should be happy he's back, but I cannot find it in myself to feel anything other than complete misery. I'm beginning to understand why Caleb descended into such madness after killing me. This is the most horrible, gut-wrenching feeling in the world.

Mateo and I stumble as the ground beneath our feet begins to shake. The rumbling is so forceful that it wrenches us apart as we fall to our knees.

Gianna.

I scream when a set of familiar sneakers appears before me. Glancing up, I find Caleb staring down at me, fear in his haunted eyes.

"She's coming for you, Sky," he warns.

My tongue seems incapable of forming a single syllable as I stare up at the ghost of my greatest love. I did this to him. He's trapped here forever because of me.

"Stop pitying yourself and run!" Caleb bellows before turning to address Mateo. "Get her out of here!"

"We have to go!" Mateo pulls me to my feet and drags me from the clearing.

We sprint through the trees as nonstop earthquakes fight to knock us off balance. Gianna's mission is clear. If she can't leave, no one can. I only hope the others made it out safe. They don't deserve to die. Like Caleb, their poor choices were influenced by the real villain in all our lives.

Vines snake up from the land to snap at our ankles, and I don't have to glance down to know the thorny tendrils have ripped into my skin. That's the last blood I'm letting this damned lake house steal from me.

I run harder, pumping my legs with all my might. Never releasing my hand, Mateo tugs me through the trees.

The sound of a purring golf cart has us both glancing over our shoulders.

I scream in horror at the sight of Samuel behind the wheel. He's barreling right toward us and showing no sign of stopping as he nears. His mission is clear. We won't be apprehended. No—he's coming to kill us.

"I am not dying again!" Mateo howls, practically wrenching my arm from its socket as he forces us to pick up speed.

The surrounding trees seem to be getting the same treatment as a fierce wind begins to pull them up to their roots.

"Watch out!" I cry as an enormous trunk teeters in our direction.

We dodge the falling oak only to hear an agonizing scream and metallic crunch from behind us. I risk another look over my shoulder and find the trunk has crushed Samuel in his golf cart. The gruesome image makes me gag, but Mateo refuses to let me stop running until the sound of a rumbling engine ahead gives him pause.

"Not more golf carts," he moans.

"No!" I shriek with relief. "It's the road."

We're nearly to the property line. I can hear cars passing just on the other side of the trees.

Gianna must realize this, too, because she throws everything she's got at us. Unruly roots raise in the path, forcing us to jump every few steps. Limbs fall overhead. The angry wind whips leaves against our faces and forces debris into our eyes. But we refuse to allow it to stop us.

I sense Caleb running alongside us, keeping a watchful eye on our escape. He'll be trapped here with his monster of a mother, but I know if there's anyone who can endure it, he can.

"I'll come back," I vow to him. "I'll get rid of her."

"It'll be okay! Just go!" he calls to me. There's no strain in his voice from the sprint.

With one final look at Caleb, I press on. I know it won't be forever.

A tall metal fence stands between us and the road. Immediately, Mateo and I release each other so we can jump onto the fence. It rattles beneath our grip, slicing into our palms, but we do not falter until we scale upward and crash down on the other side.

All at once, everything stops. There's no earthquakes or dangerous winds. Nothing to threaten us now that we're away from Camp Casper.

My partner breathes out a laugh of relief, staring back into the forest. "We made it. We're safe."

"We're alive." The words come out as a sob as Mateo pulls me against him and his arms wrap protectively around me. Resting my head against his chest, I take a long look at the woods I considered my safe haven. The horrors that linger between the trees can't reach me anymore.

Now, all I have to fear is if my heart got left behind to rot.

EPILOGUE
NEXT SUMMER

This is the last time.

I think it to myself over and over again, forcing my brain to commit the promise to memory.

This is the last time I will visit the lake house.

After last summer turned into a night terror brought to life and I barely escaped with my own life, I left Casper for good. Mom knew better than to come after me. I tracked down the only woman who would empathize with my predicament. Maggie, the old counselor who revived her brother Jonah. She's letting me crash at her little cottage on the coast of the Florida panhandle while I earn enough money for a place of my own. I promise myself I've only temporarily given up on high school. I'll find a way to complete my education eventually.

Maggie and Jonah understand why I like to keep to myself. They say it takes time to learn how to live again.

I visited Mateo in Boston during his winter break. Unlike me, he's returned to his life before death. He has to repeat junior year, so he's still stuck living with his parents. They're so petrified he'll speak a word of what they did to get their son back that they're spoiling him more than ever. Mateo says he's counting down the days until he can be done with them for good.

It was easier than expected to avoid Amelie, Zane, and Cricket during my visit. The remaining Quinn children knew to keep their distance. They live with some relatives now, but thanks to all the money their mother left them, their lives haven't changed all that much. Aside from the newfound trauma, of course.

It was nice to spend time with Mateo, but after a few months of struggling to date long-distance, we realized a relationship was infeasible. Our foundation was built on foul memories neither of us want to remember. We left things at "we'll see what happens one day after we're fully healed."

I wanted it to be him. I *needed* it to be him. However, I know my heart is capable of pounding harder than it does when I'm with Mateo. Maybe I'm being foolish and not realizing my heart simply beats differently now, but until I know for sure, I cannot promise myself to him. It wouldn't be fair to either of us.

I'm still holding onto hope that we'll find our way into that van one day; driving around the country and helping lonesome spirits pass on.

Until we're both ready for that, I'm on my own.

Shortly after this realization struck home, I started to feel the pull to the lake house. It's like someone is tugging at a loose thread in my mind, and if I don't succumb to their call, I might unravel entirely.

No matter how terrified I was to return, I had a promise to fulfill.

During my first visit in the spring, it was Phoebe who greeted me at the edge of the woods. She was the source of the tug because she was ready.

The spirit of the girl was exactly how I left her. Too young to be dead. We talked for hours, about all the things she wanted to do, be, and see. Afterwards, she sighed with relief.

"Maybe you can visit the French Riviera for me," she said wistfully.

"I promise I will."

And miraculously, that's all it took for her to pass on. The girl simply needed someone to live in her name.

It healed a piece of me to help her, so whenever I could, I snuck back to help one of the wayward souls pass on. Beau and Eve were quick. Like Phoebe, they just needed someone to listen. Camila wanted to hear all about how Amelie was suffering with regret. Pamela never stuck around, which makes me wonder just how much guilt she held for assisting Gianna. In time, I finally had the courage to face Mackenzie, and after we both apologized to each other profusely, she passed on. I even found Samuel and let him recall every last one of his happy memories from Camp Casper. Like Mackenzie, his mind had been twisted by Gianna, and once unbound, he found peace. By helping them pass on, I found some, too.

But it never made me feel whole. Not completely.

I never dared trek deeper into the property, preferring to stick to the edge of the woods. The last thing I wanted to do was test Gianna, who was known for causing quite the racket up at the empty lodge. It's a miracle they haven't torn it down yet; although, any surveyors who stop by the property are scared off pretty quickly.

A certain soul never made his presence known to me, which was just as well. I'm not sure I could face him, either.

Or at least, that's what I thought up until the first week of June, when the pull happened again.

I should've felt ashamed with how the tug made my heart skip a beat, but the organ is incapable of being anything but truthful. No matter how hard I try to banish him, Caleb Quinn is still burrowed deep inside by heart. At this rate, I'm convinced I'll never be able to evict him.

So that's how I wound up in the woods after thinking I was done with these trees forever.

The forest welcomes me back with a happy wave of their branches, showing off their fully-grown and vibrantly green leaves. I allow the wind to whisper through my strands of hair and immediately wonder if it wasn't an abandoned soul that beckoned me back, but the forest itself. If I've learned one thing, it's that these trees have a mind of their own.

As soon as I reach the familiar clearing with the undisturbed grave, the pull ceases, giving me pause. The hair on the back of my neck prickles with anticipation, and a new pit forms in my stomach.

Maybe this wasn't such a good idea. I could have very well walked into a trap. After all, as far as I know, the only spirits that remain on site want nothing to do with me.

I shouldn't be here.

But when I turn to take my leave, the sound of churning water gains my attention.

Run, my instincts plead with me, but my feet pay it no mind. They carry me through the forest, which is not so difficult of a feat, considering I can walk between these trees with my eyes closed.

Hesitantly creeping beyond the tree line, I study the vast property that used to be my favorite place in the world. Now, it's the setting of every single one of my nightmares.

The inky-black lake glints beneath the moonlight. Gentle ripples lap at the shore. But there's no one to be found.

Maybe I imagined the beck-and-call altogether, which doesn't make me feel any better because it means I was eager for one.

Before I can further analyze that sinful truth, a single light illuminating inside the lake house earns my attention.

"Now that's definitely a trap." One of Gianna's tricks to get me inside and exact whatever gruesome revenge she cooked up with all her new free time.

But what if it's not...

"You're a fool," I mutter to myself as I approach the lodge.

The floorboards of the back deck creak beneath my feet, loudly announcing to anyone or anything in the house that I'm coming in.

I shouldn't be doing this. And yet, I'm sliding the back door open. The detectives who came to the house to search for clues as to why Gianna Quinn and her eldest son mysteriously disappeared were so petrified that they didn't bother to lock it.

The case was pretty short-lived, all things considered. We were each questioned—separately, thankfully—about what happened to Gianna, Caleb, and the other missing members of the staff. Every single one of us knew better than to reveal the truth. No one can know what this campsite is capable of.

The investigators didn't believe us, of course. They brought in cadaver dogs and used an excavator to dig all over the property. All they found was dirt. Somehow, Camp Casper kept every single body hidden. The only corpse they identified was Lacy, who laid where she belonged in her grave.

I still don't know which of the Quinn siblings returned Lacy's bones to her proper resting place and buried the other bodies in the makeshift morgue. Maybe they worked together.

Around the same time, the TeQ board discovered Gianna was embezzling money for "unapproved passion projects." Without any other leads, it was assumed Gianna, her son, and her other accomplices fled the country to avoid the scandal. The case was wrapped up with a neat little bow.

But that didn't mean I earned any peace. Frankly, I'm not sure I've felt a second of tranquility since I killed Caleb. I've tried to convince myself it's the guilt, but I'm fearful my unease is fueled by something far more dangerous.

Creeping through the house that used to be my happy place, I search for any sign I'm being lured into a trap. The walls seem to hiss at my presence, but when no one makes themselves known, I press toward the stairwell. Remembering the way Gianna caused them to shake, I cling to the banister as I ascend.

The house looks the same as it did a year ago, though a thick layer of dust rests over every inch of it.

Once upstairs, I find the source of the light. A golden glow emits from the bedroom at the end of the hall. My old room.

Swallowing, I carefully toe my way to the door, praying my eager heart doesn't betray me. With every step, the air grows colder and colder, until my arms prickle with goosebumps.

Steeling myself for anything, I hesitantly push open the door.

Caleb Quinn turns from the window, his grin warm and wide.

I suck in a breath at the sight of him. He's still the most beautiful soul I ever laid eyes on, even in the afterlife. From the way his head cocks to the side, he knows it, too.

"Skyler Pierce." He says my name like a promise. "I knew you'd come back for me one of these days."

"Sorry it took me so long," I whisper. "I didn't think—"

"Now don't tell me you thought I wouldn't want to lay eyes on my girl again."

I release a shaky laugh as my hopeless-romantic heart pounds out of my chest. The traitorous thing practically sings with joy in a tune only Caleb Quinn can evoke.

My heart's always been my greatest ally and my worst enemy. But I deserve peace, too, don't I?

"I've missed you," I exhale.

And it's the truth. No matter how much I try to convince myself otherwise, my absentminded thoughts have always returned to Caleb.

Caleb.

Caleb.

I'll never be able to deny the inevitableness of us. My heart beats for him. It always has, and I'm beginning to accept it always will.

He nods like he knows, then his attention briefly flicks to something on my bedside table before he comes to stand directly in front of me. A cold hand traces down my cheek, tilting my chin upward. I shiver as I stare up at the boy I've loved all my life with awe.

He can touch me again. The fates must have shifted back in his favor. I guess if anyone could make the afterlife bend to his will, it's Caleb.

"Are you scared to be here with me?" he whispers.

I shake my head, because I'm not. "I'm relieved."

"That's my girl," he murmurs lovingly, and I feel everything inside me melt. He nods back to the bedside table before returning those ocean-blue eyes to me. I follow his gaze, my stomach clenching when I see it.

Of course, I've thought about saving Caleb. But am I strong enough to go through with it? To save him, I must damn another. One that I love.

There are so few left in this world who I can honestly say I truly love. But I'm sure Caleb and I can find a fitting pawn. I've always been quick to fall, after all. Especially for the wrong person.

Am I wicked to even consider such a sin?

It's the only way to find peace.

Caleb regains my attention with a gentle brush of his lips against my forehead.

"It's always been us," he whispers against my skin, making me shiver.

"It will always be us," I vow.

I might not yet know the finer details of our future, but I do want to offer Caleb a second chance, just like the one he gave me. We deserve to grow old together and die together.

A girl possessed by her heart, I pull away from the boy who has always had his hand wrapped around it. My mind swirls, as if in a dream while I make my way across my bedroom. The one place I ever felt truly at home. This is all I've ever wanted.

My smile never falters. Not when I'm beaming back at my Caleb.

Not even when I reach down to pick up the knife.

ACKNOWLEDGMENTS

For years, the story in Death Dates has haunted me, and by proxy, the many wonderful people in my corner.

I'd be remiss if I did not begin by thanking my best friend in this life and the next, Taylor Maloney. I'm so grateful to know you and your beautiful heart. I'll never forget the night I told you every one of this book's secrets and we screamed our heads off.

To Andie Smith, my tremendous friend and editor. I could not have envisioned a better partner to tackle publishing alongside.

To Kaitlyn Katsoupis, who also graced Death Dates with her editorial brilliance. I feel so fortunate to work with you and to call you a friend.

Thank you to the talented Marcela Bolívar for crafting the most hauntingly beautiful cover I could have ever imagined. It's like you plucked Sky right out of my head and brought her to life.

I'd like to thank the incredible readers and booksellers who have touched my life in such a special way. Your unbelievable kindness and support will never be forgotten.

To my sweet family, who make sure I never live a day without love and laughter. Mom, Dad, and Adam, you three are the biggest blessings in the world.

And finally, to my fiancé, Taylor. Thank you for listening to me work out every plot twist, teaching me how to operate a business, understanding my nightmares, believing in my dreams, and inspiring me with your never-ending compassion. Loving you is the greatest privilege and joy.

ABOUT THE AUTHOR

MADISON RUPP
writes young adult thriller and horror-romance novels. Based in Orlando, Madison can usually be found scribbling in a quiet corner of a theme park. She's a firm believer that riding a roller coaster cures writer's block. Madison is also the author of *Liarland*.

You can connect with her online at madisonrupp.com.